THE DIARY OF ANGEL MOON

KAREN CLOW

ACKNOWLEDGMENTS

This book is dedicated with love to:

Caroline Diane Evans, hope you enjoy the book!

To absent friends, Prabha & Ashok. I think of you often and I promise one day I will visit you in India.

My dear friend, Olive Rendle for all her support

The landlords & landladies at the Bo Peep Pub
Mark & Kerry, Stephen & Sarah.
Jess, Caroline, Claire & the staff.

Christian & Paul, congratulations!

Special thanks to my wonderful team.

Ian Paton, my amazing tech man and guardian angel.

Pamela O'Keefe and Sallyann Cole, my wonderful angels who edit, proof read, promote and put up with my constant calls! I love you guys xxx

---

Lastly, to everyone who has supported me, my fondest love to them.

FOREWORD

THE DIARY OF ANGEL MOON is my second book in the supernatural genre and I'm thrilled to see it in print. I really enjoyed writing it and now intend to write more in the genre.

Never in my wildest dreams did I imagine my books becoming so popular.

'Jimmy's Game' was my first eBook, which went onto the Amazon Kindle platform in April 2013. In a complete contrast to Angel Moon it's based on the murky London underworld.

I would be the first to admit how naïve I was back then. I knew my books needed editing, but financially this wasn't something I could afford, so I took a chance and hoped for the best. I was shocked at how popular the book became in just a few weeks. Thankfully, most people were kind with their reviews and loved the book, although a few did comment 'constructively' on the grammar, spelling and the need for editing. Despite this and much to my surprise, the book rallied a lot of support with people stating that despite the errors and a little overkill on some storylines, they loved it!

Due to my success, I now have two wonderful ladies who help me edit and proof read. I'm thrilled to say my more recent books in the 'Ruthless Series' have received wonderful reviews on all counts. I am now having my earlier books edited. It's a slow but worthwhile process as due to popular demand, I am currently writing Series 3.

Maybe the time and effort put in will bring me a step closer to securing an agent? I hope so, as so many people asked if they could buy my books in paperback, or if it's going to become a TV drama. Now using the wonders of Amazon Create Space, I intend to have all my books in print once ready. I've actually had my comedy 'BRASSICK' and JIMMY'S GAME converted to script. It's a series close to my heart and we affectionately refer to it as England's answer to the Sopranos. Who knows maybe one day someone somewhere will think they're worth considering.

I hope you enjoy The Diary of Angel Moon.

THE DIARY OF ANGEL MOON

CHAPTER 1

Linda Atwood and her husband Derek had just returned from yet another hospital appointment. It was one of many since moving into what was supposed to be their dream home. The dream was, now their children had left home, they could buy a large rundown property and do it up. A nest egg for their future, but things hadn't gone quite to plan when less than two months after buying 16 Albert Avenue, Derek had fallen ill.

Most of the large jobs he'd planned to do were still waiting. The new kitchen was still boxed in the garage, alongside the new bathroom suite complete with jacuzzi. Linda had tried to do as much as she could by stripping wallpaper and clearing rubbish from the cellar and attic, but the big jobs were his field. He'd worked all his life in the building trade and for over twenty years had run his own very successful business with his sons, who had followed in his footsteps. Linda had run the office side of things.

Both had decided to take a back seat when they reached their fifties and found the property they deemed perfect.

They both still kept abreast with company issues, but it was now run by their sons, Michael and Mark.

"How do you feel love?" said Linda as she placed a fresh cup of tea down in front of Derek.

His reply was the same as most days. He didn't feel well at all. Since moving into number 16, he'd suffered from severe fatigue, stomach cramps, sickness and dizzy spells. Seven months on and he was still no nearer to a diagnosis regarding his poor health.

Linda felt it affected him more because he'd always been very fit, a regular swimmer and keen runner. He'd never smoked and rarely drank alcohol except for social occasions. He'd always looked very good for his age, but now at fifty seven he looked the opposite, drawn and gaunt. His weight had plummeted from a healthy, muscular thirteen stone to eleven, which at six feet two inches made him look positively thin.

There had been times during the past months when she'd questioned if they'd taken on too much with the house although at the time of purchasing it, Derek had been in good health.

She had been drawn to the house since first seeing it advertised and from the moment she had walked through the door she knew they would live there.

Their sons helped out with the house renovations whenever they could, but running the business full time and not having Derek taking some of the workload, along with raising their young families meant their time was limited. They had knocked down several walls inside the house to open up the living space and replaced two of the five bedroom windows with doubled glazed units.

Like her, they hoped the doctors would find out what was wrong and, once treated, his health would drastically improve.

Later that evening, Linda watched Derek pick at his dinner, despite it being his favourite of ham, eggs and chips. She felt concerned for him, he was a mere husk of the man he'd been less than a year earlier.

It wasn't long after dinner when he fell asleep in the arm chair.

Linda carefully slipped his glasses off him and placed them on the coffee table. Her plan for the evening was to make some headway in the attic. She had already managed to clear some floor space, mostly by throwing things out.

After checking on Derek, she made her way upstairs. A few minutes later she was standing in the attic looking at the clutter.

Where to start was the question going through her mind. There were old boxes full of things, from old clothes, books, ornaments and photographs, some of which looked like they were taken years ago. Several pieces of furniture had been stored by previous owners which she would need help removing.

Being a book lover, she decided to tackle the pile of books first. The ones she didn't want to keep she would give to charity.

For almost two hours she sorted through books of every conceivable shape, size and topic from Shakespeare to poetry. However, it was the last box that was to rouse her curiosity. In the bottom of the box was a leather bound book. There was nothing written on the outside, but inside on the first page there was hand writing. It read 'The Diary of Angel Moon.'

Drawn to the book she began to read.

'I was taken to meet my new family. I was four years old. I didn't understand until much later that my parents had abandoned me and these people, Mr and Mrs Bradshaw were to be my foster parents. I can't remember where I lived before that.

At first the Bradshaw's seemed to like me, although their nine year old daughter Laura clearly didn't. She would often say and do nasty things to me when her mother couldn't see or hear her.

I remember clearly when I was about five years old; I'd been talking about snow after mum (as I was told to call her) read us a bedtime story about a polar bear. At breakfast the next morning I told everyone that it would snow on Wednesday that week. Laura mocked me by chanting 'liar, liar pants on fire!' Mum and dad laughed it off and said it rarely snowed even during the winter and never in August.

It was after the freak weather storm that Wednesday when it snowed, things started to change for me. Laura would tell tales on me, she especially liked telling that she'd heard me talking to someone in my room at night. I remember mum being angry with me when, after she asked about it, I told her it was the fairy that came into my room to talk to me. Things really went downhill after that. When our next door neighbour Mrs Donnelly's dog went missing, I told them she was trapped by her collar on some waste ground behind our house. Of course when they found the dog caught by its collar exactly where I told them it would be, they said I must have done it to the poor dog, otherwise how would I have known.

By the time I reached seven, I was heading for my next foster home with Mr and Mrs Bawdry. She was a formidable woman with a stare that could melt ice. I could sense she didn't like me the moment I walked through her door. Their children had left home and either joined the Forces or moved away. Mr Bawdry was a thin, chisel-faced man who was clearly intimidated by his wife, as was I.

Within a few weeks, I'd learnt that what mum said was law. If she said do something you didn't argue, you simply did it. She treated me with the contempt of a refugee who she neither wanted or cared for. I was simply a means to bringing money into the house with Social Services paying a fee for me.

I spent my ninth birthday with yet another set of foster parents, Mr and Mrs Haskins. She was actually quite nice to me, so was Mr Haskins, especially when he wanted to grope me when he asked me to sit on his lap. It was after it happened the second time, I realised I was different to other kids. I wished something bad would happen to him so he would stop touching me. Two days later he had an accident at work. I heard Mrs Haskins telling her friend a piece of machinery had malfunctioned at his works. She referred to it as a freak accident, which even the safety experts couldn't explain or understand how it had happened. All I knew was both his hands were busted up pretty bad. He was in agony for weeks; he couldn't even hold his knife and fork without it hurting. I never told anyone that I had wished him to hurt his hands. I even tried to convince myself it may have been a simple fluke, but I knew it wasn't.

No matter how hard I tried, for me things just seemed to go from bad to worse after that. By the time I was thirteen, I was considered a difficult child to place. I'd moved from foster home to foster home. It was the same every time, whenever something happened that they couldn't explain I got the blame. One family, the Robinson's, tied me to a chair and doused me with Holy Water. They believed I was possessed by the Devil after I told them about my best friend Johnathan; the fairy who regularly visited me. Knowing what they'd done to me was against the law and fearful of whom I might tell, they threatened that if I said anything they'd say I was lying and have me committed to an asylum. A week later while I was home alone, after the family had gone out to drop their daughter off at dance class, their house mysteriously caught fire. Had Johnathan not woken me, I feel I would have perished as I'd fallen asleep on my bed. From that day on I kept my psychic happenings and abilities to myself and I never mentioned Johnathan again, more for my own protection than anyone else's.

The kids at school taunted me calling me the Devil child or weirdo. They would throw stones at me and put insects in my lunch box. Although I never showed it, I felt alone with nobody to love or look after me. Most days after school I would just sit alone upstairs until I was called for dinner and then return to the room after I'd eaten and finished whatever chores had been assigned to me. I just didn't seem to fit in with anyone, regardless of how hard I tried. If I tried to show any interest in anything, like wanting to help with the cooking, I was usually told they didn't need any help. It was around that time I decided to run away. I had it all planned for that particular day. I was going to leave after dinner that evening, but when I returned home from school that afternoon, my social worker Gina was waiting for me. She told me I was moving again that afternoon.

Little did I know then, but that would be the day my life changed. The day when I met Olivia Moon, 'now mum'. In fact, she was the only foster mother who actually deserved the title of mum.

I can remember standing at her door with my social worker and thinking, I wonder how long this one will last. Then Olivia smiled at me and warmly invited me in to her house, number 16 Albert Avenue. Instantly I felt calm, I could feel a gentle kindness about her and much to my relief, there was no Mr Moon.

I settled in very quickly. Unlike with any other foster homes, I actually felt I belonged there. I didn't know if Olivia had fostered other children or if some more may be coming. Not knowing if Olivia knew about my psychic episodes worried me, but I never mentioned them; or the fact that from the moment I stepped into her house I could see and hear several spirits.

It was over breakfast two days later on Sunday morning all my questions were answered. It was as though Olivia knew what I wanted to ask. She started the morning's conversation by telling me she'd never fostered before and despite having plenty of room, she didn't intend taking any more children. In a strange way it made me feel special, especially when she went on to tell me she'd wanted children of her own, but her husband had died tragically seventeen years earlier when they bought the house. He had been putting a new aerial on the roof when he slipped and fell to his death. Olivia had been twenty six at the time and they had just started trying for a family. His passing had a devastating effect on her. For the first two years afterwards, she'd led a very quiet life with little to no socialising. I remember looking at her and thinking how attractive she was and how much younger she looked than her forty three years.

It had been a friend at work who suggested to her about fostering after reading an advert in the newspaper for carers. It had stated that even single people could apply. Knowing Social Services as well as I did, I wasn't surprised when after she'd told them she would consider taking a teenager, they signed her up. After just a few hours of being there, I knew if anyone was meant to have children it was Olivia Moon. I'd never trusted anyone and certainly not after such a short time, but she was different. I found myself talking about things I'd never talked about to anyone. How the other kids had ostracised me and how lonely I felt.

We talked for hours about life and families and how it was her belief that people met for a reason, whether good or bad there was always a reason. However, there was something she said that morning that had the greatest impact on my life. She told me it was ok to be different and the kids at school simply feared what they didn't understand. In her eyes, I had been given a gift, a God given gift no less. She talked about her Aunt who used to take her to the spiritualist church when she was a teenager. It was clear that her family embraced the idea of some people having the gift, although Olivia was quick to tell me that many psychics were fakes. Those people were like blood suckers in her eyes, they exploited the very people who needed their help and guidance the most.

That first weekend with Olivia was one of the happiest I'd ever had. She treated me like a person who had feelings. I knew then I would never leave her and in time she would become the real mum I craved.

By the beginning of the next week, Olivia had let me decorate my room with some pop posters. This was something I'd never been allowed to do before. My room was lovely, with a big four poster bed with lace drapes. I had a wardrobe, dressing table and bedside cabinet with only my clothes in. This was a first for me as I'd had to share in my other homes with other foster kids. Next to my bed, Olivia had placed a small glass dish full of sweets and next to that was a box of tissues. Everything seemed like a dream to me, a dream I didn't want to wake up from.'

Linda looked at her watch and the pile of books. Her conscience was telling her to get on with sorting the attic as time was running away, but Angel's diary had her spellbound. Telling herself she would only read for a few more minutes she turned to the next page.

'I remember coming home from school on the Monday with my blouse sleeve torn. Olivia knew I'd been bullied, but unlike my previous foster mothers she cared and intended to do something about it.

After dinner that evening we sat in the lounge talking about the bullies. She asked me how I felt about them. Her expression was one of shock when I said I felt sorry for them. I knew they were all fighting their own battles. I remember the look of curiosity on her face when she asked me to explain.

There were three girls who, since the start of secondary school, had made it their mission to make my life as difficult and unpleasant as possible. I had never done anything to annoy them, but like most bullies they picked on me because I was a loner and had no gang to back me up. Bullies are only tough when they're with other bullies. Despite hating what they were doing to me, I actually felt sorry for them. That was why I'd never wished them anything really bad. Of course if they were chasing me home, I'd wish they'd fall over and they would, but I never wanted to hurt them, just get away from them.

Rachael, the ring leader, was actually the one hiding the worse secret. I knew someone in her family called Brian was making her do sexual things against her will. He had told her that if she told anyone they wouldn't believe her and she would be put into care. It had been happening virtually every week since she was ten.

Christine, another of the girls, was living with a violent father; since her mother had left he had regularly beaten her and her brothers. To the outside world they were the perfect family. Living in a big house with a big car, but to Christine, her father's temper was something to be feared.

Lucy was the least frightening of the trio, but she also had problems. I knew she had been a fat child and due to peer pressure she had become bulimic. It was a secret even her two closest friends were unaware of.

I remember Olivia asking me if I was certain of these things. It wasn't that she was questioning my honesty; I knew there was more to it than that, but it would be the following day at school at approximately eleven o'clock before I found out what.

I knew Olivia was very good friends with the headmistress, she'd told me when I first arrived. However I had no idea she was about to open a big can of worms when I was called to her office that morning. To my surprise, Olivia was there. She had told the headmistress what I'd told her the previous night about the girls. I was amazed the headmistress didn't have me expelled, but whatever Olivia had told her must have worked because she asked me if I would have the courage to tell her what I'd told Olivia.

We were asked to wait outside when the three girls were brought into the office. We could hear the headmistress talking; she was telling the girls that some upsetting information about them had been brought to her attention. In the event of the information carrying some clout, she would endeavour to change the girls' situations. I'm not entirely sure what she said after that as she took each one of them separately to an adjoining room. All I remember from that day was each girl came out crying.

It was several days later when I was summoned back to the headmistress's office.

She asked me to sit down before she spoke.

"I don't truly understand how you knew the things you knew Angel, but Olivia can be very persuasive, so on this occasion I took a chance on what she believes in and it paid off. As a school head, I see lots of children who come from dysfunctional families but unless they talk to me about it, I'm virtually powerless to help. What you told Olivia about those girls was in fact the truth. Can I assume what I'm about to tell you now will remain just between us?"

I nodded.

"I'm happy to let you know the man you named as Brian has in fact been arrested and will be charged. Social Services are now helping Christine and her family and Lucy is going to get the professional help she needs for her bulimia. Of course I will deny ever having this conversation and under normal circumstances I would never be so unprofessional as to talk to a pupil this way, but I've known Olivia a long time and she wanted you to know. Which leaves me one more thing to ask, how did you know Angel, you're not even friendly with them?"

The look on her face was priceless when I told her a spirit named Johnathan told me.

After that day the headmistress took a liking to me and often called me to her office to ask how things were going for me. She also made a point every time of telling how well I could do academically; I was a very bright girl.'

Linda thought about the girl who had written the diary. Her heart was heavy to think that some foster parents were obviously only doing it for money. She also thought about the spirits Angel had written about. Since moving into number 16, she had often noticed strange things. On occasion when they first moved in, she would mention them to Derek, but he would always say it was her imagination. He never believed in that type of thing and she knew he'd never change. Very often she felt someone was watching her when she was alone. Things seemed to mysteriously move, yet she remembered exactly where she'd left the item only to find it somewhere different. The one place in the house she wasn't really comfortable was the cellar, although she put that down to it always feeling cold.

Closing the diary she looked at her watch and decided it was too late to continue clearing the attic. She made her way back downstairs.

KAREN CLOW

CHAPTER 2

In the days that followed, Linda found herself hurrying through her chores and looking after Derek so she could read the diary.

That morning after breakfast she had cleared up and when Derek dozed off around eleven, she poured a coffee and sat down to read while he napped.

'The first six months at Olivia's were simply wonderful for me. The school bullies left me alone and even included me in some school projects. Olivia and I went shopping together like a regular mother and daughter every Saturday, unless we had to work in her book shop. She even took me to the spiritualist's church. Oh how I welcomed those trips as we would always stay behind afterwards to talk to the psychics and mediums who had given their time to people that evening. Through Olivia, I became friendly with several of them over time. Unlike most people I'd encountered, each one encouraged me to learn more about my abilities. Olivia even invited one or two round to the house for coffee and a chat about me being psychic.

One lady, Joyce, became a very close friend to both of us, often giving Olivia messages from her late husband, Charles.

Joyce was down to earth and, in my eyes, no less than an angel herself. She helped me to understand why I was different and how best to use my gift. Although I was too young when I first met her to attend séances, she explained in depth how they worked so that by the time I reached eighteen I would be ready. However, I've since learnt that when dealing with the spirit world no matter how much you prepare yourself, there are some things you'll never be ready for.

It was a relief to be able to be myself. Johnathan would appear regularly when I was alone. Often he would say things which I really didn't understand about how he would always watch over me and if a time came when I really needed him, he would be there. He would talk about spirits and how, to them, I was like a bright light, but along with lost souls seeking my help I would encounter evil. I never elaborated on exactly what he meant, simply because I didn't want to look stupid as I didn't understand. After each meeting I would practise my abilities and talk to spirits.

Time drifted on and my first eighteen months at Olivia's passed with ease. Were it not for the fact that we share no similarities in looks, her being slightly plump with blonde hair and me being tall and thin with black hair, people would have thought she was my real mum, to me she was.

I was approaching my GCSEs my best subjects being English, Maths and Art. I knew I would pass with flying colours after Joyce told me one evening when she came to visit. That wasn't the only thing she told me.

As we sat chatting over a cuppa she started talking about spirits and especially the old lady who shared the house with us. I'd seen the old lady from the very first night I moved in, although it had been several weeks before I plucked up the courage to tell 'mum' as I now referred to Olivia. Much to my surprise mum, in a rather blasé manner, told me she was also aware of her and had been since buying the house. Unlike most of the other spirits I'd encountered, the old lady never spoke or tried to communicate with me in any way. I asked Joyce if she knew why. I was shocked when she said she feared me. I asked her why, as I meant her no harm. I can remember exactly what she said.

"I've wondered that too Angel" said Joyce with a look of curiosity, "in all the time I've been calling here not once has she tried to communicate. In fact the only time I truly feel her presence is when Charles is here. It's almost as though she's watching him."

Before mum or I could reply the lights suddenly started flickering and a strange tapping sound could be heard. It sounded as though it was coming from under the floor. Then from out of nowhere I heard Charles's voice say 'help me Angel.'

I remember looking at Joyce who had obviously heard him too, but to our surprise so had mum. We talked about what we'd heard, but we didn't understand why Charles had asked for my help. Eventually we all agreed it may have just been a coincidence or another spirit passing through.

Despite the length of time I'd lived with Olivia, she had never asked me how I knew I had the gift. That evening was to change that. Along with Joyce, she listened as I talked about my earlier life.

In the early days, I thought everyone had a friend like Johnathan. I discovered the hard way they didn't, after the families I lived with forbade me to mention him. There were lots of times when I didn't need to ask Johnathan questions, I simply knew when things would happen. The one thing I'd never told anyone was that I could move things just by concentrating on them. Ironically that evening I decided I could talk about it. Neither of them looked surprised. It was Joyce's curiosity that finally got the better of her and she asked me to demonstrate my powers. I laughed and told her to look up. There hovering above her head was a photo of Charles and Olivia. Even mum looked a little shell shocked.

Finally, I had people in my life who loved me for who I was. They didn't judge me or think I was a freak. To me it was just something I could do. I never saw it as anything unusual or great, but to them it clearly was.

Joyce went on to ask me about Johnathan. I could never remember a time in my life when he wasn't with me. They asked me to describe him. I said he was a bit younger than me with golden hair and liquid blue eyes. He was very handsome, but for me, his wings were the most amazing things.

"Wings?" said Joyce looking stunned "spirits don't have wings Angel."

I told her I knew that and Johnathan was in fact an angel. He'd told me he had been sent back to earth to watch over me. He didn't always have wings, sometimes he looked like a regular man. I'll never forget the look on their faces as they sat staring at me with their mouths open.

Joyce couldn't explain why I seemed to have my own angel, but nor did she question it.

Then mum asked me if I'd ever felt afraid.

"Oh yes" was my reply, "many times."

There had been one night about six months before I moved in with mum; I had been woken by something touching me. At first I thought I'd been dreaming, but then I saw it. A grotesque figure sitting on the edge of my bed, it was staring at me. I was frozen with fear and quickly hid under the duvet and begged Johnathan to help me and make it go away. I laid there clutching at the duvet. I could hear horrible noises and feel it moving on my bed then it stopped and I heard Johnathan's voice.

Mum asked if I knew what it was.

I didn't, but Johnathan had said something strange to me. He told me to remember it as it had made itself known to me. I didn't really understand so I just nodded.

With Joyce and mum, I found myself talking freely about everything that I'd always feared talking about. To me, having people who didn't treat me like a freak was a truly magical experience.

Joyce stayed with us until eleven that evening talking about things that to her were wonderful and not the taboo subject I'd been made to think they were.'

CHAPTER 3

Linda felt a chill around her shoulders, she hadn't realised how long she'd been in the attic sorting stuff out that evening. The time was after nine and the night air was cold.

Derek was just stirring as she made her way into the lounge.

Smiling at her he focused his eyes and asked what the book was. Knowing he held a very dim view of psychics and such like, she told a little white lie and said it was an old diary of a young girl she'd found in the attic.

Making him a cup of tea she sat and talked to him, asking how he was feeling.

"Tired" was his reply.

Despite having slept for three hours he felt exhausted. It wouldn't be long before he went to bed.

Curiously, he asked her what was written in the diary. Trying to make light of it she told him a girl called Angel, who had lived there years ago, thought the house was haunted. Laughing he said the girl was probably on drugs. Linda neither agreed nor disagreed, she simply grinned. Her gut instinct was telling her Angel was genuine, but she knew her husband wouldn't agree.

They chatted until after ten then Derek retired for the night, telling Linda not to be too late to bed.

The moment he left, she opened the diary again and began reading.

'Despite the wonderful evening I'd had with mum and Joyce earlier that week when I went to bed that night the old woman was to make herself known to me.

I had just got into my pyjamas when someone pushed me. It wasn't a friendly push like Johnathan would do; there was real force behind it. So much so, I tumbled backwards onto the bed. In the few seconds it took me to regain my composure the old lady appeared. Her face was craggy and old. She was dressed in black and her grey hair was held firm in a bun. Trying to show no fear, I asked her what she wanted.

With an evil look in her eyes she stated I must leave her house. I wasn't welcome there. Standing my ground, I said it wasn't her house anymore and I wasn't going anywhere. It was then she rushed at me, her hands outstretched like claws. Her nails were long and discoloured as were her teeth. In that moment she grabbed me, only to let me go when Jonathan's voice said "Let her go, be gone woman! Be gone!"

Instantly she seemed to glide quickly away from me as she hissed at Johnathan.

I was shaking as I asked him what had just happened.

"I'll always be here to protect you Angel, but you must be strong. Never show her any fear."

Before I could ask him what he'd meant, he was gone. Mum heard me calling him and came into the room. Her first reaction was how cold it was and that maybe the radiator wasn't working. When she looked at me, she knew something had happened.

Suddenly I felt fearful that if I told her what the old woman had said she may want me to leave. I should have known better, but fear is a powerful weapon and I'd had previous foster mothers who gained my confidence through being nice then without hesitation had me moved. So I told mum I wasn't feeling well.

I spent the night in mum's room, but never told her what had happened.

Over breakfast the next morning she told me about a man who she thought liked her. He had become a regular visitor to the book shop she owned in town.

When I asked if his name was Martin, she grinned and nodded. I went on to tell her she was right and the books he purchased were actually stored in a box in his garage.

I knew Martin was a genuine man who really liked mum and I was happy for her.'

Linda looked at the clock, the time was approaching midnight. Placing the diary down on the coffee table she readied herself for bed. After checking the house was securely locked she made herself a drink and headed upstairs. She did have an eerie sense that someone was watching her, but put it down to reading about the old woman and letting her imagination get the better of her.

Entering the bedroom quietly so as not to disturb Derek; she wasn't surprised to find him awake. He'd had trouble sleeping over the last months. She offered to go and make him a mug of hot chocolate in the hope it may help him sleep, but he declined stating he felt nauseous.

They laid there talking for a while before he finally dozed off.

Lovingly, she pulled the duvet up over him and snuggled down next to him. Lying there with her arm wrapped around him, she prayed he would feel better and be the healthy man he once was.

He was still asleep the next morning when she got up; she didn't want to wake him as she knew he'd had a restless night.

Thirty minutes later she was sitting at the kitchen table eating a slice of toast and drinking a cup of tea. Opening

Angel's diary she began reading. It was like one of those crime thrillers she just couldn't put down.

Continuing from where she'd finished the previous night she carried on reading.

'Since my encounter with the old lady I felt a little uneasy, but as the weeks passed the feeling subsided. I was still aware of her presence, but she never showed herself again.

Since the night Charles had asked for my help I had tried to make contact with him, but he never came through. I had noticed that whenever I tried to contact him the old lady's presence was stronger. I could smell her perfume; it was thick and smelled stale. I couldn't help but think maybe Joyce was right; she didn't want Charles to communicate with us. I had been able to make contact with several other spirits in the house. In particular a young boy named Joseph, although I nicknamed him Joey and he seemed to like that. He had been seven when he died of TB back in the 1930's. His family had lived in a portion of the house, but moved shortly after his death. Joey was very mischievous, often moving my personal items from the dresser. I wanted to reunite him with his family, but he was reluctant to go into the light. For the time being he would be a welcome guest in our house.

That evening we went to the spiritual church. I remember being excited because a new medium was going to do clairvoyance. He was a renowned medium who travelled the country giving much of his time to the church. We had arranged to meet Joyce there at six thirty. A new medium always pulled in a bigger crowd and that evening was no exception. All the regular faces were there along with several new ones. Joyce had saved us a seat near the back.

By seven o'clock the hall was packed.

Helen, the local lady who ran the church gave a short speech welcoming Trevor Bates, the medium for the evening. He was exactly what I'd imagined him to be. In his sixties, tall and very distinguished looking with silver grey hair and a neatly trimmed goatee type beard of the same colour. Olivia said he'd no doubt been a very handsome man in his younger days.

After picking out several people and giving them messages from the other side, he walked up the aisle to the row where we were sitting. He smiled at me and told me I had a birthday coming very soon. He was right; I was going to be fifteen the coming week. I smiled and nodded, but it was what he said next that surprised me. He told me my aura was so bright he'd never seen one like it and that something unexpected and truly wonderful was going to happen on my birthday. Although I was thrilled to even get picked out, meeting him afterwards was to be a strange event.

It was as we sat drinking tea that he approached our table and asked if he could join us. Joyce's face lit up as she replied of course he could and how wonderful he'd been that evening.

After thanking her, he sat down. We sat in awe as he talked about how he'd realised he was a medium at a young age and how it had affected his life. Then he looked directly at me and asked if he could speak freely.

I nodded.

He looked sad as he talked about my life and some of the horrible people I'd encountered, but he was glad to add those days were behind me and the best were yet to come. He looked sincere when he told me there was a special place for me in the world and I would help many, many people. Then he stopped, looked at mum and said he'd had a message for me when we were upstairs, but he'd hesitated to repeat it in front of everyone. Would it be alright with mum if he told me now?

Mum nodded and said of course, as she would assume it was something important.

"Angel," he said looking back at me "you have a very special gift, you know that don't you? I'm so happy things have changed for you now and you have wonderful people in your life. The message I received was from your mother."

I remember a feeling of sadness. I never knew my real mother was dead. I always thought I'd been abandoned. Olivia reached over and, holding my hand, asked if I was ok.

I was fine, just a bit shocked. Trevor continued.

"The message I have is very important Angel. In a few years from now someone will come to you for help. You will be reluctant to help, but people's lives will depend on you. It will not be easy, but your greatest battle has to be fought. I'm not entirely sure what that message relates to, so you can see why I hesitated to tell you upstairs. I hope I haven't worried you?"

I told him it was ok, although I didn't understand it either. We all laughed.

Trevor stayed and chatted to us for a few more minutes then went off to talk to other people who'd stayed behind for refreshments.

For a while we talked about the message until I told Joyce that mum was going on a date the following night with Martin. We all laughed when mum quickly said it wasn't a date, she had simply agreed to have dinner with him. Both Joyce and I knew Martin was meant to be in her life and in time they would be very happy. Just like mum, he'd been on his own for a few years after his wife left him for another man. I knew he felt responsible because he couldn't give her a child, but I also knew she would have left him anyway. She just wasn't the marrying kind.'

Linda stopped reading when she heard Derek moving about upstairs. Assuming he would come down within a few minutes, she put the kettle on for a fresh pot of tea. A short time passed when she thought she heard what sounded like him dragging a piece of furniture across the floor. Wondering why he would be doing that she went upstairs to investigate.

Her first thought as she entered the bedroom was how cold it was. Seeing that Derek appeared to have gone back to bed and was fast asleep, she walked over and felt the radiator. It was warm, yet the room was freezing.

Quietly leaving him to sleep, she made her way back downstairs.

It was an hour later when he came down and looking pale, told her he didn't want any breakfast as he felt sick.

Placing a cup of tea down in front of him, she asked if he wanted to go back to bed. When he shook his head, she asked him what he'd moved when he got up earlier. Looking baffled he stated he'd only just woken up and hadn't been out of bed.

"Really, but I heard you moving about in the bedroom" said Linda looking confused.

"Wasn't me, like I said I've only just got up. Old houses make strange noises. I've worked on enough of them over the years to know that."

Not convinced by his theory, she tried to put it out of her mind as they talked about his health.

Later that morning, with Derek watching the sports on TV, Linda did some housework. She had hoped he'd want lunch, but he still felt sick so he went back to bed for the afternoon.

Deciding it wasn't worth cooking just for her, she made a sandwich and sat down to eat it as she continued to read Angel's diary.

The next entry was the day of Angel's fifteenth birthday.

'Opened my presents with mum this morning, my favourite being the beautiful gold bracelet she bought for me. It had my name engraved on a small heart attached to it. There were some chocolates and a scarf from Joyce and some more sweets and a book from my friends at the church.

Sitting there with mum, I felt blessed to have such wonderful people in my life. It was then I thought about what Trevor had said at the church a week earlier, when he'd told me something special would happen. I asked mum if she thought it was because I had such lovely presents.

"I'm glad you like your presents Angel," said Olivia "but I hope what Trevor was referring to is what I'm about to ask you. How would you feel about me adopting you?"

I just burst into tears and hugged her. I was so overwhelmed; I couldn't even get my words out through my crying.

Trevor had been right; it was a truly wonderful and magical birthday.

When I finally calmed down, I told mum I loved her and I was the happiest I'd ever been. She joked she was only doing it so she'd have someone to leave the house to.

It was as we both started laughing that something happened. A vase that was housed on the sideboard suddenly flew across the room and smashed into the wall behind us.

We both sat nervously looking at one another. Mum said maybe someone in the house objected to her adopting me, but she'd prefer to believe it was Charles showing us he was happy about it.

I knew it wasn't Charles, it was the old woman. It was then I plucked up the courage to tell mum the truth about the night the old lady attacked me. She looked sad that I'd left it so long to tell her, but it hadn't changed her mind over adopting me, whether the old lady liked it or not.

It was at that moment we heard loud banging coming from upstairs. I knew the old lady was angry and I think mum did too. Thankfully it stopped a few moments later.

Mum then confessed to me she'd had dealings with the old lady in the past. When she and Charles first bought the house everything seemed fine at first then mum had started to sense things. At first she ignored it and told herself old houses do strange things to your imagination. They creak and groan and even more so when people start knocking walls and things down to accommodate the modernisations.

It was after Charles's accident all the supposedly strange things stopped.

We talked about Charles. It was clear from the way mum spoke she had been so in love with him. There were framed pictures of him all around the house. Mum fetched a box from her room which was filled with old photos. For ages we looked through them with mum telling me who all the people were. It was as she neared the bottom of the box, I saw something which sent a chill down my spine.

It was a picture of Charles painting the outside of the house. Looking closer, I could see the old lady looking out, from what was now mum's bedroom window. I had an overwhelming feeling of evil. I pointed her out to mum who, looking shocked, said she hadn't noticed it before.

We continued to talk about Charles and how he'd been looking forward to getting the house back to its former glory and start a family. His plan had been to have four children.

Mum looked sad as she said they'd been trying for a baby before the accident. She contributed her lack of conception to the bouts of ill health Charles had experienced prior to his death. For several months he'd suffered from fatigue, nausea and dizzy spells. Yet the doctors had failed to find the cause. Mum believed it was a dizzy spell that led him to fall off the roof, although he'd insisted he felt ok that day.

My feeling on his health was it was connected to the house, or more probably the old lady. I never said anything to mum though. Number 16 had been her home for years and she loved the house. Nothing I could tell her would bring Charles back and she felt akin to the house because she felt he was still there with her.'

Linda stopped reading. Could the house have something to do with Derek's mystery illness? She wanted to read more, but she could hear him calling her. Knowing he'd gone back up to bed for a nap, she hurriedly made her way to their bedroom.

On opening the door she felt an icy cold wind rush past her. For a moment it stopped her dead in her tracks. Then she saw Derek sitting on the edge of the bed clutching his stomach. Rushing over to him, she asked him what was wrong. He had terrible stomach cramps.

Lifting the phone receiver from the bed side cabinet, she dialled the doctor's number, but the phone was dead. Telling him she'd use her mobile, she quickly made her way back downstairs. Remembering she'd left her phone in her bag, she scurried through the contents but it wasn't there. She looked everywhere she could think it might be. Several minutes past, Derek was calling her and still she couldn't find her phone.

Rushing back upstairs, she could see he was getting worse by the second. His phone battery was dead, so without any more thought she helped him off the bed, down the stairs and into the car.

The hospital was a fifteen minute drive away and traffic was quite heavy.

Twenty minutes later they arrived at the A&E department. Linda rushed inside and told the receptionist her husband was desperately ill in the car. Minutes later he was being taken into the assessment unit, where a doctor was waiting to examine him.

Linda spoke about his recent decline in health as the doctor examined her husband. Unhappy with what she said, the doctor wanted to admit him so he could book scans and tests for the next day. He seemed curious as to what Derek may have eaten or drank as his symptoms were consistent with poisoning. He hadn't eaten anything since the previous day and the pains were actually going off a bit since arriving at the hospital.

After Derek was given a morphine injection to ease the pain, he fell asleep. Linda used the pay phone to ring her sons and tell them their dad was being admitted.

A nurse told Linda she would better off going home as he would probably sleep for hours.

Reluctantly, after telling the nurse to call her should there be any developments with her husband, she left.

Mark, her son, pulled into the driveway seconds after her. Like the rest of the family he'd been concerned over his dad's health and couldn't settle at home. His wife, Sophie, had told him to call the hospital, which he had, only to be told his mum had left and his dad was sleeping.

Linda made a pot of tea and talked about his dad. It was then she mentioned about the diary she'd found in the attic and how she now thought the house could be haunted and connected to his dad's health.

Mark laughed and said she was losing the plot.

Undeterred, she continued to tell him about the similarities between what happened to Olivia Moon's late husband and Derek.

Mark tried to convince her it was nothing more than a coincidence. Linda wasn't convinced and began going into detail as to Angel's accounts of things that happened at the house. Still Mark didn't think it was connected to his dad's health, but he listened as his mum talked. His advice was simple, don't tell his dad what she thought, but just wait and see what the next day's tests reveal.

Just before he left, his mobile rang. It was his brother Michael wanting to know what was happening with his dad. Mark explained he was just leaving the house and he would call him when he got home.

Kissing Linda affectionately on the cheek, he told her to rest and let him know if there was any news from the hospital.

Five minutes later she was alone.

At a loose end without Derek, she poured a cup of tea and sat in the lounge to drink it. Flicking through the TV channels she settled on a film, but she just couldn't get Angel's diary out of her thoughts. Finally, she picked it up and began reading.

'Mum took me to a solicitor this afternoon after school. The appointment was to talk about the adoption and what it would entail. I was so excited I was trembling. For over thirty minutes the solicitor talked about what would be required by law for my adoption to go ahead. It was clear from mum's responses none of it would be a problem. We signed some papers before we left and the solicitor said he'd be in touch soon.

Mum suggested we should go out to eat that evening as a sort of celebration. She invited Joyce to join us at Mario's restaurant at seven thirty.

I'd never been out to eat with any of my previous carers, but mum had taken me several times and I really enjoyed it.

The time was around five thirty by the time we arrived home from the solicitors. Mum commented that she thought the heating must be playing up as the house was freezing when we walked in. I had a strange feeling it had nothing to do with the heating, but something or someone in the house. Nevertheless, I agreed with her that maybe getting an engineer to check it over was a good idea.

We left the house at seven for the restaurant. Mum always left the porch and hallway lights on when we went out at night. Her theory was people would think we were home and therefore not break in.

After a glorious meal, we returned home around nine thirty. Joyce had opted to come with us at mum's invitation for coffee.

As we parked the car, I asked mum if she'd left the upstairs lights on. She hadn't, yet the top half of the house was lit up.

We entered quietly in case an intruder was in the house, but after a check round it was deemed safe by mum.

We sat in the lounge talking to Joyce about the adoption, despite it having been the main topic over dinner. I had an overbearing feeling that we were being watched and unless I was wrong, so did Joyce. It wasn't long before she said something to mum about the recent problems with the heating. She even said she felt the cold was more likely to be connected to the spirit world. We were both a little shocked when mum agreed and asked Joyce what she suggested doing about it.

Her advice was to hold a séance or similar to ask why the spirits were acting up. She felt it might be a good idea to ask a couple of psychics from the church to join them. I asked if I could be present. Not that I wanted to partake, more as a spectator.

Mum's attitude was as long as it was safe she didn't have a problem with me being there. Joyce agreed and said she'd try and arrange it for the coming Friday, as mum had a date with Martin on the Saturday.'

Linda's tummy rumbled, she hadn't eaten for hours. Making herself some soup, she sat at the kitchen table and thought about the diary while she ate.

The time was just after ten that evening when she remembered she couldn't find her phone. Checking the house phone, it appeared to be working. From memory she rang her mobile number and instantly felt relieved to hear it ringing. Following the sound, it led her into the lounge and directly to the DVD cabinet which the TV was housed on. Opening the cupboard doors, she rang her number again and was shocked to find the phone right at the back behind the row of DVDs. How it got there was a mystery, she knew she hadn't put it there.

Checking the TV was off, she decided to take the diary up to bed and read more.

Once settled down in the duvet, Linda opened the diary.

'Since the night we went for dinner at the restaurant, things seemed to change within the house. Joey, the little boy, didn't visit me and things in the house seemed out of sync. We had bouts of flashing lights which lasted anywhere from a few seconds to over an hour. Footsteps were heard on the stairs and in the bedrooms. We had also started to experience cold spots. These were areas in the house where the air would feel freezing cold. Joyce explained to us they were usually associated with where a spirit was. For me the worse thing was the awful smell that seemed to emanate from room to room, although mum couldn't smell it at first. For two consecutive nights, I woke up almost choking on the disgusting aroma. I will never forget the look on Joyce's face when I told her about it. I listened with a kind of dread as she explained that bad smells were often connected with bad spirits, like that of the old lady. Despite being what I now know is termed as a natural medium, who was born with the gift of seeing and talking to spirits, I realised there was so much I still needed to learn. Fortunately I had a natural instinct regarding people and it had never let me down. I also had Johnathan who had explained so many things to me and helped me accept what I am.'

Linda could feel her eyes getting heavy as she read. Although she had the feeling she needed to learn more about Angel and the house, she knew she needed to sleep. Placing the diary on the bedside table, she turned off the lamp and snuggled down under the duvet.

Despite her tiredness, she couldn't stop thinking about Derek and how ill he had looked earlier.

Something in her mind was convincing her that Derek's illness was connected to the house, or the spirits dwelling there. Her son's words were running through her mind as she laid there. Maybe she was reading more into it because of Angel's diary. Yet try as she might to consider that it was purely coincidence, she couldn't believe it. For whatever reason, she believed she was meant to find Angel's diary. For a brief moment, she considered the possibility that maybe someone in the house was helping her and that's why she'd found it.

At that precise moment she felt a breeze on her face. Feeling afraid, she peered out from over the duvet and scanned the darkness, almost expecting to see something. There was nothing there. Nervously she snuggled back down, then she heard a child's voice clearly say 'find Angel.'

With her heart pounding she lay frozen with fear. It was several moments later before she plucked up the courage, be it all from under the duvet, to ask if it was Joey.

'Yes' whispered the child's voice again. Then it sounded panicked and said 'she's here, she's here!'

Terrified, Linda thought she would have a heart attack her heart was beating so fast. Then she heard a loud bang like a door slamming and Joey screamed. It was then her mothering instinct kicked in. Throwing the duvet back she got out of bed, but the room was empty.

Terrified, she made her way to the door and into the hallway. Turning the light on she thought she glimpsed the figure of a child hurrying down the stairs; something dark and almost invisible seemed to be floating along the hall behind him. Moments later the apparitions had gone.

Too afraid to return to bed, she made her way downstairs. Turning all the lights on before entering the lounge she sat down on the sofa.

All night she sat there until she finally dozed off around three that morning.

Waking when the sun began flooding the house, she didn't feel so afraid. It was an hour later at seven o'clock before she ventured upstairs to wash and dress.

Collecting Angel's diary from the bedside, she intended to read as much as possible in the hope of finding some answers.

At eight that morning she rang the hospital to ask after Derek. She felt relieved to hear the pains had gone, but he would be kept in for some tests which the doctor had arranged for that morning. All being well, he would be discharged later that afternoon.

She sat at the kitchen table and opened the diary.

'It was Friday, the day of the séance. Despite wanting to sit in on it, I was really nervous. Joyce told me to sit away from her and the others, who were sitting around mum's table. I opted to sit on a chair several feet away.

The two mediums from the church arrived just before seven. I'd met one of them, Sheila, before. With her was a man named Alan. I'd never met him, but I'd seen him at the church and Joyce had often talked about him. He was around mid-sixties with the most amazing green eyes.

Joyce asked mum to dim the lights.

Then the four of them held hands and Alan asked if there were any spirits present. Only a few seconds passed then Joey could be heard giggling, although he didn't manifest.

"Is that you Joey?" said Alan.

Almost instantly there was a light tap on the table.

"Thank you for joining us Joey. Is there anyone else with you?"

Another knock on the table clearly meant a yes.

"Is it the old lady?"

Two knocks, indicating no.

"Tell them not to be afraid Joey. We mean them no harm. Ask them to talk to us."

Another single knock.

From where I was sitting, I could see a young woman of about twenty starting to manifest behind Joyce. I felt a little nervous as she glided effortlessly towards me.

Alan and the others, including mum, could see her by the time she reached me.

Strangely, when she stood in front of me and held out her hand, I didn't feel afraid. I knew she wouldn't hurt me. The others sat silently as I took her hand. Suddenly I was in a place that I recognised as the house, but back in time. The furnishings were from years ago; like those you see in pictures of Victorian times. A man was slumped in a chair gravely ill. The old woman was pouring something from a small bottle onto a spoon. Was I actually seeing the old woman when she was alive and living in the house. There was a wedding portrait on the mantle of her and the ill man.

The entity of the young woman who'd taken me there appeared in the scene, she was their maid.

"Mam" she said to the old woman, "you must call the doctor. Your medicine isn't helping him, it's killing him."

"Go back to your chores Mary and don't ever forget your place again" snapped the old woman "you will never speak of this! Do you understand?"

Curtseying, Mary nodded and left the room. I was instantly teleported to the kitchen where I watched and listened as Mary told the cook the mistress was poisoning the master. Before the cook had time to reply, the old woman entered and ordered Mary to her room. She then forbade the cook to listen to or repeat anything Mary had said.

Moments later, I was in a dimly lit, barely furnished room in the attic of the house. Mary was sitting on the bed crying. The door opened and in walked the old lady. She locked the door behind her and instantly ranted at Mary. I watched as Mary tried to defend herself against the physical blows the old lady was inflicting upon her as she ranted that she wasn't going to sit back and watch her husband leave her for another woman. The fight became intense. Mary was knocked to the floor, smashing her head against a large trunk. She was stunned, but breathing, as the old lady took a length of rope from another box and asphyxiated her with it before concealing her body inside the trunk.

My next memory after my vision was of mum gently tapping my face. I had passed out and fallen from the chair onto the floor. Helping me up, Joyce passed me a glass of water and asked me what happened. I talked them through the scene I had just witnessed.

Alan told me I'd channelled the spirit of Mary and at least now they knew why the old lady was there. It was clear she only wanted the men of the house and that's why Olivia's husband had suffered the type of symptoms connected to poisoning. He went on to tell me that for a young girl I was a very powerful medium to be able to do what I had and that's why the old lady feared me. Olivia questioned what he'd said and wanted assurance that I was safe. His feelings were, with Johnathan watching over me and providing I didn't do anything silly, I'd be fine.

Joyce suggested making a pot of tea and discussing everything.

Five minutes later, everyone was sitting at the table listening to Alan talk. His first thought was to do some research on the old lady before they decided how best to deal with the situation.

Everyone agreed.

He advised me until he knew more about the old lady; I shouldn't try and contact any spirits as there was a strong chance she would come through. He would leave it to Joyce to arrange a meeting with him in a week's time.

When everyone had finally left for the evening, mum suggested us looking on the computer for any information.

To our horror there were several articles referring to the house and the strange deaths connected to it. It charted several strange events from the nineteenth century. There was even a picture of the old lady Agnes Tibbs and an article about how she'd been suspected of poisoning her husband. He was a prominent business man, Horace Tibbs, although she was never charged with his murder due to lack of evidence. A key witness, housemaid Mary Turner had mysteriously disappeared before the police had a chance to interview her. Five months after his death the case was closed when Agnes Tibbs was found dead in the house. She had hung herself.'

Linda hadn't realised how much time had passed until the phone startled her at eleven that morning.

It was her daughter-in-law Sophie, calling to check she was home as she wanted to pop in for a quick visit.

After telling her she'd be happy to see her, Linda ended the call and put the kettle on.

Ten minutes later Sophie arrived to a readymade pot of tea. The two ladies talked about Derek and how Linda was hoping he'd be allowed home later that day.

Sophie said Mark had mentioned about the diary. Linda went into greater detail about the strange diary she'd found in the attic. Unlike her son, Mark, she felt it was relevant to what was happening to Derek, especially since the night she heard Joey speak.

To her relief, Sophie agreed with her, she had always been drawn to the supernatural despite Mark's mockery of it. Linda was a little surprised when she offered to help her find Angel Moon.

The two ladies debated whether or not they should and finally agreed it couldn't do any harm, but where to start was the question Linda was quick to ask.

Sophie asked her if anyone in the Avenue had lived there a long time. If they had, maybe they would know.

There was an elderly gentleman who lived a couple of houses down who Linda believed had been there a long time. She'd spoken to him when they first moved in and he gave her the impression he'd been there years.

Linda was just about to take Sophie's advice and go over to see the gentleman when the phone rang, it was the hospital. She was disappointed to hear that Derek would be kept in for another day. Although he was feeling much better the doctor required more tests. The good news was she could visit him that afternoon and, all being well, he could go home the following morning after the doctor had done his rounds.

Seeing the disappointment on Linda's face, Sophie said it was better for him to stay in hospital and have the tests rather than keep going back. Hoping to take her mind off Derek, she suggested Linda going to see the gentleman down the road.

Despite being a little reluctant, Linda decided to go after telling herself it couldn't do any harm. When she had met the old man before he had been very friendly, although she wasn't sure how he'd feel about what she needed to ask.

Her fears were unfounded when five minutes later she rang his doorbell and Victor, Mr Richardson, readily invited her in. Linda declined and explained that her daughter-in-law was waiting for her, but they would love for him to come to her house and have a cuppa. Victor happily accepted her invitation.

Back at the house, both ladies instantly warmed to Victor. The elderly man spoke with fondness about Olivia and how he'd missed her when she'd moved twelve years earlier.

Sophie was happy listening to him talk about all the people who had resided in the Avenue over the thirty one year's he'd lived there, but she wanted to know about Angel and soon she would have to go home. Without wasting another minute, she asked him outright if he knew where Olivia had moved to.

It was then his face changed to one of sadness and concern.

"Not far as it happens" he said "I see her from time to time. She pops round sometimes when she's been baking; she knows I love fruit cake. I was happy for her and Angel when she married Martin, he's a good man, but I was sad to see them move. Although after what happened I could understand it."

"What happened?" asked Sophie curiously.

"It was after Martin became ill and then that awful accident with their friend. Oh what was her name? Joyce, that was it, Joyce. A nice lady, she was always visiting them."

Sophie asked what happened to her.

"She fell down the stairs and broke her neck. It was after that they talked about moving, although there were a lot of people who questioned what had happened."

Victor noticed that both women looked baffled, they obviously had no idea what he was talking about.

"I take it you don't know?"

They both shook their heads.

"Well the night of the accident, Angel ended up in hospital too. If memory serves me correct, she'd fallen down the stairs with Joyce. I went to see her; by God she was in a state. Her face looked like she'd been ten rounds with a heavy weight boxer. She had a broken arm and some fractures to her legs; she was in plaster for weeks. Understandably, she didn't want to come back to the house. They moved into Martin's house the day she was discharged from hospital. The house stood empty for a few years until Phil and Denise, the Duckworth's bought it. They were a nice couple, but they only stayed a couple of years after Phil died. Olivia told me once the house was haunted. Of course I was a real Doubting Thomas back then. That was until the day Angel called round to me with some cakes."

"Can we assume that something happened with her?" asked Linda "only I found an old diary of hers in the attic and to say it's intrigued me would be an understatement."

"Ah yes, Angel is different alright, but in a good way. I'd heard rumours about her being weird when Olivia first took her in. Olivia herself even told me that Angel had special gifts, but like I say, I just took it all with a pinch of salt back then. That changed the day she called round. She was about twenty at the time, a very pretty girl. Olivia would always stay for a cuppa so it seemed normal to extend Angel the same courtesy. It was while we sat chatting something happened. Angel said my wife Elsa was with us. Elsa had been dead for eight years and I was quick to tell her that although I didn't believe, I had often sensed Elsa. I can still see the smile on Angel's face when she stated Elsa was always there, as was our little Maggie. She was the stillborn baby we'd had. I knew I'd never told Olivia, but Angel knew things she couldn't possibly have known. I'm ashamed to say, but even then I still had my doubts, until my lovely Elsa kissed my face. Then I saw her, she reached out her hand and touched me."

Linda and Sophie watched as a tear ran down Victor's cheek.

When Linda said she would like to meet Angel, it was with delight when he said she ran a shop in town. It had originally been Olivia's book shop, but after she married Martin she worked in his business with him. The shop was a gift to Angel. You can't miss it; it's the only one like it. The name over the door 'All things Spiritual' tells you you've got the right place. You can also find her two evenings a week down at the spiritual church, the one in the High Street. Whenever I'm in town I pop in to the shop and say hello. Nine times out of ten, she gives me a message from Elsa. She's helped a lot of people over the years, everything from finding missing pets to talking to passed loved ones."

Both ladies were fascinated with what Victor had said and Linda had a feeling she was meant to meet Angel.

When Victor was leaving, Linda said he was always welcome to pop in for a cuppa.

After seeing him out, she made a fresh pot of tea and sat talking about Angel.

It was when she said "Maybe it's all a coincidence, but do you think there's a possibility Angel could help Derek?" that something strange happened.

There was a knock on the table and a tea cup moved across it. Then Joey's voice said the word 'Yes.'

Sophie sat riveted to the chair. The hair on her arms and neck were standing on end as she asked Linda if she'd imagined what had just happened.

"No I think that was Joey, he's a boy Angel wrote about in her diary. He's been to see me before; I get the feeling he wants to help us."

Instantly there was another knock on the table.

Although Sophie felt a little unnerved, she agreed with Linda. The knocking stopped after the ladies arranged to drive into town the following morning. Their intention was to see Angel. They also agreed it was probably best not to tell their husbands.

Being alone in the house that night Linda felt a little vulnerable, she wanted to read more of the diary, but decided against and settled for a romance novel. A couple of times she thought she heard children giggling and running up and down the stairs, but when she consciously listened she heard nothing.

It was almost midnight when she settled down to sleep. Much to her surprise looking at the clock the next morning, she had slept soundly all night.

KAREN CLOW

CHAPTER 4

Linda had rung the hospital at eight that morning and spoken to Derek. Thankfully, he was feeling much better and looking forward to coming home later that day. When he asked what she would be doing that morning, she told a white lie and said she was going shopping with Sophie after she'd dropped the kids at school.

The time was approaching eight thirty, Linda was ready but knowing Sophie would not be there till after nine, she poured a cuppa and opened Angel's diary.

'Alan had been busy since we saw him last week. Mum seemed worried when he told her what he'd discovered about the house. We already knew about the old lady and the other spirits in the house, but what he'd uncovered shocked us both. During the previous week he'd done some deep research and discovered things that didn't come up on our search. According to local gossip, it was believed that the house had been used for Devil worship. A man named Darby Fawkes was the original owner when it was built.

During his three year stay in the house, several strange and unexplained things happened. Darby was rarely seen; he was very reclusive. All that was known of him was he travelled extensively in Africa. When he left the house; he never took any of his furnishings or private possessions. He commissioned agents to remove everything and have it shipped to him. He would not be returning to England. After the first day of clearing the house, one agent refused to return after the packers called him in after finding the carcasses of dead animals, along with demonic drawings in the cellar.

Mum looked really worried until Alan reassured her it was probably exaggerated gossip. His primary concern was the old lady, Agnes Tibbs. He had read what she did and also had an account of the vision I'd had through Mary.'

Linda was just about to turn the page when Sophie pulled up outside and sounded her horn.

Placing the diary down, she grabbed her bag and jacket and left the house.

During the fifteen minute drive into town, Linda told her about the entry in the diary she had read that morning.

"Ooh err" said Sophie "sounds creepy, but I dare say that Alan fella was right, it was probably just idle gossip."

They looked for a parking space as they drove up the High Street, eventually finding one several shops away from Angel's.

A bell rang as they opened the shop door and entered. Several seconds passed then a young woman appeared. Linda knew instantly it was Angel. She was very attractive with black hair and eyes of the darkest brown. The shop was full of spiritual things from crystals, ornamental angels, books and tarot cards.

Angel smiled and asked if they were just browsing or if they'd come for a tarot reading.

Before Sophie could say anything, Linda asked if they had to book for a reading.

Normally they would, but it was their lucky day as Angel's next client had just rung and cancelled, so she was free and it was too late to call another client in.

Linda asked if Sophie could accompany her for the reading. Angel nodded as she locked the shop door and put a sign up which said 'reading in progress back in an hour.'

The two ladies followed her to a room at the back of the shop. There was a small table with two chairs and a green velvet table cloth draped over the table. A crystal ball, a pack of tarot cards and a small candle were housed on the table.

Angel lit the candle and shuffled the cards. Passing them to Linda, she asked if she had a piece of jewellery she could hold.

Removing her wedding ring, Linda handed it to her. Almost at the moment of touching it, Angel froze and handing it back said she was sorry, but she didn't feel she could read for her.

"You know why I'm here, don't you?" said Linda "please help us."

"I'm sorry I can't, you have no idea what you're asking of me."

Linda pleaded with her and expressed how ill her husband was. She feared for his life.

With a serious look, Angel said if she really loved her husband and wanted him to live they must leave the house.

Both ladies could see real fear on Angel's face as they begged her for help. Despite their pleading, she refused. It was only when Linda said Joey had helped her that Angel changed her stance.

Looking confused, Angel stated she believed Joey had gone into the light the night she left the house. She looked sad as Linda talked about the night Joey had visited her and the old woman tried to stop him.

They could see Angel was thinking about Joey as tears welled in her eyes.

It was when Linda begged her to help them, Angel wiped her eyes and almost commandingly said they shouldn't have come and she couldn't help them, but they must leave the house.

Their conversation was interrupted by someone knocking on the shop door.

"That will be my mum; she's forgotten her key again. I'm sorry I can't help you ladies. Just leave that house."

Angel walked out and seeing Olivia through the glass, smiled.

Olivia apologised, she thought Angel would have finished her reading and had simply left the closed sign up as they had arranged to go for lunch.

"It's ok mum, I'd finished. The ladies are just leaving."

Olivia could sense that all was not well, but she would wait to ask Angel. It was as the ladies approached the door, Linda explained why they'd gone there that morning in the hope Angel would help her. She'd never meant to upset her and she was sorry.

At a loss as to what she meant; Olivia looked at Angel.

"They live at number 16 mum."

Olivia's face changed instantly to one of sadness and shock.

For a few moments the shop fell under a cloak of complete silence. It was Sophie who broke the deadlock when, looking at Olivia, said she knew they shouldn't have come, but her father-in-law Derek was a good man and if they didn't do something, he was going to die. Everything they had was tied up in that house.

Angel interrupted and told Olivia she was going to get her bag and jacket. She left the ladies standing at the door.

"I'm sorry, my daughter cannot help you" said Olivia sympathetically. "We've put all that behind us now, but please take Angel's advice and leave that house. There is a presence of evil there beyond all comprehension. I can understand why you wanted to talk to Angel, but it's too painful for her; you have no idea what she went through. It almost cost her life. Please don't come back here, just leave that house."

Sophie explained how Linda had found Angel's diary and so many things had happened. They believed they were meant to find Angel.

"How much did you read?" said Angel as she entered the shop area.

"I read to where Alan was telling you about Darby Fawkes."

"Then you need to read more and maybe you'll understand why I can never go back to that house. I'm sorry, but we must go now, please excuse us."

Just as they were about to leave, curiosity got the better of Olivia and she asked how they knew where to find Angel. Linda explained it was the old man, Victor, who lived in the avenue.

Olivia immediately turned to Angel; the look on her face was one of complete disbelief and shock.

They talked about how Victor told them how Angel had contacted his wife.

"Victor passed away a couple of months ago" said Olivia.

Looking afraid, Sophie insisted there must be some mistake. After all, he'd sat in the kitchen drinking tea with them.

With a look of concern, Angel asked if they'd invited him into the house.

The ladies nodded and explained how Linda had gone over to his house and ended up bringing him back with her.

"I'd be surprised if it was Victor," said Angel raising her eyebrows "he hasn't passed over yet. Maybe someone is tricking you into getting me to go back. Now I must ask you to leave and please don't come here again. Just leave us alone. If you want your husband to survive go home and pack. I can't help you, I've said too much as it is."

Reluctantly the two ladies left the shop.

Thirty minutes later, the two were back at the house. It was clear they were both uneasy with what had been said about Victor. Maybe Angel was wrong and he had passed over. Sophie asked Linda if she thought it was best to listen to what Angel had said and leave the house.

Her reply was simple; they couldn't leave. Everything they'd worked for had been put into the house. They'd used all their savings to buy the materials to do it up. It was to be their dream home and, furthermore, Derek would never believe there was something there. There was also his failing health to consider, she doubted he could survive another move at that time, he was so weak.

Sophie started to cry, she couldn't bear what was happening to them or the fact that apart from her, no one in the family would listen to Linda. Not about to give up, she gave Linda her word she would help her. There must be other people like Angel who could help them. Her first thought was to look on the internet for a local medium that may be willing to help.

Despite Linda having no choice but to agree, she knew Derek would think she was wasting her time and probably tell her not to. Her thoughts on the matter were simple; they would have to arrange it for when he was out. That would be difficult as he was often too unwell to leave the house.

Sophie came up with a plan. What if she could talk Mark into taking him for a hospital appointment or take him out without telling him the real reason. She would simply use the ruse that Linda needed some space and it would be good for Derek to get out the house for a while, even if he didn't want to.

Linda nodded. She had relied on Angel helping them, but she had sensed real fear in both Angel and Olivia when they'd talked to them.

While she made tea, Sophie fired up the PC to search for help. It wasn't long before she came across a paranormal investigators site.

Giles Beauchamp was listed as a natural medium that specialised in hauntings.

Just as Linda put the tea mugs down on the table, Sophie emerged from the study carrying a piece of paper. Looking pleased with herself, she stated she'd found someone who sounded genuine, she suggested calling him.

Linda sat quietly as Sophie made the call.

As she listened she thought the conversation sounded promising, especially when Sophie explained he would have to come to the house when Derek was out.

Curious as to what had been said, the moment the call ended Linda asked her.

According to Sophie, Giles would only need a few days' notice as he didn't do much spiritual work now, he was semi-retired. He had two other mediums that often worked with him, so one or both may accompany him. His fee was fifty pounds for the first visit and twenty five thereafter, should he need to come back. He had built up quite a reputation over the years, having done TV and radio and been in several newspapers. Hopefully he would be able to help them.

CHAPTER 5

Despite feeling better whilst in hospital, in the two days since Derek had been discharged, his health had taken a turn for the worse. Unable to keep food down, he was feeling tired and nauseous most of the time.

Unbeknown to him, Linda had arranged a visit from Giles Beauchamp that evening, yet she was now doubtful as to whether Sophie's plan to get him to go and spend time with his son Mark at their house would happen.

Sophie had obviously done a convincing job on Mark. When he arrived at five thirty that evening to pick his dad up, it was clear to Linda he wasn't about to let Derek talk his way out of going back with him.

Finally, after Mark telling him that Michael was going to pop over for a cuppa with them around seven, Derek agreed to go.

Sophie left the children at home with the men so she could spend time with Linda and the paranormal investigators.

When she arrived, she could tell Linda was nervous about Giles coming. Reassuringly, Sophie said it would be fine and they had time for a cuppa before he was due to arrive.

They chatted while they waited. Linda told her she'd read a little more of the diary, although time had been limited with Derek feeling unwell. None of what she'd read had given her any insight into the evil presence that Olivia had mentioned other than the old lady; she would clearly need to read more.

She jumped when the doorbell rang just before seven.

"Calm down" giggled Sophie "it's probably that bloke, Giles."

Both ladies went to the door. It was indeed Giles, who quickly introduced himself along with Deborah Sparks, a middle aged lady who had accompanied him. He described her as a sensitive. They were individuals who could sense spirits and the atmosphere they carried with them, sensing if they were good or bad.

Inviting them in, Sophie noticed that Deborah seemed a little nervous as she entered the hall. She seemed to be looking at something or someone on the stairs.

Linda took them through to the lounge where she invited them to sit down and offered them refreshments. Giles said tea would be nice as he wanted to ask her a few things before they started the tour of the house.

Both ladies couldn't help but think as they talked to him that he had never really dealt with anything as serious as the haunting Linda was experiencing.

Sitting there sounding confident and relaxed with his tea cup in his hand, dressed like a university professor with a stripy scarf and blazer, he waffled on about how most hauntings are simply not hauntings at all. They were simply things that happened which the residents couldn't explain. On the rare occasions when spirits were present, they were simply lost souls who needed guiding into the light.

While Giles talked, they noticed that Deborah fiddled with the cross on the necklace she was wearing. She looked uneasy and even more so when the temperature seemed to drop suddenly and their breath was like fine smoke as they spoke.

Giles, despite pulling up his collar and shivering, proceeded to take a bible and a crucifix from a small leather bag before finishing his tea and telling them he was ready to begin. He stated he would start in Linda's bedroom as that was where the most activity had been. He suggested Linda and Sophie stayed downstairs.

It was as he and Deborah stood up, something started banging on the floor above them. When Derek asked if there was anyone else in the house and she said no, he took on a worried, if not very fearful look.

Barely five minutes had passed since they ventured upstairs when the lights began flashing and the sound of footsteps could be heard running across the upstairs floors.

Sophie clutched Linda's hand through fear as they sat on the sofa.

Upstairs, the once confident Giles was trembling as he walked around the bedroom telling whoever was there to show itself. Suddenly the bedroom door slammed and the most awful stench filled the air. They were choking as Deborah told him they should leave as there was a dark presence in the room. Then they heard someone laughing, it wasn't a nice laugh like that of children, it was deep and gravelly. They were terrified when, seconds later, the same voice told them to get out.

Giles was the first to the door, followed by Deborah. Just as he opened the door something grabbed her and threw her back into the room. She screamed for Giles to help her as she struggled to free herself from whatever force was holding her.

With absolute terror on his face he shook his head and ran out the door. Whatever had been holding her let go and she ran as fast as she could out of the room.

Downstairs, the two women heard Deborah scream before both she and Giles came running down the stairs a few moments apart. Giles looked pale and was shaking violently as he rushed past the women and headed for the door. Deborah was limping and holding her thigh.

With her own heart pounding, Linda asked what had happened.

"Something bit me" she replied looking terrified, "you have a demonic entity here, we cannot help you. Take my advice and get out!"

Sophie noticed spots of blood on the floor and told Deborah she was bleeding. Lifting her skirt she looked at the bite, it was huge and looked like what appeared to be teeth marks, or more precisely, fangs. Blatantly refusing to stay another minute, she declined Linda's offer to clean the wound. Making her way to the door which Giles had left open, she could see him staring up at the bedroom window as he sat in the car with the engine running. The moment she got in he sped away, screeching the tyres in his panic to leave.

Inside the house, the lights still flashed on and off and a tapping sound grew louder and louder. The two women held hands and stood feeling terrified too afraid to move.

Sophie couldn't wait to leave the house, she was shaking as she begged Linda to come and stay with them.

Linda was crying as she said Derek would never believe what had happened that evening and he would be angry if he knew Giles had been there.

In that moment everything stopped and the house returned to a calmer state.

"Don't worry about Derek, I was here, I'll tell him! God only knows what happened upstairs, but we heard it and something definitely bit that Deborah! I wouldn't spend another minute here if I was you!"

Before Linda could reply there was a tap on the coffee table. Still in shock and feeling afraid, both women looked up. There standing in front of them were Joey and Mary, they were holding hands. Frozen with fear, the two women simply stared at them.

Tears were rolling down Mary's cheeks as she said, "Please help us, get Angel."

Then they both faded away.

"Oh my God," said Sophie "did that really just happen?"

Linda nodded and said it was Joey the little boy who was trapped in the house and who she presumed to be Mary, the old lady's maid, due to her dress.

When Sophie asked what she was going to do, without hesitation Linda stated she was going back to see Angel, only this time she would make her listen. In the meantime she was going to do what Angel said and read her diary.

Sophie thought she should leave, but if Linda was determined to stay, she would help her despite her fear.

Both women were still shaken an hour later when Sophie had to leave. She suggested Linda going with her and coming back with Mark and Derek. That way she wouldn't be on her own and they could say she simply came for the drive.

Not relishing being there alone, Linda agreed and left with her.

Derek was exhausted by the time they returned home at ten o'clock.

Mark helped him upstairs to bed then joined Linda in the lounge for a cuppa before he left. She never mentioned what had happened earlier.

When he left, not wanting to stay downstairs alone, she headed up to bed. Taking Angel's diary with her, she intended to read as much as possible.

Once comfortable in bed, she took the bookmark from the diary and continued reading.

'Despite heeding what Alan had said about not contacting any spirits, I was beginning to see and hear more things in the house. I often saw Joey and Mary, fortunately not Agnes Tibbs, but I felt the reason for that was a stronger presence in the house. On several occasions

I'd seen a dark shadow moving about. I couldn't see who or what it was, but it scared me. The hairs on my neck and arms would stand up and my legs often felt shaky.

Mum was also aware of changes. Most nights we would hear footsteps running through the house and the occasional loud bang. I suppose in a way we got used to it and on most occasions believed it to be Joey. That was until several nights later when I was woken by something climbing on my bed. At first I thought it was Joey as he often did that, but that night it wasn't him. Not only was something on my bed, but I could see smaller figures moving about in the room. There was a heavy, pungent smell. It was vile. I was petrified frozen with fear. I tried to call out to mum but no sound came out of my mouth. I felt the heavy weight of something on top of me. I was too afraid to look, but I felt its claw-like fingernail run down my face and I could hear a low growling sound the nearer its face came to mine. Just as I thought it was going to attack me a light filled my room and to my absolute relief, Johnathan appeared and told me not to be afraid. In that moment I felt the demon quickly move off me.

Sitting up and straining my eyes in the dim light, I could make out the figure of Mary. Several children were hiding behind her and she was holding a tiny baby in her arms. Johnathan told me I was safe.

The other children ranged in ages from about three to twelve, there were nine of them. All looked sad and afraid, all very thin, dressed like street urchins in raggedy clothes. Now seeing them clearer as my eyes adjusted, I beckoned them to me. Slowly they moved out from behind Mary and one by one climbed onto my bed. I asked Johnathan who they were. Sadly they were children who had been murdered in the house by Darby Fawkes. One tiny girl aged about six, held her hand out to me and asked me to help her. As I took her hand I saw a vision of her death. The place she was in resembled our cellar. There was a type of fire pit burning in the middle of the room, drawn around it was a star shape. At each point there were symbols and what looked like mathematical signs. To the far side of the room was a large table, again it had symbols on it and black candles burned at either end. The girl looked like she was drugged as she hung by a rope around her wrists from a hook on the wall. I watched as a man dressed in a black robe with the hood up, lifted her off and carried her to the table. There were four other people dressed like him in hooded robes. Laying her down on the table, he began chanting words in a language I didn't understand. The others began chanting with him before going down on their knees and praying to a ram's head that was painted on the wall behind him. Then, without compassion or feeling, he plunged the dagger into the girl's chest and proceeded to catch her blood in a chalice as it ran over the edge of the table. I watched as he lifted the cup and drank from it then passed it round for the others to drink. I felt sick to the pit of my stomach, but none of what I'd just seen could have prepared me for what I saw next.

When the ritual finished, the man lifted the child off the table and, carrying her to the fire pit, threw her in. I could hear cries and screams as ghostly figures of children raised their arms up from the flames. A few moments passed. I watched as the fire seemed to rise up from the pit. Then I saw him. In the flames stood the beast, I believed it to be Satan himself. His face instilled absolute terror in me. Resembling a grotesque but human form, with horns like that of a ram and red eyes. He gave out a roar and seemed to grow in size as fire spurted out from his mouth. The others prayed and wailed as he looked down upon them. At that moment the little girl released my hand and the vision disappeared.

The children and Mary were still standing in my room. I was crying as the little girl spoke and begged me to help them. Moments later they seemed to evaporate and disappeared. I never slept a wink that night.

Over breakfast the following morning, I told mum what had happened. After that day I couldn't bring myself to talk about it when I was in the house. I waited to tell Alan and the others when we visited the spiritual church later that week.

Alan and Joyce looked concerned; I wasn't ready for anything like this. Alan believed the children saw me as a way to escape the beast and go into the light. I'm ashamed to admit I hoped he was wrong and what I'd seen was simply a vision.'

Linda's eyes were getting heavy. Looking at the clock she'd been reading for two hours and now felt tired. Placing the book down on the bedside table, she turned off the lamp and snuggled down in the bed next to Derek. She was just drifting off to sleep when she felt something tug at the duvet. Petrified she laid frozen to the spot. Three loud taps came from above her, they were so hard she knew it wasn't Joey and loud enough to wake Derek.

"What was that?" he asked sleepily.

Linda was too terrified to answer him; she just lay there silent, speechless from fear. He obviously thought she was asleep as he pulled the duvet up around his neck and dozed back off.

Linda lay awake for hours; it was almost as though she was waiting for something to happen, fortunately it didn't. Finally she must have dozed off. She woke the next morning to the sound of Derek coughing.

CHAPTER 6

Over breakfast, Linda asked if he felt up to going shopping. She was secretly relieved when he said he felt tired, but would have no objections to her going. Her intention was not really to shop, but to visit Angel again. When she said she would be back within a couple of hours, Derek said he would have a rest and watch TV while she was gone. Over a cuppa she tried to broach the subject of the house being haunted and said she thought something was in their bedroom. Just like before, he dismissed the notion as poppycock. She knew he wouldn't listen so she gave up.

Their sons were coming later that afternoon to lay laminate flooring in the lounge for them after Derek felt too ill to do it. At least it would mean that one room would finally be finished.

Linda left the house just after nine that morning and arrived at Angel's shop twenty minutes later.

There were three people in the shop. Two young women were browsing and a gentleman was chatting to Angel. It was clear from their banter they were good friends.

Linda browsed around the shop while the two ladies bought a few items then left.

It was then Angel looked at her and smiled.

"Hello" said Linda "can I talk to you please Angel. I don't mind waiting while you chat to this gentleman."

Much to Linda's surprise Angel looked at the gentleman and said "This is the lady I told you about Alan."

The man carried a presence about him. He looked younger than his years, very upright and distinguished. His face was a mix of sadness and concern as he nodded to acknowledge her. Even more surprising was when he asked if she'd had a visit from the children in the house.

"I know who you are Alan," said Linda "I read about you. Please can you help us, I'm begging you."

Alan said he would talk to her, but he didn't feel he could help her.

Angel seemed more congenial than on Linda's previous visit; she even suggested shutting the shop for a while so they could talk in the back room.

She offered them a cup of tea as they sat down. Both nodded.

Alan spoke about the visit she'd made to Angel before. He hoped she'd heeded the warning and made plans to leave the house. Linda explained that moving wasn't an option, they would lose everything.

"Then your husband will die there" said Alan in a matter of fact fashion. "I don't think you fully understand what terrible jeopardy his life is in."

"I do and I think I'm aware of what the evil there is capable of. The children told me to find Angel, that's why I'm here. I don't expect you to help me; all I'm asking for is advice. I paid mediums to come to the house, it was terrifying. One of them was bitten and whatever bit her wasn't human! I'm terrified and if it were up to me I'd leave, but my husband thinks it's all nonsense and won't even consider moving. Please, I have nowhere else to go, please help me!"

Angel looked at Alan and nodded.

Obviously he'd wanted to say something, but needed her approval.

"What I'm about to tell you has never been told to anyone. It would have been the last entry in the diary you're reading had Angel returned to the house. The night our dear friend Joyce was killed we had taken part in a séance. Our hope was to help the children cross over into the light. You cannot imagine the terror we encountered. I came face to face with the beast before it murdered Joyce. During the séance we made contact with the entity. I asked its name, he said he was the Demon Cimiries. We had no idea it was such a powerful entity. He is the 66th demon of Satan. Very few people who encounter him live to talk about it; we were all lucky to survive that night. Had it not been for Johnathan, we would not be here today."

Linda watched as Alan's hands began trembling and tears began to well in his eyes as a look of sheer terror ravaged his face.

Angel placed her hand on his to comfort him, but instantly she linked in to what he was remembering. Unable to release his hand, she went back in time to relive that dreadful night, a night she'd hoped never to have to remember.

She could see clearly Joyce, Alan and Olivia sitting at the table holding hands with her as the séance began. Everything had started fine with Joey and the children appearing to them. Then something began which saw the children running and hiding. A dark entity entered and the sound of hooves galloping was heard as it came closer and closer. The furniture began to shake and move; the table flew into the air and smashed against a wall. The most pungent aroma filled the atmosphere almost making Angel vomit. Alan ordered the Demon to show itself. A wind of gale force moved the chairs they were sitting on, they started rocking and spinning as they were lifted from the floor. Joyce began reciting prayers as she fought against the wind. Papers and furniture were flying all around them, the noise in the wind of voices crying and screaming was deafening and terrifying. Then the Demon appeared; he was huge, sitting astride a demonic black horse that breathed fire. Black body armour covered all but the Demon's face; it was a face they would never forget. Large horns on either side of his head, piercing red eyes and huge teeth that seemingly dripped blood. He was laughing as Joyce continued to try and banish him. Suddenly she was hurled into the air. They watched as the Demon raised his hand through the air almost as though he was controlling Joyce, yet not actually touching her. They watched as she struggled to release herself from his clutches as an invisible force crushed her and she fell to the floor like a rag doll.

Alan confronted the Demon, but he was hurled across the room at a ferocious speed which sent him head first into the wall. Olivia was thrown into the air and raising his hand again, the Demon pushed her up the wall leaving her suspended several feet from the floor and unable to move as he turned his attention to Angel. He laughed at her as she stood in front of him and ordered him to leave the house.

"So you are the one who has been sent to defeat me," growled the Demon with a sniggering laugh, "is this the best your God can do? The Master awaits you with his Legions, the Legions of Darkness that will bring death and destruction to your pitiful world!"

Alan regained consciousness and, although unable to stand, called out to Angel to banish him, she had the power to fight him.

Hearing his voice, she found an inner courage. Angel shouted at the Demon that his kind would never have the power of God. She didn't understand whatever force was helping her, but within those moments she seemed to know exactly what to say and pointing her hand at the Demon she began talking in Hebrew, a language she had never learnt.

Anger from the Demon engulfed the room and absolute chaos ensued. Just when all hope was fading a bright light appeared around Angel and everything seemed calmer. The wind stopped, furniture came to a grinding halt as it landed back on the floor. Olivia slid down the wall, landing speechless and numb on the carpet.

The Demon's horse moved towards Angel and reared up, almost catching her with the force of its hooves but seemingly afraid to go closer. For several minutes she held the beast, but it was as she began to weaken, the Demon flicked his hand and Angel was thrown across the room. Quickly scrambling to her feet with her back to the wall she continued to speak in Hebrew as the Demon's horse moved closer and closer.

"You are weakening" said the Demon "I can feel it. Soon you will join me in Hell!"

With every step closer he came, she fought but he was right, she was growing weak. Then just as she feared she would die, Johnathan appeared. He wasn't how she'd been used to seeing him; he was emanating a bright light with his beautiful white wings fully spread as he confronted the Demon. He was dressed in a flowing white gown and brandishing a silver sword and shield.

Instantly the Demon showed fear as his horse backed away from Angel and he concentrated his rage on Johnathan. A tunnel of bright light appeared from the ceiling which seemed to surround Johnathan as he moved towards the Demon. They fought for several seconds before Johnathan plunged the sword into the Demon's shoulder. The screams from the beast were like a million screeches from wounded animals as a fire rose up from the floor and sucked the Demon back down to the pits of Hell.

Johnathan had blood on his gown and his body seemed limp as he was lifted into the light and seemed to evaporate into it. Angel called out to him but he didn't respond. Alan called out to the children of the house to follow Johnathan into the light. They watched as several orbs seemed to appear and float upwards into the light.

It was then Angel passed out. Although she had not been touched by the Demon and she'd felt no pain, she had broken bones and bruises to her body.

When she awoke, she was in an ambulance with Olivia who was reassuring her she'd be alright and the terrible accident she'd been in when Joyce had fallen down the stairs wasn't her fault. She had tried to save her and fallen with her.

Angel knew that was what they would tell the police. Unbeknown to her, Alan and Olivia had placed the furniture back and laid Joyce's body at the bottom of the stairs before they called the ambulance. They both felt it was the best thing to do as no one would believe what had happened.

Angel and Alan were brought back from their trance by Linda's voice begging them to help her as she felt the Demon had returned to the house.

Rallying her senses, Angel focused on her, she must have been talking, but they hadn't heard her while in trance.

"Sorry we cannot help you" said Angel "please leave the house. Make your husband listen, please."

"I can't, he won't. Can you at least tell me what I can do to banish this Demon Cimiries? Maybe the angel Johnathan would help me?"

Alan told her they had not seen Johnathan since that night.

Linda began to cry as she played to their hearts, telling them the children were afraid. Begging them, she said there must be someone who could help her. Even if she could talk Derek into leaving, they would be forced to sell, which would mean another family being put at risk. That was something which would lay heavy on her mind and heart, especially if they had children. She tried to reason with them that Angel clearly had the power to fight this demon and what happened was a long time ago, maybe now she was stronger and could defeat him.

Angel looked tearful as she shook her head and admitted she was afraid. Her thoughts on the matter were simply that if she returned to the house, she would die there.

Alan shocked them both by saying the house should be burnt to the ground.

Linda, through her desperation, was relentless as she continued appealing to their spiritual sides.

"Have you seen the film The Green Mile?" asked Angel.

Confused as to why she'd asked, Linda simply nodded.

"Do you remember the scene where John Coffey took Tom Hank's hand and showed him what happened to the two little girls who'd been murdered?"

Linda did. He'd passed on the vision of the girls' murder to him.

"Then let me ask you this, do you think that was a good thing for Tom Hanks?"

"Yes, of course, but why are we talking about a film. What we're dealing with is real."

Without saying another word, Angel reached over and took Linda's hand.

Suddenly Linda jerked and shook as she watched the events of the night Joyce died. She was still shaking badly fifteen minutes after Angel removed her grip.

Alan made everyone another cup of tea in the hope it would help calm Linda down.

Finally, Angel asked if she now understood why she could never return to the house.

Still shaking and having trouble speaking coherently, Linda nodded as the tears streamed down her face.

Everything Linda had said tugged at Angel's heart strings, but fear of the demon kept her from succumbing to her pleas.

Alan was also feeling empathy to her plight but like Angel, he also feared the demon. He knew they had been lucky to survive their encounter. Had it not been for Johnathan's intervention they would all have perished. Johnathan would not be there to help them now should they face the demon again, his thoughts on that were they wouldn't survive. However, his heart was heavy over the children who were trapped in the house, he truly believed, like Angel, that they had gone into the light with Johnathan. It was purely because of his regard for them he told Linda to return to the shop later that week. Although he made it quite clear he would never return to the house. However, he would provide her with some items that may help her, should the need to use them arise.

Linda couldn't get the vision Angel had showed from her mind as she drove home.

She tried to reason as to why the demon had picked her to bring Angel back to the house, why not any of the previous owners.

She was relieved to see her son's work van parked at the house when she arrived home.

If Derek asked what she'd bought in town she would simply say there was nothing she liked.

CHAPTER 7

It had been two days since Linda had visited the shop to ask for Angel's help. After she'd left, Angel had shut the shop and gone round to Olivia's.

Always happy to see her daughter, Olivia welcomed her and asked her to stay for lunch. She'd known the moment Angel had arrived that all was not well. She wasn't surprised when told about Linda, but her instant advice on witnessing the sadness on her daughter's face, was that Angel must never return to the house.

"I may have to mum, the children need me. I need to tell you something. I kept it from you because I didn't want you worrying. I've had visits from Joey and some of the others since the first time Linda came to the shop."

Shocked, Olivia asked what had happened.

Angel said the children were terrified and they foresaw the deaths of both Derek and Linda if she didn't help.

"No Angel, you cannot go there! You know what will happen if you do and you cannot help those children. As sad as I feel about that, they are already dead, you are not!"

Olivia could see how this was affecting Angel and continued to give her a lecture on the fact Linda had been warned and if she chose to stay there, it was her choice.

Despite knowing everything Olivia had said was true, Angel still felt heart sore over the children.

It was three o'clock that afternoon when Angel left. Olivia arranged to pick her up at six thirty that evening as Angel was doing clairvoyance at the spiritual church that night.

Walking back into the shop, Angel instantly felt a presence. A few moments passed when the smell of perfume seemed to fill the air, it was a smell she instantly recognised. Joyce always wore it, 'Opium' by Yves St Laurent.

Calling her name, Angel waited and watched as Joyce appeared.

It wasn't the first time they made contact since the night she'd died, but this was different, Angel knew she'd come for a reason.

Angel welcomed her as the entity began to fully materialize. Moments later Joyce was standing in front of her.

"My sweet Angel, do not be afraid, you know it's your destiny to send the beast back to Hell."

Yes, she was right, Angel had always known, but knowing something and doing it were two entirely different things and Angel feared for her life.

Before she could reply, Joyce evaporated into the air. All Angel heard was a faint voice which said, 'Be strong Angel, trust in your faith. Linda holds the key'.

Checking she'd locked the shop, Angel made her way upstairs to her flat. The answerphone was flashing, she had a message.

'Hi babe, I'm coming home. I'm booked on the next available flight. I'll be there tomorrow morning, love you.' The caller was James Whitney, her fiancé. He was a Sergeant in the Army. Popular with his regiment; he always put the men first. Three tours in Iraq had seen him receiving a medal for bravery after refusing to leave one of his men who'd been wounded. He risked his own life to save him. He'd met Angel four years earlier through the church, after his sister had been tragically killed by a hit and run driver. Ironically, he wasn't a believer like his mother and he knew nothing about Angel other than she worked as a medium. Had it not been for his mother begging him to attend the church with her that evening, they would never have met. He was a good man, six years older than Angel at thirty four.

From the moment Angel had taken the platform that evening, he knew she was the one for him. It was after the meeting he'd spoken to her and asked her if she would go out for an evening with him. Had it not been for Olivia's persuasions, she probably would have declined but since that fateful evening their love had grown stronger every day and now he was keen to settle down and start a family. He was extremely handsome, hardworking, loyal and faithful. Angel loved him, of that there was no doubt, but she knew the time would come when she would have to face her own demons and accept what she had to do. Until then she couldn't commit to marriage and children. James, however, was unaware of her real reason and believed her when she said she wasn't ready. He would wait until she was, because he knew he had found the woman he wanted to spend the rest of his life with.

Feeling excited at seeing him, Angel's mood changed as she prepared herself a light tea to have after she'd showered and got ready for church.

Sitting there a couple of hours later eating, she couldn't get Linda out of her mind. She also had the feeling she wasn't alone, someone was watching her.

For several minutes she experienced an uneasy feeling, one which saw the hairs on her neck stand up as the room turned cold. Standing her ground and trying not to show fear, she asked whoever it was to leave, it wasn't welcome there. Then she began to recite the Lord's Prayer. Suddenly a loud banging filled the room, it was deafening. Taking a crucifix from the sideboard she held it in front of her and commanded whoever it was to leave. A photograph of her and Olivia flew off the wall and smashed. Then as quickly as it started it became calm. The entity had gone.

Feeling a little shaky, she called Olivia and said she was going to drive and would pick her up instead.

Angel arrived ten minutes later. Martin, Olivia's husband, came in from work and chatted to her over a cuppa before they left.

Once alone in the car; she told Olivia about what had happened and that James was due home the following day.

Despite Olivia being happy about James, she wanted to know more about the entity that Angel had encountered.

"I don't know mum, but I had a visit from Joyce when I got home from your house. I think it's something trying to frighten me. This all seemed to start after Linda came to the shop. It's not the first time; I've felt it since that day. I can't explain it, but it's as though it's trying to warn me off, but for me to be right would mean it fears me. Oh God mum, if only Johnathan was here, he would know."

Olivia gently patted her arm and reassuringly said she was sure everything would be ok. Maybe Alan would have some answers when they spoke to him at the church. Angel nodded.

Angel always drew a good crowd at the church, mainly regulars who also visited her at the shop. Alan was waiting in the small room where mediums prepared before greeting the parishioners upstairs. Both women looked surprised when he told them; Linda and Sophie were seated upstairs at the back.

Olivia felt it wasn't the right time to talk about the visit Angel had, but she said they needed to speak to him after the meeting. Alan smiled and nodded.

When the first medium came off stage, Angel went on. She was always well received. Looking around the seats before she began, she spotted Linda and Sophie. With a nod and a smile she acknowledged them.

After giving several people messages from passed love ones, she moved on to telling people personal things, like the new job one man was due to start the following week. It would prove very successful for him. Several ladies looked tearful as she told a middle aged lady in the front row her daughter's pregnancy would go full term and the baby would be strong and healthy, although despite the scan, it was a little girl and not the boy they'd been told it would be. The woman cried as she thanked her and said her daughter had three miscarriages before this pregnancy and Angel was right, they had said it was a boy at the scan, but she would tell her daughter to expect a girl now. A little chuckle echoed round the room.

It was as Angel glanced around the room to see who she needed to meet next, she looked at Linda. To her horror, she could see a dark shadowy figure standing behind her. Instantly she looked over at Alan. It was clear from his face he was also aware of it. Seeing that Angel felt unsettled, he made his way to the stage and announced the next medium was ready to take over.

It was after the meeting ended for the evening and people came downstairs for refreshments, Angel had a chance to speak with him about it. Just as he was about to give his opinion, Linda and Sophie approached.

"You were fantastic Angel" said Sophie "I've never been before. We wanted to come to your shop, but thought here might be better. Only it's Derek, his health is deteriorating by the day. We used the things Alan left for us at the shop, but nothing seems to have changed. Linda still hears and smells things."

Alan interrupted and said the items he'd left, consisting of some Holy water, a crucifix and some sage, were simply tools to help them. He'd made it quite clear they would not rid them of the demonic presence in the house. It was as they talked he noticed something around Linda; it was like black molasses that swirled around her. As he watched it, suddenly a face sprang out and almost hit his face, sending him staggering back with shock.

No one except Angel had seen the entity. Everyone quickly asked if he was ok. Not wishing to bring what he'd seen to light, he simply joked and said he'd lost his balance brought on by a recent bout of vertigo.

Linda and Sophie made one last desperate appeal to Angel before they left.

Sophie's mum had watched over the children for her, so Mark could stay with Derek while the ladies went to the spiritual church. At first he hadn't been keen on Linda going to the church. He believed it was because she was reading the diary and thought the house was haunted, but after convincing him it was Sophie who wanted to go after a friend from the children's school raved over it, he'd been ok.

It was just before nine when the ladies arrived back at the house. Mark opened the door before Linda had time to take her key from her bag.

Sophie kissed his cheek and asked if he'd had a nice evening with his dad. It was then she noticed the strange look on his face.

Asking him if everything was ok, she was shocked when he told her he'd seen the ghost of a young boy. He'd run along the hall in front of him.

"That's Joey" she said in a rather blasé manner, due to his earlier scornful disbelief, "did you tell Derek?"

Mark nodded, but said his dad had put it down to imagination and joked that he'd listened too much to his mother, who was convinced the house was haunted.

Mark had just made a fresh pot of tea, so they'd stay for one and then make tracks home.

Linda broached the subject of Joey as the four of them drank their tea. Derek made fun of her again, until the tapping started. Then he stopped.

"Is that you Joey?" said Linda "tap once for yes, twice for no."

A single tap echoed round the room as Derek sat wide eyed and quiet.

"Was it you who ran along the hall earlier in front of my son?"

Two taps.

"Was it one of the other children?"

One tap followed.

"Joey, will you let us see you?"

One tap sounded just as the small boy began to manifest. Derek and his son looked terrified as Linda thanked Joey and asked if the other children were with him.

Joey nodded as several other children began to appear.

Then without warning the cups on the table began to shake and move. At the same time the lights flickered and the children quickly disappeared.

Linda quickly moved and, opening the sideboard drawers, took out the items Alan had given her. With the conviction of a professional exorcist, she held the cross and began flicking the Holy water as she commanded whoever it was to leave.

Moments later the room the room was calm and back to normal.

Linda said it was the old woman and the children were afraid of her. Derek was pale and visibly shaken as he apologised for not believing her before.

Mark and Sophie left fifteen minutes later, leaving Derek talking about the strange, if not unnerving, event which had taken place just thirty minutes earlier.

Three miles away, Alan and Angel had accepted an invitation from Olivia to go back to her house for coffee and a chat.

After apologising to their guests, Martin had retired to bed; he had to be up at five the following morning.

Alan talked about what happened to him at the church when he spoke to Linda. It was unusual for an entity to leave its place of origin, yet there was clearly an evil presence with Linda. His theory was it had come to test Angel and him.

Olivia asked what he meant as she didn't really understand.

"Angel's abilities have developed far beyond that of twelve years ago" he replied "she almost defeated the demon then. He fears us; that's for certain, although it wasn't him who showed itself. It was a much less powerful force, possibly the old woman, Agnes Tibbs."

Olivia asked what he thought it all meant, looking and feeling concerned.

"Tell you the truth Olivia I'm not really sure, but I think Linda could be a part of this. I'm not sure she's even aware, but my feelings are mixed when I speak with her. Unless I'm mistaken, which I very well might be, I think she's dealt with spirits before. Maybe something happened to her as a result of that and now she suppresses it. I'd like to speak to her, maybe she can enlighten us."

Angel said she felt the same. In her opinion Linda was clairvoyant. She decided to mention the visit she'd had from Joyce and that she'd said Linda held the key. If that were true, why hadn't she told them? Did that mean she was hiding something, or more likely as with so many people, she herself feared the gift? Maybe they should invite her back to the shop. Angel would call her in the morning and try to arrange something.

With the time approaching midnight, Angel asked Alan if he would like a lift back as he'd walked to the church that evening. Accepting her offer, the two friends kissed Olivia and left.

Fifteen minutes later, Angel was outside Alan's house telling him she would call him after she'd spoken to Linda.

Kissing her cheek and advising her to be careful, he exited the car. He waved out to her as she pulled away.

Back at the shop, she made her way upstairs. It was as she went to enter her flat she heard someone inside.

Taking a mace spray from her bag, she proceeded to enter cautiously. Making her way into the hall, she spotted James's suitcase. Quickening her step, she rushed into the lounge. He was sitting on the sofa eating toast and drinking tea. They hugged and kissed as they said they'd missed one another.

With a giggle she confessed she thought someone had broken in, it hadn't occurred to her it could be him. He wasn't due back till the morning. Explaining how he'd managed to get an earlier flight, he said he was so happy to be home.

Before going to bed, he asked after Olivia and Martin and if anything exciting had happened while he'd been away.

With a giggle, she said he wouldn't believe her if she told him.

It wasn't long after they made love that James fell asleep. Angel laid awake thinking about Linda and the strange happening earlier that evening.

CHAPTER 8

Having left James sleeping off his jet lag, Angel had called Linda and Alan and made arrangements for both of them to come to the shop at three that afternoon.

James had woken at midday and eaten lunch with Angel. It was then she told him about Linda and Alan, explaining about Linda living in her old house and what had been going on. Typically of James, he grinned. She knew he didn't share her beliefs in the spirit world, but he kept an open mind.

Just before two o'clock, she left him unpacking and returned to the shop. She had a tarot reading booked for two.

She wasn't surprised to see Olivia arrive with Alan and Sophie with Linda just as she was seeing her client out.

After locking the shop and putting the kettle on for tea, they made their way into the room at the back. Using the spare chairs stacked in the corner they sat down as Angel passed their tea.

"Can I just say Angel," said Linda "I was surprised to be invited here today, but I'm glad we were. Last night at home, Joey came, even my husband saw him."

"Then that only confirms why you needed to be here today. Alan and I feel that you're clairvoyant Linda, which would explain a lot. I remember you saying, you felt someone was helping you, like when you found my diary. Doesn't it seem funny to you that after twelve years of me moving, my diary was still there? As you know the house was sold before, yet the other occupants never came across it or threw it out."

Linda agreed and said she had been curious about that, but regarding her, she wasn't clairvoyant, her family were deeply religious and to talk of those things was banned from conversation.

Alan asked if she thought that was strange, simply because most religious people do believe in the afterlife or at least they were going to a better place provided by God.

Linda shrugged her shoulders as she went on to tell them about her childhood.

She'd grown up on a small farm in Ireland. Her family went to Mass regularly and always said grace before meals. Two of her uncles had joined the priesthood and her cousin became a nun. Except for one of the uncles, she had lost touch with the others when the family moved to England when she was about nine years old.

Alan asked why the family had moved and added it was unusual for families not to remain in touch.

She couldn't remember much when she tried to think back to that time. It was then they all noticed a change in her facial expression, it was as though she had remembered something but couldn't understand it, or it frightened her. Alan questioned her as to what she'd seen. It was clear from the way she said she couldn't remember they knew she was reluctant to tell them.

Alan asked her permission for him to try and hypnotise her. It was a type of regression which some experienced psychics could perform.

At that moment she became a little defensive and assured them she wouldn't remember anything and she didn't have any psychic ability.

It was Sophie who actually talked her into it, saying it couldn't do any harm to try and it may help.

Linda finally agreed.

Alan asked her to relax and after taking a small dowsing crystal from his pocket, began swinging it in front of her eyes. A few moments later, her eyes felt heavy.

Everyone sat silently as Alan asked her to remember back to her childhood, living on the farm in Ireland.

Linda could see the farm clearly; her parents were there with her two younger brothers. Their dad's youngest brother, Uncle Patrick, also lived with them. He was her youngest and favourite uncle. Like most Catholic families; there was often a lot of years between the oldest and youngest children. Uncle Patrick was thirteen years younger than her dad. He'd always been there, since their parents died in a house fire when he was fifteen. Linda loved him, he was kind and caring. No one was surprised when at eighteen he decided to become a priest.

The scene she was remembering was of a family mealtime. Her father was saying grace. Afterwards, Patrick was telling them of his decision to join the priesthood. They were just about to eat supper when the crockery began to shake and move on the white table cloth. No one could make any sense of it and they simply waited for it to pass. Then pictures and a crucifix fell from the walls and she remembered hearing her mum screaming. As she looked across the table, Uncle Patrick was vomiting and having some sort of fit. His face looked distorted as he tried to talk but his words were incoherent. After that day Uncle Patrick stayed in his room, but their priest, Father Doyle called in a lot to visit him, sometimes staying for hours.

Alan could see that whatever she was remembering was upsetting her, so he counted to three and told her to wake.

Linda opened her eyes and looked at him. He asked her what she had seen and to his surprise, without hesitation she told him.

It was while they talked about the day the crockery shook and Uncle Patrick was taken ill, she began remembering more. Alan prompted her to tell them but he could see she was afraid.

Olivia suggested making a fresh pot of tea.

Five minutes later as they talked, Linda asked Angel and Alan why they thought she may be clairvoyant.

"I know you are" said Angel, surprising everyone, "very few people can actually see spirits, yet you saw Victor, our old neighbour, and the children in the house."

"Sophie also saw Victor," questioned Linda "but you haven't said she may be clairvoyant."

Angel went on to say she didn't think Sophie was and Victor had simply allowed himself to be seen, assuming it was Victor.

Looking confused Sophie asked what she'd meant by assuming it was him.

"Most spirits are genuine; they are who you believe them to be, whereas demonic spirits can fool people. That's the reason why I advise people never to use an Ouija board. It's easy for spirits to say they're who you want them to be, but once you welcome them in the trouble begins. Joey knew Linda was clairvoyant, that's why he helped her find my diary. I believe something happened when you were a child Linda and that's why your family moved. Can you remember anything else?"

Linda sipped her tea and sat quietly staring at her, before she nodded her head and asked what if the things she saw weren't real events. Could they possibly be dreams or nightmares she'd had as a child. Her parents always said she had an over active imagination.

Alan was quick to say it wouldn't matter but if she agreed, he would like to put her under again in the hope she'd remember more.

"I did remember something when I woke up, but it was horrible and I'm not sure it ever really happened. It was after Uncle Patrick stayed in his room, my dad always locked the door and we were forbidden to go there. I missed him and I used to sneak upstairs and look through the keyhole. One day Uncle Patrick said he knew I was there and asked me to go into his room. I told him the door was locked and my dad kept the key, so I couldn't. I heard the door unlock and Uncle Patrick told me not to be afraid but to go and see him. I did wonder for a moment who had unlocked the door when I saw he was tied to the bed, but I didn't question it. When I asked Uncle Patrick why he was tied down, he said it was in case he had a fit and hurt himself, but my dad had tied the straps too tight and he asked me to loosen them. I had just undone one of his wrist straps when a female voice said, 'no don't.' I couldn't see anyone but I heard her. When I refused to untie him, his face changed, he looked nasty. He started shouting at me and talking in a strange voice and another language I didn't understand. I remember being afraid and was so relieved when my father walked in after he'd realised the door was open. He shouted at Uncle Patrick to leave me alone, although he referred to me 'as the child.' Uncle Patrick got angry and said terrible things, he spat at my dad and his bed started to shake violently. My father grabbed my hand and we ran to the door but just as we got there it slammed shut and we couldn't open it. I was screaming and banging on the door. Something was choking my dad, he couldn't breathe and he looked as though he was trying to stop someone from strangling him. I don't remember much after that except shouting at Uncle Patrick to stop. My dad had terrible marks, like burns around his neck.

Later that day, Father Doyle and two other priests came and took Uncle Patrick away. I could hear him shouting and swearing, which he never did. I couldn't understand some of the words he used I thought it was Gaelic. We moved to England a few weeks later. Mum and dad never spoke about it and Uncle Patrick became a priest."

Alan asked if she could remember it stopping when she'd shouted at Patrick. Linda nodded and said it did and the door opened, then she must have passed out.

Angel said something which Linda found absurd. Angel believed her Uncle may have been possessed and for some reason the Demon wanted her. Thankfully, the church intervened and her family moved. Linda laughed at the thought, stating her Uncle Patrick couldn't have been possessed; he was the loveliest man ever, except when he was ill.

"Assuming he was ill Linda? Maybe you could ask your parents?"

Shaking her head and looking sad, both her parents had passed away.

Before leaving, Linda asked again for their help only this time, despite saying no, Angel seemed more cordial, almost giving the impression she wanted to. They all hugged the two women as they left the shop.

Angel invited Alan and Olivia to come upstairs and say hello to James. It was an invitation he readily accepted. Olivia declined stating she had a dentist appointment, she would see James later.

After the men shook hands they talked while Angel made tea. James was asking him about the session they'd just had downstairs. Alan was trying to explain in brief the haunting Linda was experiencing when Angel appeared with tea and biscuits.

When the conversation resumed, James laughed and said maybe he should refer to them as Randal and Hopkirk in future. Seeing that Angel looked confused, he explained they were characters from a TV programme his parents liked in the seventies which he watched years later during some reruns. Hopkirk was a friendly ghost who only Randal could see.

They all laughed.

Angel had never told James about the night the Demon almost killed her. So when he asked if they were going to help Linda, she had to be tactful with her reply simply because he knew she would always try and help.

It was then Alan surprised her by saying maybe they should try and help. Instantly she stated she didn't feel there was anything they could do. Fortunately and, possibly because James was there, Alan accepted what she'd said and didn't elaborate on it.

CHAPTER 9

Since actually seeing Joey and the other children, Derek was not quite such a Doubting Thomas regarding the house being haunted. There had been no more visits from the children in the four days since. However, unbeknown to him, Linda was sensing a different kind of presence. It wasn't nice like the children and she feared it. At first she thought it was Agnes Tibbs, but the more she sensed it the less convinced she was. This new entity was bigger and stronger; making its presence felt whenever she was alone. For several days, she had felt something was watching her. Doors would mysteriously open and close and items seemed to be moved to different places, yet she knew exactly where she'd left them, like with her mobile phone the time she'd needed to phone an ambulance for Derek. The previous night she had felt something trying to pull the duvet off her, fortunately Derek had woken and it stopped.

Since her meeting at the shop, she couldn't stop thinking about Uncle Patrick, so much so she decided to phone him. This wasn't something she did very often, maybe once or twice a year, birthdays and Christmas being the only regular times, but something was compelling her to ask about his illness when he'd lived with them on the farm.

That afternoon while Derek slept upstairs, she made the call. After talking for several minutes to other priests at the Vatican, she was finally able to speak to Uncle Patrick. With excitement, he expressed how happy he was, if not surprised, at her call. They bantered for a few minutes about the family and how she was hoping to meet up with her brothers later in the year. Patrick knew they both lived miles away which made visiting difficult.

It was when she asked about his time at the farm, he went quiet before asking her why she needed to know. She told him about the things that were happening at the house and how she'd found Angel's diary. To her surprise, he said he may try and visit her in the near future so they could talk about things in detail. Linda knew instantly something wasn't right as Patrick never left the Vatican. Since the days he left the farm that had been his home. Now a Cardinal, he was very close to the Pope. She also knew his health was poor. Despite only being in his late sixties, he was losing his sight and had the early onset of Parkinson's disease. He asked her if she'd had a priest round to bless the house. She felt ashamed to admit she hadn't got round to it due to Derek's ill health. Patrick said he had a good friend who was in London at that time who he would ask to call round. In fact, she may even remember him; he was Father Angelo, the young novice priest who had come to the farmhouse with the older priests when Patrick was ill. Like Patrick, he devoted his life to God and the Church. He was in London on a seminar.

Although grateful, she said she didn't want to put Father Angelo, his friend, to any trouble and she could speak to her own parish priest. Patrick wouldn't hear of it and said Angelo was his dearest friend and was also very experienced with hauntings. He would contact him that very day so she should expect his call later. Patrick was confident Angelo would be in touch with her as soon as he'd spoken to him.

Unbeknown to Linda and her two siblings, Patrick had been possessed by a demon. After the family had moved to England, Patrick had been incarcerated in the Vatican. All his needs had been attended to by Angelo and the other priests, although he was confined and often restrained. It was only after gruelling and arduous visits from the Cardinals and the young and newly ordained Father Angelo, the demon was finally cast out.

Father Angelo was in fact an exorcist; despite the Church denying these priests actually exist, they were very real. Angelo had his calling to God when he was just fourteen. At the time he was living with his family in Italy. They were a devout Catholic family who always looked for the guidance of their own priest, Father Luigi.

As a boy, Angelo enjoyed spending time with the older priest, talking about the Church and being head altar boy. Often he would accompany Father Luigi on visits to local people who lived in their village. It was after such a visit, requested by Angelo's own mother, Angelo knew he wanted to be an advocate of God and fight evil.

Father Luigi was preparing for Mass the day Angelo's mother rushed into the church. Luigi could see blood on her hands as she begged him to come to her house. Something had happened to Angelo. Without hesitation, Father Luigi accompanied her back to her house.

Inside, Angelo was lying on his bed being cared for by his three older sisters. Pulling back the bed covers, his mother showed Father Luigi the boy's hands and feet. They were bleeding from small circular wounds, there was also a wound on the boy's side and blood was evident on his forehead as though something had punctured his skin just below his hairline. The boy's wounds were consistent with the crucifixion of Christ. Father Luigi knew he was looking first-hand at stigmata. He asked Angelo's mother to bring bandages and cover the wounds and for the sisters to leave the room. Alone with the boy, Father Luigi asked if he could remember anything. Without any fear, Angelo said he'd had a dream where God had chosen him to be his advocate against evil. In the dream there had been a presence of evil, yet Angelo hadn't feared it although his belief was it was the beast, Satan himself. In the dream it was a young novice priest named Patrick who was being possessed. Angelo fought the demon with the gallantry of a knight and the knowhow of an Archangel.

When Angelo was seventeen, he was told about a young novice priest in Ireland who needed the help of the church. His name was Patrick. Despite his youth and being a novice himself, Angelo was ready to travel with a Vatican priest to Ireland. The day he met Patrick, his life changed forever. He knew he was the young man from his dream and needed his help.

By the time he was eighteen, Angelo was ordained and working at the Vatican. He shares a close relationship with the Pope, who had on several occasions over the years talked of him becoming a cardinal, yet Angelo had always tactfully talked his way out of it. He knew he could best do what God had chosen him for as a priest. He neither wanted, nor needed the higher order. As a priest he could move freely to wherever he was needed to do God's work.

Patrick ended the call after telling her to expect Angelo's call and how wonderful it had been to talk to her. As always he would remember her in his prayers and ask God to watch over the family.

Making a pot of tea, she sat down to read Angel's diary. Just as she settled down comfortably and picked the diary up, Derek returned downstairs. Five minutes later they were chatting over a cuppa. Linda told him about the call she'd made to her Uncle Patrick and that his friend would come to bless the house for them. Just as Derek was about to reply the house phone rang. To Linda's surprise it was Father Anglo. Instantly she warmed to his voice and the friendliness of his words. However, she was a little shocked when he asked if he could call on them the next morning after he explained he would be returning to Rome within the next few days. They arranged for him to visit at ten the next morning before he ended the call.

It was the evening before Linda had an uninterrupted chance to read. Derek had dozed off in his chair after dinner, giving her time to settle down with the diary. Angel's next entry began.

'Since my encounter with the dark entity, I was nervous whenever anything strange happened. Had it not been for Alan's guidance, I think I may have lost my mind. In a strange way and as much as I feared this entity; I felt I was growing stronger. In my heart I hoped we could send it back to where it came from. Alan believed the house held a portal to the underworld which had been opened by the original owner and Devil worshipper, Darby Fawkes. During his satanic rituals, other dark entities had found their way in. Several times over the coming months, I felt its presence. Often I could feel it breathing on my neck, especially when I was alone in my bedroom. I wasn't experienced, but I knew if this portal Alan spoke of was there, it was in the cellar. The fire pit I'd seen made it the most likely place. Over the years it had been covered by a concrete floor, but I knew in my heart that's where it was. Mum had also experienced it presence; but recently it had actually touched her.

It was after going into the cellar to change a fuse that had blown she was to encounter it. With the lights out, mum had taken a torch with her to replace the fuse. I waited upstairs. I was watching mum go down the stairs when suddenly the door slammed. I instantly felt dread, there was no draught and no valid reason for it to shut. After fighting against the force trying to prevent me, I finally entered the cellar. Following the torchlight to where mum was, I could see her standing still. It was as though she was unaware I was there and was riveted to the spot. I could not only feel the evil presence, I could smell it. The vile odour was overpowering and making me nauseous. Mum said later she knew I was there, but even when I touched her, she barely moved. I looked at what she was staring at. To my horror, there was blood running down the wall next to the fuse box, but worse still was when I realised my feet felt wet through my slippers. In the exact spot where I'd seen the fire pit in my visions, blood was oozing through the concrete floor. I tugged at mum's arm to get her to move. It was as we made our way back up the wooden staircase something grabbed her foot through the treads, sending her face first into the upper steps. Once back in the kitchen I asked if she could have simply tripped but she showed me her leg. There were what appeared to be claw marks around her ankle. For several days her ankle was painful and swollen. Neither of us ventured into the cellar alone after that, we always went together. We never saw the blood again. Another thing I found unsettling was when I recollected a dream I had a few days before mum's accident. There was a large fire on the ground, like that of a camp fire only larger. There were, what I felt to be, African people dancing and chanting to the heavy deafening sound of bongo drums. It was as though I was invisible to them as they danced. It became quite frenzied. They were wearing voodoo type masks and on their bodies were paintings and symbols. The women were topless with symbols painted on their breasts. A young girl was brought out by four African men, she was screaming and kicking. Then the drumming stopped suddenly and everyone closed ranks into a tight circle before the men released the young girl. Frantically she tried to break out of the circle, but they laughed and pushed her back as they taunted her. It was as she got up and ran at the wall of natives, a man wearing only a ram's head and covered in painted symbols like that of a tribal witch doctor emerged from the crowd and grabbed the girl. She passed out as he dragged her into the middle of the circle next to the fire and laid her on the ground. A cockerel was brought out to him. Holding it by its legs, he took out a dagger from the waistband of his kikoi (loincloth) and slit its throat as he stood over the girl. Everyone began chanting as the animal's blood ran onto her body. Moments later, he plunged the knife into her chest before gouging out her tongue and eyes which he threw onto the fire. As horrific as this was, what was to follow was the most sickening sight. With blood oozing from the dead girl's wounds, he laughed and said 'fees, kinders fees'. I watched helplessly as the people got down on their knees and, like wild animals, began eating the flesh of the girl. Never was I happier to wake up than after that vision. My bed was damp from sweat and my heart was pounding. It played on my mind so much that the following day I researched the words 'fees, kinders fees.' It was African for feast children feast. Mum, I and Alan felt it was connected to the drumming sound we'd heard in the house and more specifically, Darby Fawkes.'

Linda closed the diary as Derek roused. After making him a drink she talked about the diary and what she'd read that evening. Despite having actually seen the spirit children, he wasn't sure he believed everything she told him. However, they were both wondering what Father Angelo would make of the house when he arrived the following morning.

That night Linda went up to bed the same time as Derek, just before ten because despite sleeping most of the evening he felt tired.

With Derek fast asleep, she had laid awake thinking about her Uncle Patrick. She could remember quite clearly the day the door unlocked on its own and Patrick had asked her to loosen his restraints. The more she thought, the clearer her memories became. She could now remember the door being locked as they tried to leave the room and how she had ordered her Uncle to unlock it. At that moment the door had unlocked and opened on its own. Once safely outside the room, her father ordered her to leave and tell her mother to call Father Doyle. He returned to Patrick's room, but like a curious child she didn't leave straight away. After her father had closed the door behind him, she listened and watched through the keyhole the terrible scene that followed. As her father secured Patrick's restraints, Patrick spat and hissed at him and spoke in what was to her a foreign language. She'd watched as her father took a bottle of Holy water from his pocket and after flicking it at Patrick, ordered the demon to leave. Most disturbing was every time the water hit him, Patrick's skin tore open and caused him to scream and vomit. Objects were being thrown around the room by an invisible force, almost as though a great whirlwind was inside. Moments passed then she heard Patrick's voice, it sounded pitiful as he begged her father to kill him. Without consciously thinking, she had gone down on her knees and prayed to God to help her father and Uncle Patrick. Moments later all was quiet and she moved quickly away from the door as her father began to unlock it.

Despite trying to sleep, she couldn't stop thinking about her childhood in Ireland. She remembered hearing their priest, Father Doyle, who visited Patrick daily, talking to her parents. Often she was supposed to be feeding the chickens, but instead she'd hidden behind the door. It was the day after the incident with her father and Patrick, the priest was telling them Patrick would have to be moved to the Vatican. There he could be properly cared for, he added Linda would not be safe while Patrick was at the house. She listened as the priest went on to say Linda's visions must never be talked about for her own safety.

Finally, she dozed off to sleep with Derek's arm around her.

When she woke around eight the following morning, her first thought was to tell Alan and Angel what she'd started to remember. Were Father Angelo not coming to bless the house, she would have called them that morning.

The time was approaching nine o'clock when Derek finally came downstairs. He looked pale and said he felt nauseous so he didn't want any breakfast, just a cup of tea.

Father Angelo arrived by taxi five minutes early. He was just as Linda had imagined him, in his sixties but nevertheless a handsome man. His once black hair now streaked with grey, but his most striking feature was his beautiful blue eyes. The very moment she opened the door she warmed to this gentle man who instantly said hello with a smile. His face did actually look familiar to her, despite all the years which had passed.

After introducing him to Derek, she offered him refreshment.

While they sat drinking tea, Father Angelo caught her staring at him and instantly smiled and said he remembered her from Ireland. Searching her memories, she began to remember the handsome young novice who had played with her while the older priests had been with Uncle Patrick. He listened as she talked of that time and they shared distant memories. She couldn't help but notice the scars on his hands, two tiny round marks on his palms but she never mentioned them.

It was a few minutes later, Linda noticed he looked away from her and into the corner of the room. Not wishing to appear rude, she never asked what he was looking at; she simply left to make another drink.

When she returned; Father Angelo was placing on the table the items he needed to bless the house.

"Thank you for doing this Father" she said "Uncle Patrick insisted on asking you. I hope we haven't interrupted too much with your day? Only I'm sure you have plenty to do before returning to Rome."

"My dear friend Patrick was right to ask me to come and there is always time for the Lord's work. I'm certain Patrick would have come in person, but he rarely leaves the Vatican. I'm very much looking forward to seeing him on my return. If there is anything you would like me to take for you, please let me know."

Linda grinned; she had already written a letter to Uncle Patrick which she had intended to ask Angelo to take back with him.

Thanking him, she mentioned it.

After he finished drinking his second cup of tea, he stated he would like to begin blessing the house but again he looked over to the corner. Linda's curiosity got the better of her and she also looked. She wasn't surprised to see Joey and Mary.

"Can you see them Father?" she asked.

"Yes" he replied, almost as though it was a normal occurrence.

Derek interrupted and told the priest he wasn't comfortable with the entities like Linda was. They were both shocked with his reply.

"Not many people are Derek but like me, Linda has a gift, no doubt from God. Patrick and I have many conversations about her. Having met her again this morning, I can see why he's so fond of her. Now I really should begin."

He asked them to wait downstairs for him as he began in the lounge walking with a crucifix in one hand and a small silver fob filled with Holy water in the other. He sprinkled water as he asked God to bless the house and clear it of any evil presence. Repeating the words, he made his way slowly through the ground floor. It was after he'd made his way upstairs the empty cups began to rattle in their saucers on the coffee table in front of Linda and Derek. Then the TV mysteriously came on but there was no picture, just static flicking across the screen. When the lights flashed on and off, Derek reached over and took her hand. Knowing he was afraid, reassuringly she said it was probably the children playing tricks, but she knew it wasn't.

Upstairs, Father Angelo was now sensing a dark presence as he moved along the landing. Beads of sweat were massing on his forehead and the hair on his neck rising as he made his way to the master bedroom. When he entered, he felt the temperature drop rapidly and the door slammed behind him. Most alarming was he could feel something standing behind him. It was breathing on him, its foul breath making him feel nauseous.

"In the name of Christ, I compel you to leave this house" he said as he slowly turned around.

There before him stood a grotesque creature. Of no sexual gender, its body twisted with cloven hooves and two horn shaped bones protruding from its head. Despite Father Angelo being six feet in height the beast towered above him, its piercing black, soulless eyes staring at him. Long filthy nails that resembled claws reached out to touch him. Showing it no fear, Angelo flicked the water at it and commanded it to leave.

"You denied me once Priest, you will not deny me again," said the beast as its long forked tongue reached out and licked the side of Angelo's face. "I want the one you took from me. He will come and I will be waiting! Tell Patrick if he does not come, I will take his precious Linda in his place!"

Standing firm and despite his inner fear Angelo commanded the beast to leave, stating this house was a place of God and the beast was not welcome.

From downstairs Linda had heard the door slam and raised voices. Concerned for Father Angelo, she had run upstairs and was banging on the door but failed to open it. In that moment a mighty wind, like that of a twister spun around the demon and seemed to suck him down through the floor. Angelo could hear it laughing as it said they would meet again.

Moments later, the priest appeared looking unnerved. There was a red mark on his face where the beast had licked him, it looked like a burn.

Derek looked concerned when they returned downstairs. They both noticed Father Angelo's palms were bleeding and asked if they could help him. As though it was nothing unusual, he asked for a bowl of water and some bandages.

With his wounds cleaned and covered, they chatted. He decided not to talk about the demon he encountered due to Derek's failing health after Linda mentioned the cups shaking and how it had unnerved him. Instead, he asked her to tell him about the people she'd talked to Patrick about, namely Angel and Alan.

Linda talked freely about how both Angel and Alan were very talented mediums. She spoke candidly about how Angel once lived in the house and how finding her diary had led her to find Angel. They spoke about the shop Angel owned and how she and Alan often did mediumship at the local spiritualist church. Being a Catholic, Father Angelo wasn't supposed to believe in the likes of clairvoyants and mediums, but he wasn't like other priests, having witnessed first-hand the gifts that certain individuals possessed and knowing Linda was among them. Although she didn't know it, he knew it was no coincidence that she had bought the house after falling in love with it.

It was forty minutes later as Father Angelo stood up to leave; Linda said she would walk him to his taxi.

Once outside, she thanked him for not speaking of the demon he'd encountered because Derek hadn't quite come to terms with the strange happenings in the house.

"I know Linda, but how did you know I encountered anything?"

With a grin she reflected back to her childhood and how her Uncle's door had mysteriously slammed shut when she'd tried to leave his room, also the voice she'd heard when Patrick had attacked her father. Whilst banging on the door, she'd heard the same voice talking to Angelo.

"Patrick was right, you have the gift Linda. He also told me the woman Angel fought the demon Cimiries. In my opinion she successfully banished him. This demon is called Beelzebub. I first encountered him as a young man; he was the demon I helped exorcise from Patrick. I hoped never to meet him again, but your presence in the house has changed that. I would ask you not to tell Patrick as I fear he would come here. Were he in good health, I would welcome him, but his time is limited and he needs to rest."

"Oh my God Angelo, I never knew. He never mentioned it when we spoke. I know he has the early stages of Parkinson's, but people can live for years with that. Is there something he hasn't told me?"

"Unfortunately yes, he has a rare form of bone cancer and it's very aggressive. He's declined from having any treatment. He just wants to end his days at the Vatican surrounded by God. Against the Pope's wishes, he is still carrying out his duties as a Cardinal, but every day he grows weaker."

Linda was shocked that Patrick hadn't mentioned it to her.

Father Angelo kissed her cheek as he opened the taxi door and said he would no doubt be in touch and he would see her again very soon.

Walking back to the house after waving goodbye to Father Angelo, she glanced up at the window. The old woman was standing staring at her. Despite her heart pounding, Linda stared back for a few minutes until the old women disappeared. In a strange way she felt she had won a victory, simply because she'd stood her ground and in her mind the old lady had backed down.

Entering the house, she was overwhelmed by the foul smell that greeted her when she'd opened the front door. Feeling quite nauseous, her first thought was Derek as she hurriedly made her way to the lounge.

It was clear from the relief on his face when he saw her, he was glad she was back indoors. While she'd gone to see Father Angelo out, he'd heard strange noises from upstairs and the TV had again come on, the words GET OUT appeared on the screen. Linda noticed he was trembling and reassuringly sat on the arm of his chair and placed her arm around him.

With a look of fear, he asked her what was going on.

Not wanting to alarm him as to the absolute truth, she simply said their house was haunted, but hopefully Father Angelo had sorted it out for them. With a look of fear he shook his head and told her what had happened when she was outside.

She decided to tell him all the things she knew and about her Uncle Patrick. Derek looked stunned; especially that she'd been remembering things from her childhood. However it was when she spoke in detail about Angel's diary, he seemed interested. Maybe Linda had been right all along, maybe his illness was connected to the house and the old lady. Worried as to what he might say next, she was relieved and thankful when he said he was sorry he hadn't believed her in the beginning and it was up to her whether they stayed there or not. He would stand by any decision she made, unless he really felt their safety was in question.

Hugging him, she expressed how she feared for his health, but she knew they both loved the house and maybe that's why she'd been drawn to it. One thing was certain, she wouldn't let anyone or anything run her out. She would fight for it, but not at the cost of his life.

"I've never believed in ghosts Linda, you know that, but now I'm convinced something in this house wants to hurt us. We've always stuck together and I don't intend to stop now! I just wished I felt well enough to help you."

Linda hugged him and said she felt the same, but his wellbeing must be the priority.

CHAPTER 10

Father Angelo made his way through the vast corridors of the Vatican. His mission was to find his friend Patrick. Finding him praying, he rested his hand on his shoulder to let him know he was there.

Patrick looked pale and gaunt since their last meeting two weeks earlier. Standing up he embraced his dear friend and asked how things had gone in London. Angelo talked about the seminar and his visit to bless Linda's house as they walked. He'd talked for almost fifteen minutes before they reached a large dining hall. It was quiet with very few priests using the room.

The two friends sat down and, moments later, a young novice priest came over and asked if they'd like some refreshments. Both men thanked him and said a cup of tea would be very welcomed.

Father Angelo continued to talk about his time in London. Patrick asked him about the blessing he'd performed at Linda's. Angelo tried to sound convincing that all was well, but he knew he hadn't been successful when Patrick grinned and said.

"Now tell me what really happened Angelo. We don't have secrets from each other. I may be losing my eyesight my dear friend, but I can tell you're holding something back. I noticed the mark on your face, it was a mark I saw many times on Father Doyle and the other priests, yourself included, when I was a young man in Ireland. So come on, tell me what happened because I know something did."

Reluctantly, Angelo began telling him the truth about his visit to Linda's.

Patrick listened. He'd known this day would come and knew he had to put an end to it, once and for all. He told Angelo he intended to visit Linda and rid her of the demon. Angelo felt afraid; he knew it would probably result in Patrick's death. He wasn't a well man and he certainly wasn't strong enough to fight this demon. It would have killed him the first time had he not been a strong young man.

Angelo begged him to let him go in his place, but Patrick wouldn't hear of it. This was his calling, his chance to rid the world of an evil presence that would possess anyone who wasn't strong enough to resist him. Angelo was quick to point out he would need the approval of the Pope. His hope was the Pope would decline his request and send him in Patrick's place.

"There are things I should tell you my friend," said Patrick "my memories of my youth are as clear to me now as they were then, but there is much I have kept to myself to protect Linda. Now I feel the time has come for me to tell you Angelo."

The priest listened as Patrick began telling him a story which even he had been unaware of.

When Linda was five years old, her father had expressed his concern to Father Doyle that she was different to other children. Since the death of Patrick's mother and father and him moving in with the family, Linda had seen things. Unbeknown to anyone at that time, a month before the accident, she had drawn a picture of it. When her father had found it, he asked her about it. With the innocence of a child she told him a man who came into her bedroom told her it would happen. As she was the eldest child and only daughter; her parents decided not to make too much of it. They hoped it was just the overactive imagination of a child, but they were wrong. Often at night, Patrick, at the time a boy himself, heard her talking to someone in her room. Often he would get up to check on her, but he never saw anyone. For a while after she started school everything seemed to calm down. It was after Patrick told the family he wanted to join the priesthood a couple of years later, things started up again. Linda was around seven years old by then and her closeness to Patrick was clear to everyone. One evening he returned with the family from Mass and was talking of his calling from God when Linda started crying. Her mother asked what was wrong. In a tearful voice she said 'he would hurt her if Patrick left.'

The family were shocked when, after Patrick asked who would hurt her, she spoke of the monster who wanted her. At first they wondered if she simply didn't want him to leave, they all knew how close she was. Her father explained that although Patrick might have to go away she would still see him when he came to visit. Instantly she had begun screaming and begging him to stay.

Finally, Patrick managed to calm her down and told her he would read her a bedtime story.

Angelo asked what happened after that time. With a look of sadness, Patrick told how the demon tried to possess Linda.

There had been several times when the family were aware something evil was present. Often there were cold spots in the farmhouse and crockery and ornaments would fly across the room. It became apparent these strange occurrences always seemed to happen when Patrick was with Linda.

"Father Doyle had blessed the house, but that just seemed to make things worse. Linda's parents were in turmoil. The Church had been reluctant to get involved other than Father Doyle's blessings. I knew if the demon did possess her, she would die unless someone helped her. Over the weeks she became withdrawn, she didn't want to eat and her mood was often hostile towards her younger siblings. I had read about demon possession and everything seemed to fit with Linda. Father Doyle also thought it, but he was powerless to help without the Church's backing. Two weeks before the demon possessed me, I had gone into Linda's room to check on her. She was asleep in bed; she looked so ill, so frail. Her mother hadn't left her side for days. The doctor had visited but was at a loss to diagnose what could be wrong with her. He had arranged some hospital tests for later that week. I told her mother to go downstairs for something to eat and drink while I sat with Linda. There had been no change and she'd been unable to get Linda to eat or drink anything. It was only a few minutes after she left the room; Linda opened her eyes and smiled at me. Taking her hand, I tried to comfort her. Then he showed himself and I was no longer looking at my sweet niece. Her face contorted and she spat at me. Then he spoke to me, telling me she belonged to him. The crucifix her mother had placed on the pillow flew at me with such force it cut my face. I don't mind admitting how afraid I was Angelo, but I couldn't run or just stand by and allow this to happen, I was young and lacked experience. Linda began to levitate; I just sat there praying to God to help her. It was when I grabbed her leg to bring her down she turned on me. I cannot begin to tell you the strength she had Angelo. I was thrown across the room. Everything began shaking, the bed was banging up and down and I could barely move against the force of the wind. I feared for my life, but still I prayed and begged God to help her. Her parents heard the noise and came running into the room. Linda was suspended, crawling along the ceiling; she hissed and spat at them below her. Her mother was hysterical and began screaming; the demon laughed and vomited green pus down on her. In the moments that followed, Linda swooped down on me and attacked me. I looked into her eyes, they were no longer the eyes of a child they were red and soulless. I knew it was the demon. As we fought I said 'in the name of God leave this child and take me!'

My brother told me I passed out and Linda collapsed. She had no recollection of what had occurred the next morning. Her appetite returned and for the first time in weeks she looked happy. I believed God had helped us and heard our cries for help, but the following day as my brother said grace, I felt the demon inside me. The rest is history."

CHAPTER 11

Angel was enjoying spending time with James that evening. Over a glass of wine, he talked about them getting married. Although she loved him with all her heart, she didn't like the idea of him being away so much, or the fact his life was in constant danger. It would never be her intention to ask him to resign from the career he loved, but she feared for his life and she would want him home raising any children they may have. She also felt that until her past was put to rest she could never commit to marriage, especially as she knew he wanted children. Her heart was telling her she should tell him of her past, but her head was questioning how he would react. All he knew was she was a medium who made a reasonably good living from her gift. Ironically, she had never read for him due to his lack of belief. He rarely accompanied her to the spiritual church and only on rare occasions mentioned her gift.

Catching her staring at him as she pondered, he smiled and asked what she was thinking. With a smile, she said he probably wouldn't believe her if she told him.

Placing his wine down, he snuggled up closer to her on the sofa and said she should try him, she may be surprised.

He noticed a look of anguish on her face as she began telling him about the happenings at number 16 Albert Avenue. He knew she'd been fostered and then adopted by Olivia, but he had no idea about any ghosts, why would he, he hadn't met Angel until she moved out.

She went into great detail about how Linda finding her diary had stirred up issues and feelings she'd hoped would never surface again.

James listened and watched her face go through stages of happiness when she talked of Joey then fear as she talked about the old woman. However, he hadn't bargained on what she would say about the night the demon Cimiries manifested. She had never talked about Johnathan, her guardian angel, either. The only thing she didn't talk about was Joyce's death; she decided it wasn't in her best interests to tell anyone.

"Doesn't all this stuff give you the willies Angel? I know I've never really been into it, but if those things really happened and that's not to say I don't believe you, but I think I'd give up doing it. Your guardian angel, Johnathan, do you think you'll see him again?"

Angel shrugged her shoulders, she hoped she would but she had no way of knowing. Taking everything on board, he asked what she thought would happen with Linda and her husband.

Looking sad, it was her belief if they didn't leave the house, Derek would die and she had no idea how Linda would fare. Although Alan was convinced she had seen and heard things for a reason, he also believed they had a moral and spiritual duty to help them.

"Ok Angel so all this hocus pocus aside, what do you think about us getting married?"

Angel playfully picked up a cushion and hit him with it for making fun of the supernatural. She giggled and said if she did agree to marry him, she would expect him to go down on one knee and in future not mock what she believed in.

Promising he would on both counts, they kissed and cuddled.

Three hours later, after making love, they were cuddled up in bed together. James was fast asleep, but Angel's mind and heart were heavy. It was as she lay there, she felt she wasn't alone. Something was watching her, but it wasn't a good feeling. It was a feeling of something evil. Her heart was pounding as she scanned the room in the dim light. Suddenly something caught her attention; a black shadowy figure was standing at the bottom of the bed.

When she commanded it to leave, she heard a sinister laugh then the bed started to move on its own. Travelling at speed, it shot across the room and smashed into the dresser. James immediately woke and, gathering his senses, asked what the hell was going on but before she could reply, the bed moved again even faster only this time hitting the mirrored wardrobes, shattering the glass over them.

James was shouting for it to stop, but all he heard was the same terrible laughter. Suddenly a bright light filled the room and the demon vanished.

"Johnathan, is that you" called Angel, but there was no reply.

Still in shock, James asked what had just happened and was he having a nightmare, because if he was, it was very real to him. The room was wrecked, there was broken glass everywhere including on the bed. Angel looked at the table lamp lying a few feet from her and using all her psychic power made it come on. In the light, the full devastation of what had happened hit them both and especially James.

Looking quite ashen, he asked her to explain what the hell was going on.

Still trembling and worried to what he would think, she said it was a dark entity connected to what had been happening with Linda. Maybe Alan was right, maybe they were supposed to help, but she was afraid. Once before it had almost cost her life and she didn't want to ever go back to the house.

She felt thankful when James hugged her and said he would be with her and it would take more than a demon to keep them apart. He loved her and he wasn't about to give up on her.

The atmosphere changed again suddenly as Angel felt a presence. Even James could feel the temperature dropping and a strange eeriness seemed to engulf them.

Then something happened to James, he cried out as he felt a searing pain on his back. Angel instantly tried to protect him by commanding whoever it was to leave. With James writhing in pain, she knew whatever was attacking him wasn't going to stop. With all her strength she asked God to help her and protect James. A few moments passed then another attack followed, only this time Angel saw the old woman, Agnes Tibbs. It was clear from her frightened look she had hoped to remain invisible. With Angel looking at her and threatening to send her to Hell for all eternity, Agnes Tibbs hissed at her. With James's blood on her nails, she seemed to glide backwards across the room. The door slammed as she moved through it.

Angel tended to James's back and arms. Deep scratches were bleeding from where Agnes had attacked him.

As she bathed him with antiseptic he winced. The scratches were deep like cuts and it stung as she cleansed them. Apologising, she never thought for one minute he would be attacked or even at risk. Her theory was that after he'd said he would stand by her, the demon sent Agnes to frighten him off.

"I told you Angel, I'm here for you, but tonight has opened my eyes to the dark side of what you do."

Fully understanding how he felt, she asked if he wanted to leave and stay somewhere else.

Shaking his head, he stated he couldn't leave her but they needed help.

Angel nodded in agreement and said she would speak to Alan. Although he agreed in principle, James thought a priest may be a better option.

They spent the rest of the night in the guest bedroom after deciding to clear up the broken glass in the morning. Neither of them slept, but there were no more strange incidents.

First thing the following morning, Angel called Alan and spoke of the strange events from the previous night. Her timing was perfect; he'd already arranged for Linda to come to his house for coffee at eleven that day. She'd called to say she had information from her Uncle Patrick and Angelo and she was remembering more. He suggested Angel and James joining them.

James wasn't as keen as Angel would have liked, but nevertheless he would accompany her. They spent the early part of the morning clearing up the mess in the master bedroom. It was obvious James was still stunned by what happened and in a strange way she was glad he'd seen first-hand how some spiritual forces acted. Although it wasn't common, it could happen again.

By ten fifty they were at Alan's.

Greeting them at the door he said Linda was already there.

After he made drinks they all listened to what Linda told them Father Angelo had said when he blessed the house and how they believed Angel had successfully banished the demon Cimiries, but now another dark entity, Beelzebub, was causing devastation. While they chatted, Alan looked up the demon and discovered he was one of the most feared demons, commanding the grand order of demons. He was also referred to as the Lord of Chaos. This demon appeared to be far more powerful than Cimiries.

The friends looked on in horror as James lifted his T shirt to show them the wounds the old lady Agnes Tibbs had inflicted on him.

Alan was in no doubt Agnes was fearful of Beelzebub and was simply doing his will.

Angel reached over to touch Linda's hand in a reassuring manner after seeing the look of fear she had. It was as Linda reciprocated and squeezed her hand, Angel had a vision. Despite trying to let go of Linda, it was like holding an electrical cable, a force was preventing her from releasing it.

Suddenly she was back at number 16 Albert Avenue, but she wasn't alone. Two priests, Linda, James and another man were there with her. She was standing in the master bedroom; it was almost as though they were expecting someone. For a few seconds she just stood there then everything came over dark and the foulest smell filled the air. Moments later they encountered the demon Beelzebub, he was there for the old priest. The frail old man tried to fight, but Angel saw his death. Before the vision finished, unbeknown to Angel, James had prised her hand from Linda's after both women began to shake violently.

With both women badly affected, Alan made tea and then began asking Angel what she'd seen, but before she could reply, Linda said they'd foreseen her Uncle Patrick's death.

Surprised she had witnessed the vision, Alan asked her to tell him exactly what she'd seen.

Angel agreed with everything she said. Alan had a theory that Angel's vision was something that would happen in the future. Angel asked if he felt James was at risk.

With a worried look, Alan said after the attack by Agnes, he wouldn't rule it out.

CHAPTER 12

Linda had been busy working on the house, stripping wallpaper in the bedroom. Derek had felt unwell and slept most of the day in the armchair. Not having read Angel's diary for a while, she decided that after dinner she would take a couple of hours off and read.

The time was almost eight when she finished clearing up from dinner. Derek watched the TV while she read.

'After hearing the drumming noise for a few weeks things seemed to calm down. I should have known it wouldn't last long. I began experiencing nightmares. This was rare for me. Of course I had bad dreams, but this was different. I had the same nightmare for several nights. In the nightmare it was dark, night time. I was running through a wood. People carrying flaming torches were chasing me; they were wearing long black hooded robes. It was just as they surrounded me, a voice would come from nowhere. I could never make out what the voice said, but it had them running back into the woods. Then I would wake.

I didn't tell mum the following morning over breakfast that it had happened again, simply because I knew she had some important news to tell me. I was so happy for her.

Martin had asked her to marry him, although I knew he would. Despite only having been seeing one another for a few months it was clear the way they both felt. He sent her flowers with beautiful notes attached and took her out for dinner at least once a week. Best thing for mum was that I liked him; he was a good man who I knew would make her happy. I wasn't surprised though when she stated it would be a long engagement, she wasn't the type to rush into anything as serious as marriage. Or when she added she wasn't keen on them living there after what had happened to Charles. Martin had made it clear he would be quite happy for her and Angel to move in with him and sell the house. We chatted about Martin and their wedding as we ate, but mum looked sad and asked if I thought Charles would approve. What followed made her happy when there was a knock on the table and the cups rattled. Confident it was Joey, I said hello. Moments later Mary and Joey appeared. We could both see them clearly as though they were real. With a smile, Mary seemed to curtsey before telling mum Charles did approve. A tear ran down mum's cheek as she looked upwards and said 'thank you Charles that means a lot to me.'

A gentle breeze seemed to come from nowhere and it carried the smell of roses. Mum knew it was Charles; he always bought her roses and had planted some rose bushes in the garden just before he'd died. Neither of us had noticed Joey and Mary disappear; we were both in awe of what was happening. That beautiful moment was then marred by the presence of Agnes Tibbs. I couldn't see her, but I'd recognised her smell, it was thick and pungent like formaldehyde. The atmosphere instantly went to one of loathing and suppression. We knew Agnes was angry that Charles had managed to make contact. Nevertheless, mum let it pass, happy in the knowledge that Charles had given his blessing.

It was the school holidays so I was going into work with mum that day at her book shop. I loved it, I could read, chat to mum and serve customers. I loved the smell of the shop, like old books. People would come in and ask if she had a particular book by a certain author and she always knew exactly where to look. Little did either of us realise how different that day was going to be when we left the house for the shop that morning.

Mum knew a lot of her customers. They were avid readers or collectors of old books.

I was sitting at the counter reading while mum made us a cuppa in the back room when the bell above the door rang. I smiled at the little old lady who entered.

Every now and again I looked up from my book to watch as she pondered the books on the spiritual shelf. Almost an hour passed and several people had come and gone by the time she selected a book. Mum had just popped out to the baker's two shops along, to buy us a filled roll for lunch.

Finally, the elderly lady came up to the counter; she was carrying a leather bound book. Thanking her as I took it, I attempted to make conversation by asking if she was looking forward to reading it. To my surprise she smiled and said it wasn't for her, it was a gift. I told her the price and she handed me the correct money as I asked if she'd like a bag. With a sweet smile she shook her head and stated the book was a gift for me and I should pay particular interest to the inscription inside the cover and page 178. A little shocked, I offered her the money back telling her I could simply read it then put it back on the shelf. It was as I attempted to open the book to read the inscription; she gently placed her hand on mine to stop me and said 'you need to answer that.' Answer what I thought, but at that precise moment the phone rang. I turned to pick it up then quickly turned back to tell the lady I wouldn't be a moment, but she was gone. The phone was just static with no caller. Replacing the receiver, I looked around the shop but she was nowhere to be seen, yet I knew the door had not been opened because the bell hadn't rung.

Mum appeared and seeing the confused look on my face, asked if I was ok. I explained what had happened. She asked me which book I'd been given. I passed it to her but there was no title or author's name, yet I could have sworn there was when the lady had given it to me. Mum opened the book and promptly told me it wasn't from her shop, she knew every title there and this book wasn't one of hers.

She read the inscription inside the cover which was written beautifully in gold italic scroll.

'Embrace your destiny without fear Angel.'

Mum and I just looked at each other with raised eyebrows. A few silent moments passed then I asked her to look at page 178.

It turned out to be the last page, but more unnerving was the fact the previous pages were blank.

I asked mum why anyone would give me a blank book. Mum's reply was maybe I was meant to write in it. After all, I had said a while back I'd thought about keeping a diary.

Mum was right, so much had happened during my earlier years. The best being the day I met mum. Yes, maybe I would write a sort of diary.

For the rest of the day, I thought about the sweet old lady. Despite the strange circumstances of me being given the book, I felt good about it.'

Linda stopped reading when Derek asked her what the time was, after having dozed off in the chair.

Looking at her watch she was surprised it was almost eleven. He nodded when she suggested a nightcap then heading for bed.

Ten minutes later as she lay in bed, she thought about Angel's diary. She felt intrigued by the old lady who'd given it to her and the inscription that was written.

CHAPTER 13

Despite wanting to spend time with James, Angel had the shop to run. That day she had three tarot readings booked for the morning.

With James still in bed, she kissed his cheek and said she was only downstairs if he needed her, but for him to enjoy his lie in.

Downstairs, she flipped the closed sign to open and unlocked the shop door. Outside, the school traffic was less manic; it was just after nine. Her first customer was booked for ten; it was a gentleman she saw quite regularly. He'd lost his son in an accident a few years ago and although a total non-believer, he believed in Angel. His wife had gone along to the spiritual church after losing their son and couldn't wait to get home and tell him about the young medium that had picked her out. The things Angel had said gave her hope and helped her accept her son's death. John, the boy's father, wasn't the type to go to a spiritual church. A detective in the Police Force, he believed in right and wrong and seeing was believing. That was until he met Angel.

Due to his wife's nagging he had finally agreed to go, but not to the church, he was far too private a man for that. That was four years ago and since then every three months he visited her shop. Angel always had messages for him.

In fact she had met two of her day's customers, but the last had booked by phone. Her name was Grace and she'd never had a reading before. Angel always liked new people; it kept her business going when, after they'd seen her, they'd recommend her.

James had popped down with a coffee for her just as John was leaving.

They didn't have time to chat as her next customer was already waiting.

Before going back upstairs, he told her he'd rung Olivia and he would be taking both ladies out for a late lunch.

Grace had arrived at exactly twelve for her reading. Angel welcomed her and quickly showed her to the reading room at the rear of the shop.

There was something familiar about her, leaving Angel wondering if they'd met before. In her late sixties to early seventies with a bright smile and a kind face, Angel sat down to read for her.

Through curiosity she asked if they'd met, stating she looked familiar.

"I have one of those faces dear" said Grace with a smile "I've travelled the world several times over, so I've met thousands of people, but you're right dear we did meet once."

Angel's curiosity got the better of her and she asked where and when.

"Let me check" said Grace as she opened her bag and took out a small note book and scanned through its pages. "Ah yes of course, it was here in this very shop dear, although it was a book shop at the time. November 1st 2003. You were very young, sixteen I believe. I gave you a gift, a book."

Angel suddenly realised she was the sweet old lady from the shop all those years ago. Despite feeling a little nervous she didn't show it and asked Grace who she was and why she was there as it was clear she didn't need a tarot reading.

"I've come to talk with you dear and I have something for you from your mother, she is such a lovely woman."

Intrigued more than nervous, Angel said she never knew her mother and Olivia was her mum.

"Yes dear I know, Evelyn chose her for you and I must say it was the perfect choice."

"Evelyn, who is that? I don't know any Evelyn" stated Angel. "You need to tell me why you're here Grace, if your name is Grace?"

"Yes its Grace dear," chuckled the old lady "no matter how old I get this never gets easier. I'm never really comfortable doing this work with people. You'd think after six hundred years I'd be used to it, wouldn't you."

Now feeling totally confused, Angel simply stared at her for several seconds before replying.

"No wait, are you telling me you're six hundred years old? Don't mind if I laugh, will you, only you'd be dead and then I'd see you as spirit and believe me you look very real. So unless this is some sort of a joke can you please tell me exactly what's going on!"

"Oh fiddlesticks, I knew I'd make a mess of this. You see Angel, there are some babies born who go on to do great things. You are one of those babies, as was Evelyn, your mother. Just like you she never knew her real mother, but she loves you so much and that's why I'm here dear. She would come herself, but she holds a very special place in what you would refer to as Heaven. The book I gave you wasn't really for you, but Evelyn knew if you took the time to write your story someone who needed your help would read it. I can tell by your face you think I'm a nutty old woman who probably has Alzheimer's, believe me I'm not. Everything I've told you is the truth. The reason Evelyn asked me to come is to tell you that time is now. Soon you will have to face the biggest challenge of your life dear. A terrible evil is spreading and you have no idea how powerful it will become if you don't stop it. You know what I'm talking about, don't you dear?"

Angel nodded; she knew she meant the demon that waits at 16 Albert Avenue. In her mind she had a million questions about her mother, her life, her future, yet she sat quietly and listened as Grace continued.

"The house is a portal from Hell dear, but you know that. We know you fear this demon and you are wise to, but you can defeat him. You won't be alone dear. Never lose your courage Angel and show Beelzebub no fear."

Still slightly in awe of Grace, Angel took comfort from her words, although she really wanted to ask about her real mother.

Almost as though Grace knew this, she opened her bag again and took out a small piece of material which appeared to have something wrapped inside it. Placing it down on the table she told Angel it was from her mother. Just as Angel reached over to pick it up, she heard the shop's doorbell ring, yet she remembered locking the door. With a smile, she said James must have gone out and forgot to lock up. She would just check to make sure.

Less than a minute had passed when she walked back into the reading room after checking the shop and finding the door locked. Grace was gone, but Angel wasn't surprised.

Sitting down she looked at the small piece of material still sitting on the table. Inside was a small locket. Prizing the sides apart it revealed a photograph of a beautiful young woman who bore an uncanny resemblance to her. On the other side was an inscription 'Evelyn with love.'

She was looking at a picture of her mum. Tears welled in her eyes and spilled over onto her cheeks.

"Has she gone?" asked James looking at her from the doorway.

When Angel looked up and nodded, he noticed the tears and instantly made his way over asking what was wrong.

Without replying, she passed him the open locket.

"That's lovely babe, when did you get that taken and who's Evelyn?"

"That's not me; it's Evelyn, my mother. I'll tell you all about it when we pick mum up. Now I have to freshen up. I'll only be five minutes."

Looking baffled, he said he would check everything was in order with the shop and he'd wait there for her.

At the restaurant, Oliva looked at the locket. There was no doubt it was Angel's mum.

They talked about Grace and whether they believed her to be a spirit or an angel. Then Olivia talked about Evelyn. When she fostered Angel the details around her biological mother were sketchy at best. The fact Angel never talked about her mother meant Olivia never felt a need to bring the topic up, even when she adopted her.

They could both see Angel was thinking about Evelyn. It was Olivia who suggested them trying to find out about her, even though they knew she had died. It may be nice for Angel to know a little about her past.

James agreed; he'd help her search records while he was home.

Angel thanked them, but stated she didn't need to know about Evelyn. Olivia was her mum and nothing would change that. There was also what Grace had said about Evelyn choosing Olivia and that told Angel the type of mother she was. She knew she was a good person who loved her.

CHAPTER 14

Angel had just opened the shop when Alan walked in. Always pleased to see him, she offered him a coffee.

Knowing she'd hear the doorbell if she had a customer, they sat in her reading room. She had forty five minutes before her ten o'clock client arrived.

Before Alan started talking, she knew he had something important to tell her.

"I'd like you to come and meet an old friend of mine Angel. I've been talking to him and telling him about what's been happening. He's an expert in demonology. He seemed a little concerned when I spoke of the attack on James. I just think it would be time well spent making the trip. I've said I'd speak to you, but he thinks the sooner we visit him the better."

Angel knew he wouldn't have suggested it were it not important to him. She had also been concerned regarding the attack on James, along with the visit from Grace.

With a smile she asked when he'd like to go. She was shocked when he said as soon as possible. The friend he wanted her to meet, Nathanial Williamson, had in fact been a priest once, but he'd left the Church many years ago. Since then he lived the life of a recluse. The very fact he had requested the visit told Alan they needed to go.

Angel nodded and asked what day would suit him best; she would cancel her readings and shut the shop. She hadn't expected him to say, tomorrow.

They would have talked more had her ten o'clock client not have arrived ten minutes early.

It was lunch time before she spent time with James. They had lunch together in the flat.

Knowing he would probably want to accompany her and Alan, she stated it wasn't necessary for him to go with them if he had other plans.

Taking her hand he smiled, what would he rather do than spend time with her was his reply.

Fortunately she only had two readings booked that afternoon.

Kissing him on the cheek she made her way back to the shop for her two o'clock reading. James would cook for them that evening.

The afternoon passed quickly with her readings going well.

By the time she shut the shop, the aroma of dinner was wafting down the stairs as she made her way to the flat.

Thirty minutes later she sat down to a feast of lasagne, garlic bread and salad.

As James poured her another glass of wine, he asked her more about Nathanial Williamson.

It was as she began telling him the room seemed to take on a cold atmosphere; so much so, he asked if the window was open. Before she had time to reply the crockery began to shake. A knife flew from the table barely missing James. When Angel stood up and ordered the spirit to leave, everything became quiet.

"What the Hell was that Angel?"

"I don't know, but I'm sure it has something to do with us talking about Nathanial. I've never encountered anything like this James. Alan seemed keen for us to speak with this Nathanial chap since hearing about the attack on you. Maybe something is trying to frighten you off.

Whatever it is, I'm not sure if I'm strong enough to deal with it alone."

Despite feeling nervous, he told her nothing would scare him away from her, he was with her all the way.

Neither of them slept particularly well that night. Visiting Nathanial the following day was heavy on their minds.

Alan's car horn sounded outside the shop just before eight the following morning. He'd suggested leaving early to avoid the rush hour traffic. They had a four hour drive ahead of them.

James was full of questions about Nathanial as they drove.

"I met him by chance through a friend many years ago" said Alan "he's quite a character. In my opinion he's the undisputed expert on demonology. His knowledge on the subject is quite extraordinary. He was a priest for ten years before leaving the Church and becoming a world authority on demonology. I'm not sure why he left the Church, we've never spoken about it, but I'm sure it wasn't without good reason. I think you'll be quite surprised when you meet him, he's not what you'd expect."

The entire journey was taken up with talk of Nathanial and the strange events around Angel.

After leaving the motorway, Alan turned into a country road. It seemed to go on for miles before he told them they'd be there any minute.

In front of them was a rundown house, which was really more of a mansion. There was rambling woodland to three sides and a gravel drive leading up to the house via the front. Two evil looking stone gargoyles seemed to look down on them from above the front door as Alan rang the bell.

After what seemed like ages, but was barely a few moments, the door opened.

Nathanial hugged Alan and greeted them as he invited them in. He was a ruggedly handsome man in his early forties and looked more like a body builder than a demonologist. Like Angel, James had envisaged him being a much older man.

Inside the house was a far cry from the overgrown exterior. Old paintings which looked to be worth money lined the hall walls.

Following him through to the lounge the first thing Angel noticed was the rhino's head mounted on the wall above the large open fire.

"Grotesque isn't he" said Nathanial "I hope poor old Horace didn't suffer before his death. It belonged to the previous owner who left me the house. I've often toyed with the idea of taking him down, but I'm used to him now. Anyway enough talk of Horace, we need to concentrate on matters pending. So Angel, you must tell me of these events Alan has spoken to me about."

Over the next two hours they drank tea as she told him about her life. When she finished, Nathanial looked at James and asked if he believed in God. When he shook his head and said "Not really," Nathanial smiled and stated it would be a good time to start believing because the demon had marked him.

"Marked me?" said a clearly disbelieving James.

Without replying to his question, Nathanial said there was something they should see.

They followed him through to the drawing room. The items they saw there would have been worthy of a place in a museum. The table was littered with scrolls and parchments. Maps, along with pictures of the solar system, covered the main wall.

Unrolling a large old scroll, Nathanial told them to secure the edges with a weight. There were several items to choose from including candles, paperweights and small carved boxes.

Once opened out, the scroll showed the solar system. There were many strange symbols and writings in what appeared to be a type of hieroglyphics.

"Right" said Nathanial "according to Alan this was around the time you were born Angel. See how the planets cross there? This is a rare occurrence; in the Hebrew calendar it represents the birth of a Holy child. Now that doesn't mean you are a super being, on the contrary, it simply means you have been smiled upon by God. You possess certain skills which most of us do not. Of course, as with all good things to descend upon the earth something bad descends with it, that's just the way it is, good versus evil. After speaking with Alan, I tried to calculate the day of your birth along with a change in the planets. These are a series of photographs I took. Now look at the areas I've enlarged which I've copied onto disc."

Reaching behind him, Nathanial picked up a lap top and quickly brought up the picture of the scroll. Zooming in on planet earth, he crossed over several map references until they became an exact fit over one another. Then, taking the middle and one definite point, he typed in the grid reference.

"I believe that is the house where you lived Angel" said Nathanial "16 Albert Avenue? Now if I go back for a period of one hundred years, I can pinpoint every child who was born who now has a link to number 16."

He moved the mouse to another set of references.

"By putting in the day and time of each birth, I have all the information I need. The area you're seeing now is the farmhouse in Ireland where Linda was born."

He moved the grids again and on stopping, said it was the house where her uncle Patrick was born. Moving them again he marked the spot where Father Angelo had been born. Lastly, he referenced James, Olivia and Alan's birth.

"So do you see what this all means, none of you have met by chance, number 16 is the reason. It's a doorway from Hell and every ten years a new demon is sent. I should tell you Angel, you are the first person to fight and successfully defeat your demon and live to talk about it. Now as wonderful as much as strange all this may seem; I came across a very worrying fact."

He used his lap top to show them another map, explaining to them it was marking a series of unnatural phenomena which happened throughout the world.

"Firstly, you may remember reading about an incident in Israel where hailstones fell in the desert for exactly one hour. That happened the day Linda was born. Some years prior to that in Rome, the Vatican experienced hundreds of dead birds dropping from the sky. That happened the day Patrick was born. I remember reading at the time it was due to pesticides. It had nothing to do with pesticides. I've logged every event for the past hundred years, using all the grid references to mark the exact places. Every birth coincided with a phenomenon. Now look what happens when I put all those reference numbers together."

They watched as Nathanial clicked the mouse and rotated all the grid references into one. Then zooming into the spot where the combined total marked. It was 16 Albert Avenue.

Alan asked what it all meant.

"Well my friend, I believe it's the coming of the Anti-Christ. The legions of Satan have increased their numbers. Believe me, something big is about to happen. For ten years I've kept a secret watch on the occult. I'm not referring to kids who dabble with Ouija boards and stuff; I'm talking about real devil worshippers. Many of these people hold high stations in life."

Using his lap top, he brought up a series of photographs of different people and clicked onto the first photo.

"This is Hermann Klaus; he's a dealer in religious artefacts. For the last ten years he's travelled extensively, buying rare items. On his last trip to the United States, he spent time with Damien Fargo."

Nathanial clicked to the photo of a young man in his thirties.

"Meet Damien Fargo, homosexual billionaire, who inherited a fortune when his father died. For a pastime he deals in antiquities and artefacts. Was investigated by the FBI three years ago after two young boys accused him of kidnap and holding them against their will. The media at the time stated these boys had been subjected to terrifying rituals. Due to Fargo's wealth, their families settled out of court, but I managed to acquire the police statements about the boys. They recalled seeing people dressed in black robes, chanting and calling upon Satan. From the information I was able to obtain, it was clear to me they were to be sacrificed. Somehow they managed to escape. They were found naked huddled together in an alley. They had scratches and bite marks covering their bodies. The police found them in the nick of time. They were so traumatised it was weeks before counsellors could speak to them."

The next photo was of an older woman, heavy makeup covered her face.

"Leticia Lemaitre, fourth wife and now widow of the late and famous billionaire jeweller, Wentworth Lemaitre. She's been married four times and outlived three of her husbands. The one who survived has spent the last forty years locked up in an asylum after two failed suicide attempts. Details of why are not really clear, but his psychiatrist's records state he saw the Devil and was convinced something was coming for him. Leticia moves in very high circles. Has properties all over the world, but spends most of her time at her luxury mountain retreat in Zurich. Recently she's had lots of visitors including Hermann Klaus and Damien Fargo along with several other high ranking occultists."

James asked why he thought these people had bearing on what was going on at number 16.

With conviction, Nathanial explained that several known high priests of the occult had met up within the last three months. He had secretly listened to telephone conversations between them and he was confident they would meet in London before the 25th of March which was in two weeks' time. His solemn belief was they were gathering for the Apocalypse.

Walking over to a glass cabinet, he removed what looked to be a very old scroll. Taking it back to the table he rolled it open. There were symbols and text which looked like a story in drawings. Nathanial told them the scroll was thousands of years old. It had been discovered on an archaeological dig in the 1950's. He didn't tell them how it came to be in his possession and they didn't ask.

Slowly he took them from the first drawing to the last, reading the inscriptions, which were written in Hebrew, that depicted the story.

The story and writing told a tale of demons who were successfully banished to Hell. Centuries passed then some of these demons rose from the Underworld. Bloody battles with Angels sent from God were fought. A black hole showed demons re-entering the world. A group of what appeared to be mortals were shown to be fighting them with two angels helping them. The final picture showed a golden hand reaching down from heaven.

Nathanial firmly believed it was depicting the hand of God.

Despite not really understanding all the alignments with the planets and how he'd managed to find out so much information, there wasn't one of them who disbelieved what he'd said.

Rolling the scroll back up and placing it back in the cabinet, he asked if anyone had any questions.

"Yes, I do" said Angel "what happened the day you were born Nathanial?"

With a smile, he told her that a lake in Canada turned red with blood and all the fish died.

James was the only one who couldn't understand his part in everything. He definitely wasn't religious and he'd never experienced any strange events as a child. His only connection to any of this was Angel.

Nathanial believed that was why he'd been chosen. Angel had already faced a powerful demon and successfully banished him. There was no doubt in his mind she was the one the occultists feared the most. In his opinion, the night she'd met James was no coincidence. God knew she would be targeted and he needed someone strong, without fear and with total love for her here to protect her when the time came.

"I would die for her" said James "I'll do whatever it takes to keep her safe."

Angel clutched his hand. She knew, if the time ever came, he would die protecting her.

They were all nervous and surprised when there was a knock on the drawing room door. Nathanial grinned and stated it was his housekeeper, Nancy. He had asked her to prepare a buffet lunch for them before they returned to London.

After calling out to her, the door opened. They had all expected his housekeeper to be old, yet Nancy was a beautiful young woman in her twenties. With a broad smile, she told them lunch was ready and if they required anything else she would be in the kitchen.

Nathanial asked her to stay and join them for lunch.

With a smile she nodded.

A few minutes later they were all sitting at a large dining table with a veritable feast in front of them.

Angel found herself staring at Nancy. She carried an air of gentleness about her. It was as she watched her she began to experience a vision from Nancy's past.

Angel was seeing her as a young girl. She was lying on her bed. The room was full of people who Angel believed to be her family. Nathanial was there, but he was a young priest. Nancy was experiencing a demonic episode, she was spitting and hissing at him and talking in tongues. The room was in chaos as furniture flew around and an older priest was hurled against the wall. Yet it was Nathanial, the young priest, who stood his ground and commanded the demon to leave her.

"Angel where are you babe, the pepper?"

The vision stopped as Angel realised James was touching her arm, asking her to pass the pepper.

Re-joining the conversation, she was a little shocked when James asked Nathanial why he'd left the priesthood and even more shocked when Nathanial told him to ask Angel, because she knew.

In an effort to laugh his suggestion off, she giggled and said like a lot of priests he possibly realised it wasn't for him.

"Why do you doubt your abilities Angel" asked Nathanial, "did you not just see the reason why I left? Maybe you would prefer me to tell everyone?"

Angel nodded.

During his time as a priest, he'd found himself drawn to the work of an old priest, Father Michael.

He was the priest who researched demonic possession. It was while spending time with him Nathanial became fascinated and wanted to know more; almost as though it was his calling.

Father Michael would often moan about the length of time it took the Church to agree and accept that demonic possession was active in certain individuals. Often this delay resulted in deaths and, more often than not, in children dying.

Father Michael never lost his faith, no matter what evil forces he encountered. When Nathanial was twenty four, he accompanied him to a house where the family were convinced their elderly mother had been possessed by a demon.

Nathanial witnessed this elderly woman, who was riddled with arthritis, levitate and then attack her family with the strength of an elite athlete. He'd watched as she screamed and hissed the vilest of profanities at her family and them. Although he was terrified at the time, Nathanial took courage from Father Michael who never once faltered in his belief that God would rid the woman of the curse.

After that day, he became Father Michael's personal attaché, travelling with him and answering many calls for help.

Over time and, due to his mentor, Nathanial became an expert on demonology and the occult. Like Father Michael he was an exorcist. That was how he'd come to meet Nancy after her family turned to the Church for help.

Then a child of nine, she was possessed by a very strong and powerful demon. Had Father Michael not helped she would most certainly have died. The Church had been reluctant to acknowledge and confirm it was a possession, only agreeing to send Father Michael because the family were benefactors of the Church. After their first visit to Nancy's parents' house, they both knew this demon was deadly and they would need the help of other priests if they were to banish it, but the church disagreed. By the time the Church finally admitted they had been wrong, it was too late. Father Michael and Nathanial stayed with her day and night until she was freed from the demonic possession.

Nancy's parents couldn't cope with the events of her possession and asked Nathanial to take her. Her grandfather had given him the house; she'd been there ever since. When she reached eighteen, she could have left but she stayed. Her love for Nathanial was so strong she would never leave him.

It was when James asked what became of Father Michael, Nathanial smiled and nodded at Nancy.

Everyone waited as she left the room. When she returned a few moments later, she was pushing an elderly, white haired man in a wheelchair. There was no colour to his eyes, they were completely white. On his lap was a small chalk board, in his hand some white chalk.

"Thank you Nancy," said Nathanial before leaning over and gently touching the man's hand and saying "Michael, these are the friends I told you were coming today."

Father Michael began to shake as he tried to communicate. With the love of a son, Nathanial gently raised Michael's hand to the chalk board so he could write.

Everyone sat silently as he scribbled the words, 'Angel and tell them.'

Nathanial smiled and said Angel was there as he looked at her and beckoned her over to Michael.

Without hesitation, she moved round the table and gently took the old man's hand.

"Hello Father Michael, I'm Angel, it's so nice to meet you."

Nancy gently wiped the old man's face as tears began to flow down his cheeks.

Angel squeezed his hand and in that instant began to see what happened to him.

It was the evening he banished the demon from Nancy. During a struggle with the child, the beast had shown itself. Father Michael held his ground and not once backed down or showed the fear he was experiencing. The demon threw him around the room like a leaf caught in a storm. Had it not been for Nathanial, he would have perished.

That was the day his back was broken and his sight lost.

Angel had tears in her eyes as the vision ended.

Father Michael began tapping the blackboard with his chalk.

Nancy gently took his hand and secured the chalk between his thumb and fingers.

He began to scribble, but his hands were shaking and Angel couldn't make out what he'd written.

Nancy lifted the board and reading out loud said "Show him no fear, God is with you."

Moments later, Father Michael's head dropped to one side. Nathanial was the first to gently check he was alright.

Feeling Michael's pulse, he knew the old priest was dying.

With Father Michael's life slowly ebbing away, Nancy suggested taking him to his room. She would stay with him until Nathanial could come.

Alan instantly said they would leave to which she replied there was no need to hurry, she would care for Michael.

Before she wheeled him back to his room, Angel took his hand and gently kissed his face.

Once Nancy had left Angel said they should go, so Nathanial could be with them.

"He waited to meet you Angel" said Nathanial "he should have died long ago, but he always knew you would come. He'll be at peace with God soon. There are some things I need to tell you all before you leave. You all need to take extra care and you must convey this to Olivia. The beast knows you have been chosen and he will send his legions to destroy you before you can harm him. Like the old woman who attacked James. Be aware and trust no one except each other, but always remember evil has many guises. Alan you must advise Linda. Unless I'm mistaken, her husband's health will start to improve. The beast knows if he dies, Linda could leave and he's waiting for her Uncle Patrick, so the old woman will be forbidden to harm her husband. I have some things for you."

He lifted an old fashioned water flask made from animal hide from a shelf then proceeded to fill several bottles from it.

"It's holy water from Lourdes. In 1858 a young girl, Bernadette Soubirous, saw a vision of a white robed lady. On the day of the 16th apparition, the robed lady revealed herself as the Blessed Virgin Mary. That day was March the 25th, so it's important for you to use this water as the date is significant."

Nathanial proceeded to take a dagger which was wrapped in an old cloth and passed it to Angel.

"It was given to St David. It was believed stolen after Vikings pillaged the churches, but it has been safely hidden until now. Note the small emblem on the handle. It's a dove. Guard this with your life Angel, it may save yours. Now I must go and spend time with my dear friend Michael and give him Last Rites. I will see you all again very soon and remember what I said, trust no one. Nancy will come to see you out."

Quickly telling him that wouldn't be necessary, Alan said they would make their own way as he shook hands with him.

Moments later they were back in Alan's car. He suggested Angel telling Olivia the following day and he would tell Linda.

Angel was noticeably quiet during the drive. Everything Nathanial had said was going through her mind. Why was she the chosen one, she never asked to be nor did she want it. Her concern was more towards James and Olivia; they were simply involved because of her. What if this demon was more powerful than the last one she had encountered? She just didn't feel she was cut out for all this and believed people like Nathanial were more suited to it.

It was seven o'clock when they arrived home. Alan waved out to them as he pulled away.

James suggested sending for takeaway rather than having to cook. Angel nodded.

Forty minutes later they were tucking into a Chinese. James said he had a surprise for her and he was just waiting for the right time to tell her about it.

Excitedly, she asked what it was and with a giggle said she didn't mind if he gave it to her then.

"It's not something I can give you babe, it's something I want to tell you. I've resigned from the Army. I'm now a civilian."

Shocked, she threw her arms around him and asked why. The army had been his life since enlisting when he was eighteen.

"Why because I want to marry you babe and have a family; I always knew that was half the reason why you wanted to wait. I've seen so much death and pain; I want change babe. I don't think I'll have a problem getting a good job and I've got savings to tide me over so I don't need to start looking until after March 25th."

Taking a small box from his pocket, he went down on one knee and asked her to do him the honour of being his wife.

Tearfully she held out her hand and nodded as he took the ring out and slipped it on her finger.

"If Nathanial was right, I may not survive the 25th none of us might. James I'm so sorry I got you involved in all this. I'd understand if you wanted to leave."

With a broad grin, he stated he wasn't going anywhere; he was going to make sure she survived. He loved her more than anything and if need be he'd die protecting her.

CHAPTER 15

Linda was thrilled when Derek came downstairs that morning and for the second day running said he was feeling better. Even his appetite had returned.

Alan had texted her earlier to say he would like to meet up later that day, if it was convenient for her. She had arranged to go shopping that afternoon with Sophie so they would pop in on their way home.

She didn't expect the call from Father Angelo when he rang. Apologising to her for the delay in arranging Patrick's visit, he explained how the Pope wasn't happy about him undertaking such a long journey. However, Patrick had convinced him. The Pope had finally granted Father Angelo the good fortune of accompanying him.

They would be arriving in London the morning of March 23rd and they would stay at a rectory where Patrick's medical needs could be addressed if necessary. They would come to Linda's on the 25th.

Derek could see the mix of excitement and sadness on her face as she said goodbye to Father Angelo and that she was looking forward to seeing them.

With Patrick's failing health it would most likely be the last time she saw him.

After finishing their breakfast, she suggested him watching a bit of TV while she caught up on some reading. It was only ten o'clock and Sophie wasn't picking her up until one.

Derek was dozing in the chair while an old film ran on TV. Linda picked up Angel's diary and removed the bookmark.

'Since the incident in the basement things seem to have gone from bad to worse. Often I have a sinister feeling that something or someone is watching me. Today I went into work with mum at her shop. It was always busy on Saturday with lots of people just coming into browse.

It was as we pulled up outside we noticed what appeared to be a homeless man sitting in the doorway. His head was hanging down between his knees.

As mum approached the door, she politely asked him to move on. It was as he lifted his head I felt a sudden fear. He had a long dirty beard and piercing eyes that seemed to look straight through me.

We hoped he would just move on, but as he stood up he grabbed my arm and said "He's coming for you."

Mum grabbed his hand and, prising him away from me, said if he didn't leave she would call the police.

He scurried off along the parade of shops and we quickly entered the book shop.

I was still trembling ten minutes later. I knew it had also worried mum; so much so she called Alan and told him. Neither of us was surprised when he walked into the shop an hour later.

Mum told him about the homeless man and, typically of Alan trying to reassure us, said he was just trying to frighten us because he'd been asked to move. We all knew that wasn't the case, but nobody said it.

By two that afternoon, Alan had left and we had all but forgotten the homeless man that was until he walked into the shop. Mum was quick to tell him she would call the police if he upset me.

Looking a little less menacing than before; he stated he wasn't there to frighten me, but to warn me. Something was coming and it was coming soon.

That was it, mum had heard enough. With a stern voice she ordered him to leave.

"Just doing the Lord's work" he called as he shuffled out the shop.

Mum suggested shutting the shop early and going home. I didn't hesitate to agree, it was a great idea and especially when she said maybe we should invite Joyce and Alan over for dinner. She had originally planned to go out with Martin, but he'd been put out of action by a flu type bug. Our friends arrived just before eight. It was so good to see Joyce after she'd been away visiting family in Canada. We spent the evening talking about her holiday along with the strange events connected to the house. Joyce was very keen to do a séance, she had a feeling something just wasn't right. What was occurring in the house went beyond a normal haunting; we could all feel an oppressive evil. It felt to all of us that something was growing, a terrible presence seemed to hang over the house. Even the children in the house seemed to be keeping a low profile, Joey hadn't been to see me for days.

It was just after dinner when we all sensed something; the room took on an instant coldness. Then the banging started, it was quite deafening. The crockery shook and pictures fell from the walls. On Joyce's advice we held hands and prayed. Finally it stopped.

Alan surprised us when he said maybe we should consider selling the house. Mum was the first to say she loved it there and she wasn't about to be driven out by Agnes Tibbs.

With a serious look, Joyce said she didn't think it was Agnes Tibbs, it was something far more powerful and sinister and the children were trapped in the house by it.

They saw Angel as a way into the light, but whatever the evil was, it wasn't about to let the children go.

Like me, everyone wanted the children to cross over so it was agreed that later that week, Joyce and Alan would have a sitting and hopefully cross the children over and into the light.'

Linda closed the diary to get ready to go shopping with Sophie.

Twenty minutes later they were parking in the precinct.

It was whilst having a coffee in a cafe, Linda asked if Sophie would mind calling at Alan's on the way home.

Sophie was happy to see him, she really liked Alan.

It was as they headed for the car park an hour later they both noticed a homeless man sitting next to Sophie's car. It was unusual to see people like him, especially in the car park.

Approaching the car cautiously they hoped he would move when Sophia used the automatic key to open it and the lights flashed. Still he sat there.

Linda had a strange feeling about him and looked around the car park to see if anyone was there. To her dismay there wasn't a single person either parking or leaving.

The man was sitting near the passenger door which saw Linda having to squeeze past him to get into the car.

Thankful to be inside and for the automatic locking system once Sophie put the key in the ignition, they put their seatbelts on. It was as they pulled away the man knocked on Linda's window, he was shouting something about she had been marked and she couldn't run or hide. Quite shaken, Sophie pulled away. At the barrier she stopped and spoke to the man in the booth, stating there was a tramp that scared them, he was shouting things at them and if a young woman with children encountered him, he would frighten them. The man called through to security as Sophie pulled out of the car park.

Believing they'd seen the last of him, both women were horrified when, after stopping at a set of traffic lights, they spotted him standing on the side of the road. He was smiling at them.

Relieved when the lights changed to green; Sophie sped away.

They put the incident behind them when they arrived at Alan's. That was until they told him about it and he said Angel and Olivia had also seen him.

"Oh my God" said Sophie, "what does it mean Alan, we thought he was just some alcoholic or something!"

Alan stated he wasn't really sure, at first he thought he was someone bad, but when he went back into the shop he was different. It was then Alan told them what Nathanial had said. That had been his reason for wanting to see them that day.

Both women looked concerned and even more so when Alan said Derek's health was likely to improve. It was after he explained why, Linda said his health had improved, but she was concerned for her Uncle Patrick. He was due to arrive in England on March 23rd and to them on the 25th.

"Your Uncle is one of the people Nathanial spoke about Linda. He knows he has to be here to defeat this demon as does Father Angelo. This evil is far greater than any of us imagined and it will stop at nothing to harm you. Nathanial was right, you must take extra care."

Sophie was the first to suggest they simply left the house for everyone's safety. Alan instantly disagreed, stating that if Nathanial was right and he had no reason to doubt him, the best time to fight this evil was March 25th.

Sophie looked concerned and asked if there was no way Linda could not be involved. She was concerned for her and Derek.

Alan explained about the alignments of the planets and how everyone's birthday had coincided with a religious phenomenon. Everyone had been chosen and it was their destiny.

"But Linda doesn't know anything about these things, surely there must be people who are better qualified. I've seen films where people deal with demons!"

Alan grinned. Films were fiction, these events were real. People usually mock the supernatural until it happens to them.

Linda was full of questions about Nathanial and how he thought this could all end. Like Angel, she didn't feel she had the knowledge to be a party to this. Alan was quick to reassure her she did.

She confessed to him that when Angel had showed her the vision of what had taken place at the house the night they encountered the demon, she was terrified and had she been there she would have been frozen with fear. More to the point she wouldn't have a clue as to what to do. Alan disagreed, but suggested it would be a good thing if they all met at his house later that week. Linda was happy with that.

The ladies talked about all the strange things that were happening, but their main topic was Nathanial.

CHAPTER 16

James was in the bathroom getting ready for an interview. It wasn't the type of interview where he would need a CV. Since putting the word out that he was now a civilian, one of his friends had contacted him about some private security work. It wasn't the type of job you'd see advertised. It was as a bodyguard to a diplomat who would be visiting Britain for one month from April to May. The man was a high assassination risk so they needed someone they could entrust his life to and that was James.

Angel smiled as he walked back into the bedroom; he looked so smart and handsome.

Throwing her arms around his neck she kissed him and wished him luck, not that he'd need it. With his track record the job was his for the taking. She never told him, but since telling her about the job offer, she'd had a strange feeling about it.

It was as he reciprocated the kiss and said he loved her, the bedroom door slammed. They both knew it wasn't from a draught and instantly became alert.

James spotted the bed sheet moving and walking quickly to the bed threw back the cover, but it was empty. The bed sheet was wrapping itself into a rope. Suddenly it whipped out knocking him across the room. The sheet moved with the precision and speed of a striking cobra as it lashed out at him and only stopped when it was wrapped around his neck.

Angel rushed to help him, but the loose end of the sheet threw her backwards onto the bed. Standing up she began talking in Hebrew. James, although now in a semi-conscious state watched as beams of light seemed to fly across the room at the sheet. There was a piercing shrill cry then all was still, the sheet dropped lifelessly to the floor. Angel rushed to James who was holding his throat, gasping for air.

"What the Hell was that Angel and those words you were saying and those sparks flying from you!"

Looking terrified she cried as she held onto him and stated she didn't know.

Finally they calmed down after Angel poured them both a drink.

Now thinking and talking more rationally, they both agreed it was probably what Nathanial had told them. Angel was a threat and they would do everything they could to stop her. With James out of the way it would be easier.

He would call his friend to reschedule the interview for a couple of hours later. That would give him enough time to drop Angel at Olivia's; there was no way he was going to leave her alone in the apartment.

Before they left, Angel dropped a mace spray into his pocket. With a grin he said he didn't need it and she should keep it. Angel smiled and stated she'd just feel safer knowing he had it. More to please her, he left it in his pocket.

Olivia was always pleased to see her. Like any good mother she'd realised instantly when James had rung to tell her he would be dropping Angel off, something had happened.

James declined her offer of coffee, he needed to meet his friend and the traffic was building up.

Kissing both ladies on the cheek, he said he would be back as quickly as possible.

Olivia looked concerned when Angel told her what happened. Like Angel she had some news of her own which originally she hadn't intended to worry her with, but under the circumstances, she felt she should. The previous night, she had been woken by something tugging at her hair, but when she had tried to sit up something had pushed her down with force and bitten her. Taking her cardigan off, she showed Angel a large bite to her forearm.

"Oh my God mum, why didn't you call me?"

"What could you have done darling? It all happened so quickly, even Martin slept through it. Alan warned us this sort of thing might happen. He called me earlier to arrange for all of us to meet at his house; I think it's a good idea. If what you said before about the 25th being significant is right, we only have two weeks to go and due to recent events, things are going to get worse. I believe he was going to ask that Nathanial fellow to try and come. I must say, after what you said, I'm intrigued to meet him."

Angel talked about Nathanial and what an unusual man he was.

Across town, James was walking into a hotel. He'd arranged to meet his friend in the bar. They had served in the Army together, but now Colin recruited mercenaries and bodyguards for high profile people. He'd made contact with James after hearing he'd left the service.

The two friends shook hands as Colin thanked him for coming and how good it was to see him. Due to the nature of their meeting, Colin didn't want to discuss business within earshot of anyone, so he suggested once they finished their drink they would take a drive somewhere quiet.

While the two friends talked, James had a strange feeling they were being watched. Casually glancing round the bar lounge, he spotted someone he thought looked familiar.

The man caught him staring and subsequently raised his glass to acknowledge him. In that second, James realised he didn't know him but he had seen him, it was Hermann Klaus. Ignoring him, James turned to Colin but his thoughts were on Angel.

Asking Colin to excuse him and using the ruse he needed to use the toilet, he stood up. The moment he began walking away, he called Olivia's house phone. There was no answer; so he called her mobile and then Angel's, both went straight to answerphone. He didn't like the feeling he was getting. Regardless of the job, he knew he had to drive home.

Back in the bar, Colin smiled as he approached and asked if he wanted another drink before they left to discuss business.

"Sorry Colin, but I need to get back home. I'll drive; we can talk in the car. I just want to check on something."

Colin had no objections; he'd never met Angel and was looking forward to it.

James watched as Hermann Klaus spoke into his phone as the two friends stood up to leave. James had a feeling he was calling someone to have them followed.

Colin was full of questions about Angel, too many questions for James's liking. Then Nathanial's voice came into his mind, 'trust no one.' Suddenly James felt he needed to go alone.

Turning to Colin, he said on second thoughts it was probably best if he went alone and met him back at the bar in an hour.

When Colin totally dismissed the idea, James thought quickly and stated the traffic would be heaving, so maybe it would be best if they stayed there and maybe talk about the job in Colin's car which was in the hotel parking lot. He would just call her again; eventually she would pick up the phone.

It was when Colin too readily agreed, James considered maybe Nathanial was right and Colin wasn't the trusted friend he'd believed him to be. Considering he'd been so keen to meet Angel just a few minutes earlier, yet had instantly agreed not to go made James suspicious.

Now he needed to offload Colin and get back to his car. Just as they reached the lift, James used the ruse he needed to use the toilet again before leaving. He would meet him in the parking lot in a few minutes. Colin insisted on waiting for him, stating they would go to the car together.

Trying to act casual, James nodded as he began walking towards the toilets. He was aware however that Colin was also walking in the same direction.

It was inside the men's toilet he used the urinal, not that he really needed to pee, but because he had a strange feeling Colin would come in.

A few moments had passed when the toilet door opened. It was Colin, but he wasn't alone. A heavily built oriental man was with him. The atmosphere instantly let James know something was very wrong, especially when the other man stood silently with his arms folded blocking the door.

"Just coming Col," he said in a blasé manner "I can't get a reception here, so I'll call Angel from the lobby."

Colin just stared at him before replying he couldn't let him do that.

James knew beyond doubt they weren't going to let him leave. So he asked what was going on.

"You need to come with us James. We don't want to hurt you, but we will. You see we need you as bait, so let's just take a nice walk out to my car."

Sounding angry, James stated he thought they were friends and he wasn't going anywhere with him.

"I am your friend James, but I need you to come with us. My friend, Chin, will kill you if need be, so let's not do anything stupid."

Hoping to lull them into a false sense of security, James asked where they were going.

Colin declined to reply, but stated they had to go.

Keeping up the act he would go with them, James began walking towards him then without warning threw a punch. Instantly winding Colin, Chin intervened, grabbing James from behind and holding him in a bear hug. The strength of the man was immense. Lifting James off the floor, he was crushing the life out of him. James knew he had only seconds before he passed out as Colin rallied and stood in front of him but as Colin went to say something, James kicked him with such force it threw him against the urinal. Using the strength of his legs he then pushed against the toilet wall crushing Chin between him and the toilet door. No matter how he struggled, Chin would not let go. Then James remembered the mace spray Angel had dropped in his pocket. If he could move his hand slightly he may be able to reach it. Struggling and using anything he could to push against with his legs, momentarily he felt Chin lose his grip slightly. This was his chance. He struggled like a man possessed making it impossible for Chin to keep his grip. Managing to free one hand, he reached into his pocket finding the mace. Now he needed to free his entire arm so he could spray Chin. In those moments he fought for his life against the might of his opponent until his arm was free. Raising his hand above Chin's head, he sprayed down on him. Instantly, Chin began releasing him as the spray hit his eyes. Colin was stirring as James made haste to leave. Without thinking he sent a crushing blow to Colin's head with his foot.

Still blinded, Chin had managed to move to the hand basins in an effort to rinse his eyes. Seizing his opportunity, James caught him off guard and with all his strength smashed his head down onto the basin. Leaving both men out cold, James carefully opened the door and looked to see if anyone was waiting for him. Spotting a man standing just a few feet away with his back to him, it gave James the impression he was on guard.

Carefully closing the door and locking it, he made his way back into the toilet to look for a way out.

Colin and Chin were still unconscious on the floor.

There was a small window at the rear of the room. Using his jacket he wrapped it around his hand to protect him from breaking the glass. A few minutes later he was in an alley behind the hotel.

Putting his jacket back on, he casually walked back to the main street and joined the flow of people as he made his way to his car.

Driving to Olivia's, he continuously checked his rear mirror to ensure he wasn't being followed.

Pulling into Olivia's drive, he noticed her car was gone. Panic stricken he called Angel's phone and felt relieved when she answered.

She was surprised when he said he was back. Then she heard the panic in his voice as he asked where they were and that they should come home immediately.

Before she had time to tell him they had met Martin for lunch, he insisted they came home and to make sure nobody followed them.

Angel knew something serious had happened. Telling him they'd be home within thirty minutes, she ended the call. Olivia and Martin looked concerned when she told them; so much so Martin wouldn't return to work, he would follow them home in his car just in case they were followed.

It was nearer to forty minutes due to traffic before they pulled onto the driveway.

James was standing by his car, looking concerned.

Hugging Angel as she exited the car, he spotted Martin turning into the road.

Telling the ladies to go inside, he waited for Martin to park his car.

Once they were all in the house, Angel asked what was going on and why was he back so early.

After explaining to them what happened at the hotel and how he'd seen Hermann Klaus, he said they had to leave. London wasn't safe for them.

Olivia protested that she and Martin would stay, but he should take Angel away.

James was quick to say they would be used as bait to lure Angel out, so they were coming whether they liked it or not.

Olivia expressed concern for Alan and Linda, but he reminded her Nathanial had said they wouldn't harm Linda or Derek because they need her Uncle Patrick to come. Regarding Alan, she could call him and ask if he wanted to go with them.

Like everyone else, she knew Alan wouldn't go before she even spoke to him, but she felt better having asked.

James told them just to pack a few essentials. They could stop on the way at the flat so they could collect a few things. Of most importance was the Holy water and the dagger Angel had been given. The people who wanted Angel would no doubt check the flat once they realised they'd left.

Less than forty minutes later, Martin and Olivia waited in the car while Angel and James packed a few things from the flat.

Several times during the drive, Martin asked where they were going.

Finally and only once they were forty miles away from London, James said he was taking them to Nathanial's.

They never stopped throughout the four hour drive. James just wanted to get there without any pit stops.

They had been driving for over three hours when they reached the rural countryside quite near to Nathanial's.

James had been vigilant, checking they weren't being followed.

It was as he turned into a narrow country lane a tractor pulled out in front of his car from a field. Instantly he felt panicked, but knowing he couldn't pass it he had no choice but to slowly follow behind it. His hope was it would turn off.

Several minutes passed as he continued to try and pass, but his efforts were futile. Looking in his rear mirror, he noticed a Land Rover coming up behind them at speed. Only seconds had passed when he knew they weren't going to stop, they were going to ram him. Quickly telling the others, he shouted for them to brace for impact. The tractor stopped and the driver jumped out, quickly moving away from the vehicle.

In those split seconds, he watched as the rear driver rammed into the back of them, pushing them into the tractor. The rear of the car crumpled with the force and pressure. Everyone was thrown forward from the impact. Unable to open his door and hindered further by the air bag, James struggled to get out. His hope was to get to the range Rover and disable the driver. Smoke was coming in through the dashboard. Unable to open the windows, he shouted for Martin to break the window.

Then everything came to a sudden stop. James could see another car pull up behind the Range Rover. He'd hoped it was another motorist who would help them.

It was when Olivia screamed they realised the car was surrounded by men. One was aiming a shotgun at Olivia's window. Within seconds more guns were pointing at them as a large man used a crowbar on the passenger side door to open it. James was shouting until a shot was fired.

The man managed to open Angel's door and grabbing her arm tried to drag her from the car, but James was holding her and shouting at him to let her go.

Another warning shot was fired.

Angel calmly looked at the man and asked if she went with them would they leave her family alone. The man nodded. She told James to let her go, if he didn't they would all die. There was something about the way she looked at James, she knew they could find her but he'd be no good to her if he was dead.

With a menacing look, he threatened the man if they hurt her, he would kill every single one of them. Slowly releasing Angel's hand he said he loved her and he'd find her

Tearfully she said she loved him as she got out of the car.

They watched as she was taken to the rear car and pushed onto the rear seat.

Two men remained and at gun point ordered them to throw out their mobile phones.

Olivia was shaking so badly, Martin had to find her phone in her bag and throw it to them.

When James threw his out they ordered him to get Angel's from her bag.

Moments later they were gone.

James managed to get out through the passenger side, but after failing to open the rear doors, he instructed Olivia and Martin to climb over from the rear.

Olivia was inconsolable over Angel to the point of becoming hysterical.

It was James who shouted at her to pull herself together. With no usable car they had no choice but to walk the rest of their journey. James was confident they could get to Nathanial's in thirty minutes but he was Army trained, the others weren't and Olivia had heels on. Martin suggested James going on ahead and sending someone back for them.

He reached Nathanial's in twenty minutes once travelling alone.

Nancy looked shocked when she opened the door and instantly knew something was wrong.

The moment she closed the door behind them, she called Nathanial.

Nancy had her jacket on and the car keys in her hand ready to leave to pick the others up by the time James had explained what happened.

James followed him to the drawing room to discuss what they should do. As they passed by the lounge, he noticed a coffin.

Nathanial said it was Father Michael, he'd only passed away the previous day.

James had just finished telling him what happened when Nancy and the others returned.

After being introduced to Nathanial, Olivia broke down in tears. She feared for Angel's life.

Nathanial quickly calmed her fears by telling her they would not kill Angel. They would take her somewhere and hide her until the 25th.

Olivia asked what would happen on that date. She looked terrified to hear she would be sacrificed then. The atmosphere quickly became frantic when Olivia started crying.

James kept his wits about him and told Olivia to stop; crying wasn't going to help get Angel back. Looking at Nathanial, he asked what they should do.

Asking Nancy to make some tea, Nathanial began asking questions about the people who had taken Angel. He wanted descriptions of the men.

While they gave details, Nathanial placed his lap top on the table and brought up a series of photographs.

After listening to the description of the man who had dragged Angel from the car, he scrolled down to the photo of a man and asked if he was the man they'd seen.

Instantly James said yes and asked who he was.

"His name is Murray Donaldson. He's an antiques dealer who owns a shipping company, deals mainly abroad. To the outside world, he's a family man. His twin daughters attend Harvard. He lives in a converted farmhouse in Surrey. His wife, Monica, runs her own very successful business breeding and racing horses. Her stable boasts a Grand National winner. Money is certainly no problem for the Donaldson's. I've been watching them for the past two years. No real evidence to link them with anything sinister, but their circle of friends is a concern. Leticia and Hermann have recently visited them. I knew they were into the occult; I just wasn't sure how involved. The fact he was involved in Angel's abduction makes me think they're big fish."

James asked if he thought they'd have taken her to their farmhouse.

Nathanial shook his head. They knew it wouldn't take long for them to identify the abductors. It was unlikely they'd use the houses of any of the people involved. They had simply been used to do Hermann's dirty work. His guess was they would take her as near to Albert Avenue as possible. They would want to avoid a long journey on the 25th of March.

He suggested they looked through the photos he had to see if they could pick anyone else out. Once they knew exactly who was there, he could look to see who had properties near to number 16.

Between them they managed to identify three of the five men.

It was some time later when Nathanial asked why they were coming to see him that day. He listened as James spoke about the events at the hotel with his ex-army friend Colin and his accomplice, Chin.

Nancy was talking to Olivia and Martin in the lounge. Nathanial checked the names of known occultists along with any properties they owned in or around London while he talked candidly to James.

By chance, he came across a derelict property which had recently been purchased by Leticia Lemaitre. It was an old theatre, unfit for habitation. It needed complete refurbishment. No planning application had been submitted so the building was empty.

Nathanial had no way of knowing it would be where they would take Angel, but his gut feeling was telling him they might.

Nathanial Googled the blueprints of the theatre and printed them out. There were only two entrances shown, but a large disused drain system ran directly underneath. There were several manholes that linked to it from adjoining streets.

James was eager to go and check out the theatre but Nathanial said they must wait. If the people who had taken Angel had the slightest inkling they were on to them they would move her, assuming she was even there.

He suggested leaving Olivia and Martin with Nancy and then he and James driving back to London.

After convincing Olivia it was safer for them to stay, Nathanial took James upstairs to a dressing room. It clearly hadn't ever been used; it was full of boxes and chests. There were several mannequins, some were naked, but some had wigs and clothes on.

Nathanial explained the room hadn't been touched and the man who gave him the house entertained a lot of actors and actresses. He was certain they could find something to disguise themselves as he was confident the people who took Angel would have spies out looking for them. Unfortunately, both men were clean shaven, heavily built and James had short cropped hair.

Nathanial sifted through a large chest and found a false beard for himself and a shoulder length man's wig for James. Had the situation not been so serious the two men would have laughed.

Before leaving the room, Nathanial opened another box and removed two handguns, along with a box of bullets. Passing one to James, he looked serious when he said he assumed he knew how to use it. James nodded.

Nathanial also gave him some Holy water and a crucifix.

The two friends left the house five minutes later.

Leaving his car in the drive, Nathanial walked to an outbuilding at the property.

Inside under a canvas sheet was a small, hand built sports car. James was amazed when it started with the first turn of the key. Nathanial had only finished building it one month earlier. He hadn't yet registered it, so technically nobody knew he had it.

CHAPTER 17

Linda was unaware what was happening with Olivia as she settled down to read Angel's diary.

'Tonight is the night of the séance. Joyce and Alan plan to arrive early which is nice. It will give us time to chat. I haven't mentioned to them that since Joyce arranged for them to try and help the children cross over into the light things have happened. I'm debating whether to say anything tonight. One thing that is really bothering me is that Joey came to see me last night. He was clearly afraid until Mary joined him. What they told me gave me serious cause for concern. It was Mary who said there is a dark presence in the house, its neither Agnes Tibbs or the man who terrorises us. This presence is like no other and it's lying in wait for me. I could defeat it, but more will come.

I asked Mary how she could be sure this would happen. She simply said she knew, the house's core was pure evil and they would never be allowed to leave.

Suddenly there was a loud banging which seemed to echo around the room. It became quite deafening. Mary shouted he was there and for me to run. The furniture began to rock and move as a terrible wind seemed to swirl around the room. The door slammed shut. In those moments I experienced real fear as I witnessed a large clawed hand appear in a ring of fire. I stood helplessly at first as it gripped the children and the flames engulfed them. Knowing they needed me, I tried to free them but as I moved towards them I was thrown across the room by a strong invisible force. They were screaming as they were sucked down through the floor and disappeared from view.

In all the chaos, I hadn't heard mum banging on the door. She had obviously heard all the noise and had come running to help. She looked quite frantic as the door opened and she saw me lying on the floor.

We went downstairs and talked about what happened and whether I should tell Joyce and Alan when they came to the house later. I believed something terrible would happen if they went ahead with the séance because this entity wasn't like anything I've ever experienced. I knew it was a powerful demon. We talked about it over a cup of tea then mum asked me if I wanted to leave the house. Of course I did, but the children needed me and so did her husband Charles, he was trapped in the house too. We were both aware that since my first day in the house when I saw the spirit children things had changed. My gift had become a powerful force and for a long time I'd wondered if my meeting Olivia (mum) was because I was meant to be there. Although the love and affection we have for each other is very real.

Over several cups of tea, we debated whether or not to cancel the séance. In the end we both agreed to tell Alan and Joyce what happened and let them decide.

It was as we sat there the cups began to rattle in their saucers and a foul smell seemed to fill the room. We both had a feeling something bad was coming, but neither knew what. I stood up and asked whatever it was to leave us alone. Suddenly I felt as though I was being strangled. Mum could see the life ebbing out of me, but was powerless to help. Whatever this force was it had pinned her to the chair unable to move. I believe I saw my life flash before my eyes as the demon's grip grew tighter and no matter how I struggled I couldn't get free. Never in my entire life was I more pleased to hear Johnathan's voice when he commanded the demon to let me go. I never saw Johnathan, but his voice carried on the air as he said, 'be strong Angel'.

Mum was crying as she hugged me and asked if I was alright. She had also heard Johnathan's voice.

In a strange way it made us realise that telling Alan and Joyce was the right thing to do. This demon was powerful and should they decide not to do the séance we would understand.

When I said to mum trying to help the children was the right thing to do, we heard Joey say 'please help us Angel'.

His words decided it for us, we would hope Joyce and Alan would want to help but the choice had to be theirs.

With both of us feeling a little calmer, mum suggested us going into town for lunch. When I nodded, she smiled and suggested I wore a scarf as there were marks and scratches around my neck. She joked saying she didn't want people thinking she was a bad mother who abused her daughter. Nobody would ever think that, she was the best mum in the world and I felt lucky she was mine. When I said I would go and find a scarf, mum looked sad but serious when she said she didn't know why all this was happening to me. She felt I was too young to have so much responsibility and although she admired the way I handled everything, she feared for my safety and if I wanted us to move she would understand. No matter how much she loved the house, her love for me was paramount. It was the sentence that followed which made me realise just how wonderful a mum she was. With sincerity she said she would be willing to give her own life to protect me. I never dared to imagine or believe that anyone would feel so deeply for me. Her words brought tears to my eyes, because I knew she meant them.'

Linda was in no doubt of the love Angel shared with Olivia.

Closing the diary she pondered over the demon that attacked Angel. She could only try to imagine the fear Angel had experienced.

CHAPTER 18

Angel could smell chloroform as she started to regain her senses. For a moment she had no idea where she was, her head felt muzzy, her vision was blurred and there was a gag over her mouth. It was several minutes later when she realised she was suspended by her wrists from heavy chains. Her feet were barely touching the cold floor beneath them. The place she was in was cold and dimly lit, with just a tiny light shining through a small window above her.

As her senses slowly returned, she realised someone had undressed her, she was now wearing a long white cotton gown. The pain in her arms was immense; her hands were numb through lack of circulation.

She tried to move her hands, but the chain was so tight around them it was futile.

With her vision now clearer she looked at her surroundings. The walls were plain brickwork and it was damp. The small barred window appeared to be just above ground level as she could hear traffic and people as they walked past. That told her the building was in a built up area. On the far wall there was what looked like scenery boards. They were old and faded, but the front one looked like a street scene. There were broken chairs, newspapers and such cluttering the floor.

Feeling her situation was desperate, she prayed for God to help her. To her surprise she heard a woman's soft voice say, 'be strong Angel, you are not alone'.

Then something caught her eye amongst the debris. Focusing her eyes on it she saw the locket Grace had given her. It must have fallen from her neck when she was chained. It was open showing the picture of her mother. It appeared to be shrouded in a light as it began to move. Then as if lifted by invisible hands it rose up from the floor and floated towards her. She felt it roll over her hair before it gently slipped down onto her neck. In those seconds she knew her real mother was there with her and that gave her hope.

With tears rolling down her face she felt someone gently kiss her cheek. Moments later she was alone.

The hours passed, her body was shivering with the cold and she could feel herself falling into a dream state, like the type people are said to experience due to hypothermia.

As her mind drifted she thought she heard voices and then the door unlocked.

Too disorientated to lift her head, she could see several peoples' legs and feet. They were standing in front of her. Sudden shock rallied her senses when someone slapped her face several times and ordered her to look.

It was Leticia Lemaitre, wearing a fur coat. Thick makeup covered the deep lines and wrinkles on her face. Her teeth had a slightly yellow tinge. Her whole demeanour was that of a sinister woman.

She ordered two men to get Angel down and put a coat on her. The master wanted her alive.

The chains she was suspended from were attached to a pulley.

One of the men freed it off and after simply letting it run, he watched as Angel hit the floor with a thud.

The other man grabbed her by the hair and lifting her up threw her onto a chair. The weight of the chains now dangling down between her legs made it hard for her to lift her hands.

"We are all supposed to fear you" laughed a man with a German accent "yet you don't look very powerful to me. So maybe you would like to give us a demonstration of your supposed powers?"

Angel seemed to find some strength as she lifted her head up and just stared at him. Then almost as though he was afraid, he stepped back and dropped his head so as not to give her eye contact.

Leticia moved forward and in an arrogant tone said Angel was nothing and no one was afraid of her. Angel noticed she was staring at her locket. Leticia moved closer and said, "What is this trinket?" but as she tried to pull it from Angel's neck something happened. The locket burnt into Leticia's flesh and try as she might to let it go, it stuck to her skin. Finally, she wrenched her hand away and ordered one of them to give her a handkerchief.

Hermann Klaus removed a clean one from his jacket pocket and passed it to her. When she opened her palm to wrap the handkerchief around it, she saw the casing design of the locket burnt into her flesh.

Leticia ordered one of the men to remove Angel's gag.

"No one will find you here and escape is impossible," said Leticia "so do not even think about it!"

Angel never replied she simply stared at her. She could tell Leticia was intimidated.

"Our only order is to keep you alive until you meet the master. Now we are going to move you, do not give us any trouble or you will be sorry."

Still, Angel never spoke, not that she didn't want to, but simply because she knew her silence was unnerving them.

The two men yanked her up from the chair by her arms a third man removed the large chain from her, but replaced it with a smaller neck collar which he padlocked. After securing a small chain like a dog's lead to it, they manhandled her through the building, taking her to the basement where one of the men lifted a trap door in the floor. There was a set of wooden steps. Without any regard for her safety one of the men waited until she was on the top rung then aggressively told her to hurry up as he pushed her.

Falling down the steps she landed on the cold damp floor. Before the hatch was closed she tried to look at where she was. There was no light and nothing to sit on; it was simply a barren hole in the ground with shutters of wood holding the dirt back preventing a cave in.

When the hatch closed completely, she was alone in the dark. She tried to strain her eyes but she could see nothing, it was pitch black.

For the first time she felt really frightened. Her arms, although free, were excruciatingly painful, in particular her left arm. She had landed on it when she fell. There was no water and she was thirsty.

All manner of things were going through her mind, what if her captors simply left her there to starve to death. No one would find her.

Tears rolled down her face as she thought about her family and how much she loved them, the children she'd hoped to give James.

Feeling such despair; she laid down on the damp ground and through sheer exhaustion and pain she fell asleep.

Waking what seemed like several hours later, she tried to move to stand up but the pain in her arm was worse. Managing to use her other arm, she levered herself up to a sitting position.

To add to her plight, she remembered what Nathanial had said about the 25th of March and if he was correct that was eight days away. Logically she knew she would be unlikely to survive that long without water, but Leticia had said the master wanted her alive, so maybe they would give her some if only enough to keep her alive.

As the hours passed she lost all concept of time, she wasn't sure if it was day or night, but it was getting colder and despite having been given a coat, she was shivering.

CHAPTER 19

Olivia was pacing up and down the lounge. Despite Martin and Nancy telling her stop worrying as they were confident James and Nathanial would find Angel, she couldn't settle. It was only when Nancy's mobile rang Olivia stopped.

They listened intently as Nancy spoke; it was obvious she was talking to Nathanial.

The moment the call ended, Olivia was full of questions. Her hopes were dashed when Nancy said they hadn't found Angel yet, but they were going to watch the abandoned theatre. They had come across an empty building across the road from it, so they were going to watch it from there. They had managed to contact Linda and Alan. Fortunately, Nathanial's theory about Linda being safe seemed to be correct. She had told them there had been nothing suspicious and Derek's health was still improving. Nathanial had declined from telling her where they were as he couldn't be certain her phone wasn't being tapped.

Alan had a different story to tell, one which Nathanial found concerning. Alan was convinced he was being watched and followed. A dark coloured transit van with tinted windows had been parked outside his house for two days. It had followed him that morning when he went into town. When he parked in a multi-storey car park, the van had parked several spaces away. He had expected someone to get out, but they didn't. Once he reached the lift a man appeared. He never said anything and simply got out on the same floor, but Alan had spotted him several times later as he shopped.

Nathanial told him to take care and if he was able to give them the slip he should try and go somewhere safe. As with Linda; he didn't tell him where they were, simply that they were safe. He would have said for him to go to his house, but he couldn't take the chance they were being listened to. His hope was Alan would know that's where he meant and make his way there unnoticed. The last thing Nathanial wanted was to put the others at risk. For years he had gone to painstaking lengths to keep his address secret. It wasn't even his name on the deeds; it was his mother's maiden name.

Not wishing to stay on the phone too long, Nathanial had ended the call after a couple of minutes.

Nancy suggested Olivia making a cup of tea, not that she really wanted one, she just hoped it would take her mind off Angel for a while.

They talked about Nathanial as they drank. It was obvious how much Nancy loved him. Olivia believed she was actually in love with him.

Along with Martin, she listened as Nancy said he was the bravest man she had ever met. He always made her feel safe.

When Olivia asked if there was any romance between them, Nancy looked sad. Although he was no longer a priest, he still believed in his faith and the vow of celibacy he'd taken. It had been the Church who let him down, not God. Had God not have been with him the day he banished the demon from her, they would all have perished.

Olivia asked how long she intended staying there with him as she was young and could meet a good man and raise a family. With a look of genuine love on her face, Nancy replied she would never leave him.

Martin had a sense that Olivia really wanted to say more so tactfully he asked to be excused, stating he was going to take a bath.

With Martin gone, Olivia talked about Nancy's love for Nathanial, even stating they would make a wonderful couple. Nancy simply smiled and said he would never give up his faith for her nor would she expect him to, even though she knew he loved her and felt the same way she did.

While the ladies talked about Nathanial, he was in London keeping watch on the theatre. For hours they had watched, yet there had been no one in or out. He had just said to James that maybe he was wrong about Angel being there when James noticed something.

A car had pulled up on double yellow lines outside the theatre, letting two men out before driving away. He instantly recognised one of the men as Chin, the man who had attacked him in the hotel toilets.

Nathanial told him to keep out of sight. They would keep watch to see what happened before they decided on a plan.

They watched as the two men used a key to enter the building.

Twenty minutes later, two different men came out. They must have been in there before they'd set up their surveillance. Nathanial was convinced Angel was there, but they would bide their time.

Over the next four hours eleven more people turned up, including Hermann, Damien and Leticia. Despite Nathanial's thoughts on Angel being kept alive until March 25th now he was having doubts. Why were so many people going into a derelict building at eleven o'clock at night?

James had seen enough and stated he was going over there. Had it not been for Nathanial's calmness and reasoning, James would have gone, but Nathanial knew they couldn't fight everyone and would probably end up dead or captured. However, he did want to ensure Angel was unharmed so he suggested he would go over and try to find a way in at the back of the theatre. Hopefully he could sneak in unnoticed and assess the situation. If Angel was in any real danger, he would call James.

Not really happy with being left behind, James suggested he should go, but saw the logic when Nathanial said if he got caught he'd need him to come to his rescue. If he wasn't back within the hour, James should expect the worst.

From a broken window pane; James watched as his friend made his way across the street keeping out of the car headlights that passed him. James watched until he slipped out of sight down a small alley two buildings along from the theatre.

Time seemed to drag as he waited for Nathanial to return. He was just about to go over and look for him when he noticed three men hurriedly leaving the building. It was as though they were looking for someone; his thoughts were it was probably Nathanial.

Keeping a firm watch on them as they split up and went off in opposite directions, he was convinced they were after someone as they began running. A few minutes passed when he spotted two more men as they appeared from the alley, one of them was Chin. His one consolation was they hadn't caught Nathanial or they wouldn't still be looking.

Then James's phone bleeped and a text came through.

"Don't reply or move. I'm safe inside, now delete."

It was from Nathanial.

James kept watching the theatre and forty minutes later all of the men had returned.

It was three that morning when all except two people had left. All he could do was wait for Nathanial.

Another hour passed before Nathanial appeared back in the room.

James was eager to find out what had happened.

"They were there for a black magic ritual. Angel is there, she's unharmed. Two men fetched her from another part of the theatre. She was tied to a makeshift altar. They held a chicken above her and cut its throat. They're preparing her for sacrifice, but if I'm right it won't happen until the 25th and then it will be at the house. Two men have been left to guard the place; they're armed so we need to proceed with caution. I think the best chance we have of finding her and getting her out is now, under the cover of darkness and while there's only two guards."

James couldn't wait to leave, but Nathanial expressed the need for caution. He knew the guards wouldn't hesitate to kill them. His hope was they could sneak in and take them by surprise.

They continued to watch for another hour in case anyone came back.

Finally, Nathanial said they should go.

Making their way into the street they kept out of the headlights and street lighting as they made their way to the side alley.

Nathanial had already found a way in so their entry was quick and quiet.

Moments after entering they heard voices, the two guards were talking.

Nathanial indicated he would distract one of them, leaving James to deal with the other.

Picking up a piece of broken glass, Nathanial threw it in the direction they had just come from.

Instantly the two guards stopped talking and listened for any further noise. Nathanial threw another piece and this time his ploy worked.

One of the guards told the other to stay put while he checked out the noise.

The two friends hid and watched as the guard left the area then Nathanial followed him, leaving James to deal with the other one.

Only a few moments had passed when there was the sound of a struggle followed by a loud thud.

The guard sprang to his feet and called to the other one. When there was no reply he rushed off in the direction of the noise. That was James's chance. As the guard passed by him unnoticed; James caught him with the element of surprise. With a fierce blow to the back of the guard's head the man fell forward. James was straddled over his back the moment he hit the floor then with a power hold, broke his neck.

Nathanial appeared a few moments later. It was obvious he'd either killed or seriously wounded the other guard when he told James he wouldn't be bothering them anymore.

James suggested they split up to look for Angel. It was a large building and she could be anywhere.

Twenty minutes passed. James was growing desperate until he heard Nathanial calling that he'd found her.

Moving quickly through the building, he followed the sound of Nathanial's voice. He hadn't expected to see him placing a small ladder into a hole in the floor when he found him.

James felt fearful when he looked down into the darkness and saw Angel lying deadly still on the ground.

"Is she alive" he called.

Relief rushed through him when Nathanial called back, "Yes, help me bring her up; I'll pass her to you."

Angel groaned and began to rally as they removed her from her prison.

Once out of the hole, James held her in his arms and gently stroked her face.

The white robe she was wearing was soaked in the chicken's blood. Her lips were dry and swollen as Nathanial passed him some water for her that one of the guards had left.

Swallowing too quick through sheer thirst, she coughed almost to the point of choking.

Waiting until she stopped, Nathanial said they had to leave.

Scooping her up from the floor, James followed Nathanial through the building and out into the street, taking care not to be seen.

Nathanial's car was parked in the next street. Moving quickly and as safely as they could they reached it a few minutes later.

After gently laying Angel on the back seat, James sat with her, holding her in his arms. She barely spoke a word for the first two hours of the drive; she just slept with her head on James's chest.

The latter part of the drive saw her more alert and wanting to tell them what happened to her.

She cried when she told them she thought she was going to die when she was tied to the altar, but worse was her fear of being left in the hole to die a slow lingering death.

Reassuringly, James said he would never let anything happen to her, he would die protecting her.

It was daylight by the time they arrived back at Nathanial's. Taking extra care to ensure they weren't noticed, he told James not to exit the car when he pulled up, but to wait for his signal that it was safe.

He spotted Nancy watching from the window as he stopped the car as near to the door as possible. Moments later, she and the others were rushing out to help them. Olivia looked shocked when she saw the blood on Angel before placing her arms around her and asking if she was hurt.

Hurriedly they made their way into the house. Nancy checked they hadn't been followed before driving Nathanial's car back to the outbuilding and covering it.

CHAPTER 20

Linda was expecting her family that morning. Since Derek's health had improved she had invited everyone over for lunch.

It was just after midday when they arrived.

Their son, Michael, had recently acquired a dog from a friend who was emigrating. He hadn't actually planned on having one, but he knew it was a great dog, house trained and good with kids.

Despite the dog being a large German Shepherd, Linda made a real fuss of it before placing a bowl of water down on the floor for it.

She had missed spending time with her grandchildren. Before Derek's illness they would often come to see them.

After lunch her sons talked about the house and if the strange occurrences had stopped.

For the best part they had, although Derek was the one who said they still heard the children and often there were bad smells and cold spots, but other than that all seemed quiet.

Sophie was surprised after she asked how she was getting on reading Angel's diary and Linda said she'd finished it.

Curiously, Sophie asked what she'd read and frowned when told it was only page 178 which wasn't the end of the book.

It was as she spoke about the last entry; Sophie interrupted stating that must have been the night of the accident Alan had told them about.

Instantly the men asked "What accident?" as neither woman had mentioned it to them.

It was Sophie who went over the events of the night of the séance to cross the children of the house over into the light. It was the night Linda's neighbour, Victor, had spoken to them about and how he'd been to visit Angel in the hospital.

They stopped talking when Mark asked his brother what his dog was doing. They all watched as the dog began wagging his tail then rolled onto his back as though someone was rubbing its tummy. Linda said it was probably one of the children from the house, although they couldn't see anyone.

"Here boy," said Michael, but the dog ignored him and continued to give the impression someone was petting him.

The atmosphere changed from one of wonder to one of fear when Michael, clearly unnerved by the dog's behaviour, suggested his parents leaving the house. The crockery began to rattle followed by the dog getting up quickly and growling.

They sat silently as the dog seemed to be watching something or someone move across the room. Its teeth were bared and the hair on its back was raised.

Suddenly, the dog leapt into the air almost as though he was attacking someone. Everyone watched helplessly as the dog was thrown through the air by an invisible force. Landing with a thud it yelped and lay on the floor momentarily unable to get up.

In those few moments, everything had turned to chaos. Then the banging started and it got louder and louder. The grandchildren started crying, although they were really too young to understand the implications of what was occurring.

Mark shouted for them to get the children out of the house, but in that second the door slammed shut.

Panic stricken, the two younger men tried to open it but whatever was keeping it shut was stronger than both of them.

Michael's wife was too terrified to move or speak. Sophie held her hand although even she was afraid.

The dog began to move and a few seconds later began barking at the door, whatever was on the other side was pure evil.

The atmosphere changed instantly after Linda heard a voice tell her to order it to stop.

Mustering all her courage she shouted "STOP IT!"

Instantly everything became calm and the door opened.

The dog ran through the hall. Stopping at the basement door he began barking and growling as her family made haste to leave the house.

They all begged her and Derek to leave with them but Linda refused, stating it was their house and Uncle Patrick was coming soon. He would sort it out for them.

"Mum" said Michael "whatever that is, Uncle Patrick is not going to be able to get rid of it! You saw what it did to the dog! For God's sake mum, come home with us! Look at the dog, there's something here!"

Reassuringly she rubbed his arm and said they would be fine.

"He's right mum, listen to him" said Mark "we knew the house was haunted, even I saw things, but that today was something evil! You need to leave!"

Linda was adamant she wasn't leaving. She knew she had to finish what Angel had started and free the children that were trapped in the house. Derek's health was improving by the day and she absolutely believed something in the house was responsible for it.

Michael was angry that she wouldn't seem to listen. It was as though she felt she had the ability to stop whatever was happening. She talked about Uncle Patrick and Father Angelo like they were her saviours and after their visit everything would be fine, her sons didn't share her belief.

With Michael's wife still shaking, she begged him to drive them home. Asking his parents one more time to go with them and Linda refusing, they left.

Sophie hugged her and pleaded with her to come with them while Mark secured their kids in their car. She was the only one who really understood why Linda refused. Having met Angel and Alan, like Linda they had both had a profound effect on her. Maybe she was meant to be there and maybe Uncle Patrick would be able to help, but nevertheless, after the events of that day like everyone else she wanted Linda to leave.

Everyone knew that Derek would leave in a heartbeat but he was staying for Linda.

With their family gone, before going back in the house he tried to reason with her. The kids were right, they should leave.

Inside she made them a cup of tea but suggested taking it into the garden and drinking it in the summer house. Derek nodded.

Fifteen minutes later they were drinking tea. Derek looked round at the summer house. Like the house it needed work, but despite the chill in the air and missing a glass pane in one of the windows it was quite warm.

Knowing he was only staying there because of her, she tried to justify her reasons for needing to stay. She talked about Angel's diary and the evil presence she'd told her about. The visit from Grace when she had given her the diary, but most surprising to him was when she said that during his time in hospital, she had visited Angel and Alan had suggested hypnotising her. Derek looked shocked when she talked about her childhood on the farm and how her Uncle Patrick had been possessed. During their marriage he had only met Patrick a few times and found him to be a very devout priest who was also a very nice man.

Although he didn't share her belief in the supernatural, he did have to admit since living at number 16 his views had changed and as much as he wanted to support her, he was afraid of what was actually there. He'd seen programmes where houses were supposedly haunted, yet none came even close to the things they had experienced. It was then she dropped the bombshell about the house allowing his health to improve because it didn't want them to leave before her Uncle Patrick visited.

He asked why she hadn't told him all this before and said he was really concerned now, not only for them but for Patrick. Perhaps it would be better to cancel his visit and just sell the house. Another concern was that since her friendship with Alan and the others, her head was being filled with nonsense. All he knew for certain was there was something in their house that terrified him.

"I know how you feel Derek, but don't you see it's my destiny to be here? I've never told anyone this and didn't think I ever would. When I was a child growing up on the farm, I saw things. I have tried all these years to forget them, but since Alan hypnotised me I'm remembering more. There was a river that ran behind our property. I remember once being there with my mum and my brothers. We were throwing bread in so we could watch the fish come up. As I watched, I saw a small boy lying on the bottom; he was tangled in the weed. I screamed for my mother to help him. She looked, but saw nothing and told me it must have been a trick of the light or my brothers' reflection. It was neither, I saw him as clearly as I'm looking at you. He was wearing a red knitted sweater. Being a child I believed what my mother had said until later that day when I heard her talking to my father about it. I heard her telling him I'd seen the O'Malley boy. Then they talked about a young boy who had drowned three years earlier. I would have been about four when it happened. My father told her she'd done the right thing telling me it was a trick of the light and forbade her to talk about it to anyone. There have been lots of times since then I've seen things that weren't real. I never told you or anyone for fear you'd think I was going mad."

Ironically he'd often wondered if she was psychic, simply because over the years different things had happened. Not major things, just simple things she'd said. Being a non-believer, he'd simply let everything go over his head. She was a wonderful wife and mother and that was all that mattered to him.

His main concern was how all this would turn out, especially after what Sophie had said about what happened the night Angel left the house.

It was obvious to him Linda was also concerned, but for some reason she felt compelled to stay. For whatever reason she knew the evil in the house needed to stop and she couldn't sell it knowing what could happen to the next owners. Clearly convinced it was fate that she'd met Angel and the others and although she didn't know why, she was certain that her Uncle Patrick would play a vital part.

They both agreed it was best not to talk of leaving once back inside the house.

CHAPTER 21

Nathanial had spent most of the day going over astrological charts. It was over dinner that evening he talked about his findings.

Angel, although still a little traumatised, was looking and feeling much better.

Nancy had been a rock to her, maybe because she had experienced evil first hand.

After dinner, Nathanial said he wanted to show them something. It was a secret passage which ran under the house to one of the outbuildings. Only he and Nancy knew of its existence, it wasn't on any blueprints of the house.

Angel was the first to ask if he thought they would need to use it.

"I hope not Angel, but we cannot simply assume the day you were taken was by chance. It may have simply been you were followed from London, but it could also mean they knew you were coming here. To the best of my knowledge nobody knows about my house, but it's a big coincidence if your abduction was random."

The secret passage was behind a false wall in his drawing room. He showed them how to open it by moving a sequence of books. Once they reached the outbuilding there would be a car they could use. In the event they did get found, James's primary concern would be to get Angel to safety. Under no circumstances was he to wait for anyone, but simply to go.

Father Michael was due to be buried the following day. The hearse would arrive at one. While they were gone he suggested they watched the CCTV closely for anyone approaching the house. It covered every possible angle. Should any unexpected visitors turn up, his advice was to hide in the secret passage and not come out until he or Nancy returned. For safety, he suggested they used a password for any messages or calls, just in case they were taken. The password would be 'Maybe.' If any of them used that word anywhere in a message the others would be alerted to the fact they'd been captured. It was a good and easy word to incorporate into any sentence. Nathanial also showed them a list of places he and Nancy could be taken to should anything happen to them at the funeral. There were also the three phone numbers. They were listed under utility suppliers, but the people would help them should the need arise. All they needed to say was Nathanial gave them the number.

"You think they're coming for me, don't you Nathanial" said Angel "I don't want to put anyone's life at risk. Maybe I should just go somewhere until the 25th that way you'll all be safe."

Nathanial quickly stated her leaving would put everyone in jeopardy. The safest place for all of them was to stay there together. Despite believing that, he also knew the forces of evil would find them, he just hoped it wasn't soon.

It was around midnight when they finally turned in for the night.

Nobody was going to sleep well and especially Angel, she'd had a strange feeling since going to bed.

Finally she dozed off, but at precisely three o'clock that morning she was woken by someone calling her name.

Straining her eyes in the darkness she could see clearly Father Michael standing next to the bed.

Something about him looked different. He was younger, healthier and most noticeable were his eyes, he was no longer blind.

"They will be coming for you Angel, show them no fear and no mercy. God is with you; let him be your strength."

Before she could reply he'd vanished.

Snuggling up next to James, she felt a little fearful over what Father Michael had said, yet at the same time she felt calmer. Moments later she was asleep.

Fortunately the remainder of the night passed without incident.

The atmosphere was one of desperation and fear over breakfast the following morning.

Nathanial knew everyone felt safer when he was there and that afternoon he and Nancy had to leave for Father Michael's funeral. They would be away a few hours.

After they'd finished eating, the women cleared up while the men went into the drawing room.

It was then Angel told Nancy and Olivia about the visit she'd had from Father Michael.

Nancy felt they should tell Nathanial and leaving the kitchen, she headed off in the direction of the drawing room.

After apologising for interrupting, she asked to speak to Nathanial. Walking her back out into the hallway, he asked what she wanted.

His face took on a serious look when he heard what Father Michael had said to Angel.

Asking her to tell the ladies to join them in the drawing room, he went back to join the men.

Several minutes later, Nancy and the others entered.

The two men looked surprised when Nathanial spoke to Angel.

"Angel, I need you to tell me for certain that you actually saw Father Michael or could it have been a dream?"

Shaking her head she said it definitely wasn't a dream, he was there.

"Then we must assume he came to warn us. We need to make preparations. We need to keep you safe for the next six days. I wasn't going to tell you this as I hoped we'd be safe here, but now I feel I must. You all need to know how important it is to protect Angel. The ritual they were performing isn't complete, it has three parts. The blood from the chicken was the first part. The second part they will strip, wash her and cut her hair. Lastly they will leave her for two days without food or water before she is dressed and marked for death."

Martin tried to comfort Olivia as she began to cry before asking if there was anywhere Angel could go where they wouldn't find her.

Nathanial said he had a friend who may be able to help. The man in question was in fact a priest; he knew everything there was to know about satanic rituals. Nathanial would see him at Father Michael's funeral. Until then they must wait.

They were interrupted by the house phone. Nancy answered it and told Nathanial it was the funeral director, he wanted to speak to him.

They all listened as he gave several one word replies; like, yes no and really until saying "No it will just be the two of us. Can I ask why you assumed that had changed?"

When the call ended, he told the others the director seemed a little too curious as to whether it was still only him and Nancy travelling in the funeral car. Nathanial had a bad feeling about it.

CHAPTER 22

At one of her London houses, Leticia was mingling with a group of people, including Hermann and Damien. The champagne flowed freely as waiters walked amongst them offering a fresh glass.

A young woman of no more than twenty approached Leticia and whispered something to her. Moments later, Leticia clapped her hands together to call silence.

"I've just been told that our guest of honour has arrived. Please welcome Baron Henrik Von Schaffer."

The room erupted into clapping and cheering as a smartly dressed, tall man looking to be in his fifties with a terrible burn covering the left side of his face, entered the room. He was flanked by two heavily built guards.

Leticia bowed her head humbly as he approached and lifting her hand he kissed the back of it.

"This is such an honour for us Henrik" she said "I hope you had a pleasant trip. Please let me offer you some refreshments."

Henrik accepted her offer and took a drink from the waiter she beckoned over.

It was clear everyone wanted to be noticed by him despite his disfigurement. The women tried to act seductively in his presence.

Several hours had passed when Leticia called order and told everyone to get ready; she and Henrik would join them shortly.

Slowly everyone filtered out to the lower floor of the house.

Leticia stayed to talk privately to Henrik.

"So tell me Leticia, have you located the girl?" asked Henrik "the Master was angry at the incompetence of the guards. I assume the information I received was correct, it was the priest Nathanial who was instrumental in her escape? His days of meddling in our affairs will soon be over and he will feel the master's wrath."

Leticia looked a trifle uncomfortable with his words, but quickly tried to appease him by confirming they had found Angel and yes, his information was correct, she was with Nathanial. However he wouldn't be able to protect her much longer, as that very afternoon plans were in place to stop him.

Despite feeling that Henrik already knew, she told of a plan to take Nathanial and Nancy when they attended the funeral of another priest. At the same time, Angel and the others would be apprehended and brought to London.

"I hope everything goes to plan this time Leticia. You were put in charge of these issues because you were deemed to be capable of executing the master's wishes. Should you disappoint us again, it will be you who feels his wrath."

The look on her face told him she feared his words despite her trying to make light of it and assuring him there would be no more mistakes.

She suggested them getting ready and going to join the others.

In the basement of the house was a large room with no windows. It was completely barren of furnishings except for a black altar table. There were no electric lights only wall torches which burned from metal casements. Drawn on the centre of the floor was a large pentagram which everyone stood around.

All the guests wore black hooded robes as they stood waiting patiently for their hosts.

The room fell silent as Leticia and Henrik entered. His face was covered by a horned mask of a ram's head. His attire was a black robe with a pentagram design on the back. She wore a red robe as she walked behind him.

Taking his place behind the altar, he raised his hand and ordered them down on their knees before their master. Flames appeared in the pentagram, growing larger the more everyone hailed the master. The silhouette of a horned, red-eyed demon could be seen and heard as it growled and made what sounded like animal roars. The followers wailed and prayed to it. Finally the flames died down and vanished into the floor.

Henrik called Leticia to join him and, once standing next to him, she called out a name.

The young girl who had told her Henrik had arrived walked slowly through the crowd. Henrik held out his hand to help her step up to the altar.

She smiled as he untied her robe and it fell at her feet, leaving her naked in front of him.

Again he offered his hand to steady her as she willingly lay down on the altar.

Nobody made a sound. Henrik then took of his robe, but leaving his mask on stood naked in front of them. The full extent of his disfigurement was now apparent with his entire body covered in burnt flesh. Except for his hands and the right side of his face there was no unburnt skin.

Leaning across the altar, he began fondling the girl before moving on top of her and having intercourse. She cried out and clawed at his back making it bleed as he thrust into her.

The crowd jeered and chanted as they began stripping off. Men and women of all ages began engaging in sex together. Leticia had singled out a young stud and, although she was repulsive in every sense of the word, he willingly had sex with her. It had turned into a frenzied orgy which went on for hours until they stopped through exhaustion. The young girl who Henrik had chosen was dead; her throat had been cut when he finished with her.

CHAPTER 23

The hearse carrying Father Michael's body pulled into the church grounds followed by the car with Nathanial and Nancy in.

Nathanial had expected a good turnout of people paying their respects. Father Michael had touched the lives of many, especially during his days working as a priest. He recognised many old friends from the Church as they exited the car and a few minutes later walked behind the coffin as it was carried into the church.

Although it was expected, Nathanial wasn't really comfortable with him and Nancy having to sit in the front row of pews. They would have preferred to sit at the back where they could see everyone.

The service was, as expected long and drawn out. It was in fact Nancy who read the eulogy which Nathanial had written. Between sentences she had tried to glimpse the mourners to see if anyone looked out of place. She spotted several faces she didn't recognise which gave her cause for alarm.

Outside after the internment, everyone stood and talked about Father Michael's life.

Another priest made his way over to them.

"It's good to see you Father Nathanial" he said as he embraced him and then Nancy.

With a smile, Nathanial was quick to reply it was just Nathanial; he was no longer a priest.

"You will always be a priest to me Nathanial my dear friend. In fact you are more worthy of the title than most of us. You are without a doubt one of the best and most dedicated priests I've ever known."

"And you my dear Benedict will always be a spy, but also a wonderful priest."

Before joining the priesthood, Benedict had worked for MI5, even living undercover in Northern Ireland for six years during the seventies. Like with anything of a secret nature, he had witnessed things he wanted to forget. His faith had helped him to get through those years. At forty five he resigned from the Secret Service and became a priest.

Once he confided in Nathanial and Father Michael he wanted to repent for all the bad things he's been party to, despite successfully stopping several terrorist attacks and no doubt saving hundreds of lives.

"I should warn you Nathanial there are people here who are watching you. I know about the girl, don't ask me how but like you said once a spy always a spy. Do not turn around, but there are six people standing to the right of us, who have no reason to be here. There are four heavily built men and two women. I assume they mean to prevent you from returning home to the girl which makes me think they already have people on their way to your house. May I suggest Nancy sends word to them while we have our backs to them? We should continue talking while she sends a message. After that's done we should take a walk into the church. I can show you another way out. I will do everything I can to give you a head start."

While the two friends talked, Nancy discreetly took her phone from her bag and sent a text to James.

'Maybe a little late coming hope you don't mind waiting.'

She hoped James would realise she'd used the word maybe to alert them and they would hide in the passage.

The three friends walked towards the church, stopping every few minutes to talk to people in an effort to make it look natural.

Nathanial was aware the six strangers were following them when every time they stopped, so did the six.

Reaching the church doors, Benedict waited for them to enter before following them inside and quickly taking a floor-standing candle holder wedged it through the door handles to prevent anyone from following. Only a few moments had passed when they heard someone trying to open the door. Had it have been a parishioner they would simply have thought the church was temporarily closed. They knew it wasn't a parishioner when they heard heavy banging on the door as someone tried to force it open.

"We must go quickly" said Benedict as he passed Nathanial a set of cars keys. "You can take my car; it's the white Renault Megane parked behind the church."

Behind the curtain at the back of the church was a small, half sized door which gave the impression it was simply for storage. Benedict unlocked it and removed the shelving, which came out in one piece.

"Just follow the passage; it will bring you out at my car." Before Nathanial could thank him, there was a loud crack as the church doors were forced open.

"Go my friends. God's speed be with you! I'll stall them as long as I can."

They thanked him as they disappeared down a stone hall and he shut the door behind them.

With only a few seconds to spare, Benedict had just replaced the dusty old shelving, locked the door and pulled the curtain back in front of it when the six strangers appeared.

One of the men approached him.

"Where are they?" he asked arrogantly.

When Benedict said he didn't know what he was talking about the man hit him, knocking him to the floor.

He hadn't anticipated Benedict getting back up and returning the punch. Despite knowing he wouldn't be a match for four men he fought gallantly. He was certain they would have killed him had two mourners not come into the church. Instantly seeing what was happening one ran towards the men while the other went back to the door and called for help. Within moments several people were running towards the church.

The assailants couldn't risk being caught should the police have been called so they made a run for the door, reaching it as the people from outside entered. Pushing their way out, the assailants ran towards their car. Moments later they sped away.

Inside the car, one of the women shouted they must find the priest and the girl or they would all suffer. They couldn't have got very far and they would obviously drive back to Nathanial's house. She suggested they drove there and with luck they'd find them.

The driver reminded her that Leticia already had people going to the house.

"Good then maybe they'll need our help if that's where they are all hiding. It's because of your incompetence they managed to escape. I told you we should have followed then straight into the church, but you hesitated and said to wait!"

Arrogantly he told her to shut her mouth.

Back at the house James had suggested hiding in the passage after he received Nancy's text. He would stay and watch the CCTV and join them if he spotted anything suspicious.

He didn't have to wait long. Two attractive young women pulled up in a convertible. Exiting the car they approached the front door and looking up into the camera asked for help as they were lost.

James didn't reply and hoped they would simply go away. His instinct was telling him they were a decoy sent to find out who, if anyone, was there.

He watched as they looked through the window before moving around the house. It was clear they were looking for a way in. It was when he heard the sound of breaking glass as they smashed a window that he turned off the monitors and made his way to the passage. He hoped they would believe the house was empty.

Angel hugged him as he joined her and the others on some blankets which Nathanial had left for them, along with some food and bottled water.

Time seemed endless as they waited. Then James placed his finger to his lips to indicate they must be quiet because he could hear something.

They all sat silently as they listened to the voices outside the passage. They could hear clearly a male voice ordering everyone to search the house, check everywhere including the outbuildings. It was clear whoever was talking wasn't convinced the house was empty, especially when he stated they were likely to be hiding.

For hours they could hear people ransacking the house. It was obvious they were also looking for any secret hiding places as they could hear them knocking on the walls. Fortunately, Nathanial had taken the time to build up and insulate the area behind the drawing room panels. Obviously he'd anticipated that someone may try to find it.

Eventually everything went quiet.

After waiting for twenty minutes, James said he would use the passage to get out to the outbuilding. From there he could see if they'd gone.

Telling the others to stay hidden, he made his way out. At the other end, he listened before opening the trap door in the outbuilding.

Making his way carefully and quietly, he ventured outside. The convertible was gone from the drive. He couldn't see or hear anyone, but as he looked out to the road he spotted a car. Staying out of sight, he watched as it drove closer, it was a Renault Megane.

Relief was how he felt when, as it drove closer, he could see Nathanial and Nancy.

Still acting cautiously, he waited until they had stopped and exited the car. Although he hadn't seen anyone, he couldn't be certain they weren't simply lying in wait. He waited until they'd entered the house before making his presence known.

With a look of concern, Nathanial immediately asked where Angel was. Both he and Nancy were relieved when James said she was safe.

Nathanial suggested checking the house before assuming it was safe for Angel and the others to come out of hiding.

The house was in complete disarray. There were charts and papers scattered over the floor. The CCTV monitors had been sabotaged with all the wires having been cut and ripped out.

Food from the kitchen cupboards was all over the floor, jars and bottles smashed.

Finally, Nathanial deemed it was safe.

"Oh my God," exclaimed Olivia as the panel opened and she saw James "we thought you'd been caught! We heard people moving about."

Reassuringly, he said they were just checking the house was safe.

Angel hugged Nancy and asked what had happened at the funeral.

Nathanial stated it was no longer safe for them to stay there. He suggested leaving during the night, it would be safer then.

Nancy managed to make everyone a drink, despite most of the crockery having been smashed.

They talked about Father Michael's funeral and how they'd been attacked. It was when Nathanial spoke about Father Benedict and how he hoped he was alright after helping them to escape that Angel interrupted.

"Benedict is fine Nathanial."

Although they all believed her, Nathanial asked how she knew.

"Father Michael told me, he's here."

Everyone looked to where she was looking. Sure enough there was Father Michael.

Nancy had tears in her eyes as she looked at him. He looked so healthy, just how she remembered him before he risked his life for hers when she was a child.

"You must leave here" said the Priest "go to Brother Daniel, he will help you."

"Wait," said Nathanial as the priest began to disappear, but he'd gone.

Brother Daniel was from an order of old Benedictine monks. Nathanial had met him only once after Father Michael went to him for help and advice on Nancy and the demon she was possessed by.

The Abbey was in London which didn't sit well with Nathanial, his hope was to keep Angel away from London, but nevertheless if Father Michael wanted them to go he had no reason for doubt.

The time was approaching two o'clock that morning when he suggested they should leave. There would be minimal traffic due to the hour. His hope was they could arrive at the Abbey unseen. He gave Martin the address. In the event they were followed they could meet there. Angel and James would travel with him and Nancy.

The same password would be used should anyone run into any trouble.

Angel hugged Olivia and told her to take care; she would see her at the Abbey in a few hours.

James and Nathanial checked outside before ushering the others out.

They never stopped during the drive.

Typical of any Abbey, it was in private grounds and approached via a long driveway. The main building was impressive and imposing, built in the eighteenth century. It had a wealth of characteristics, yet like many old religion-based dwellings it had an air of mystery about it.

The time was just after five thirty when Nathanial drove through the gates.

The huge front door was made of solid oak with beautiful iron work sculptured onto it.

Nancy pulled the old fashioned doorbell; it was the type with a rope attached to the chime.

It was a nun who answered the door. She was quite young with a pretty face and a warm smile as she asked how she could help them.

"Good morning Sister" said Nathanial "our apologies for the early hour, but we've come to see Brother Daniel."

With a smile she said her day had started at four that morning and she believed Brother Daniel was expecting them.

James looked at Nathanial with raised eyebrows, how could he have known they were coming?

They followed the sister through the large corridors of the Abbey, passing several classrooms and libraries.

Despite Benedictine monks being renowned for preferring peace and time for quiet reflection and prayer, the Abbey was in fact a Catholic school boasting almost one thousand pupils.

The sister opened the door to a large study room and glanced around at the monks there to see if Brother Daniel was amongst them. Spotting him reading, she asked the others to wait for a moment while she told him they were there.

Closing the door behind her, she returned a few minutes later with a very elderly monk.

"Do my eyes deceive me" he said looking at Nancy "or is this the young girl I met many years ago?"

Having a very vague memory of him, Nancy smiled and said hello.

"I heard Nathanial was still looking out for you and I must say he's worthy of the task."

Nathanial patted the old man on the shoulder and said it was good to see him again.

"Let us take a walk, the garden is my favourite place for a chat" said Brother Daniel as they began walking.

They walked past several monks tending the gardens as they made their way to a seated area.

"Here should do us" said Brother Daniel as he sat on a picnic type bench table, "unfortunately the walls in the Abbey have many ears and what we have to discuss is not for everyone."

Nathanial formally introduced everyone to him. When Angel was introduced, Brother Daniel held her hand and with sincerity said how blessed he felt to meet her.

She asked how he knew they were coming.

"It was Father Michael; he came to me in a dream and told me you would need my help. I think we should go to my quarters, there are things I need to show you."

It took almost fifteen minutes to reach Brother Daniel's room. It was sparsely furnished, yet the shelves were full of books.

Asking Martin to ensure the door was shut, Brother Daniel proceeded to move his bed and remove several floorboards.

The others watched as he reached into the floor and took out a book wrapped in an old blanket.

Taking it over to the table, he apologised for not having enough chairs for everyone to sit on, but suggested the two ladies having a seat.

He opened the book to a specific page where he'd left a bookmark.

The pages were worn and discoloured, written in italic scribe.

Stating that his eyesight was no longer sharp and much of it was written in Hebrew, Brother Daniel asked Nathanial to read the page.

It was written that in the time of the second millennium a terrible curse will happen. Satan's army will rise from the underworld and those unwilling to swear allegiance will perish. Angels would descend from heaven to stop this blasphemy, but the fate of mankind will rest in the hands of a mortal. This mortal will possess gifts given to her by the Archangels.

There was a drawing on the page, it depicted a terrible battle. Yet the most curious of issues was the woman in the picture looked just like Angel.

Brother Daniel said they could stay at the Abbey.

CHAPTER 24

With March 25th just two days away, Linda had sensed a change in the house. For the past four evenings she had seen a man standing on the opposite side of the road. He didn't appear to be doing anything and he had a slightly sinister look about him. He was dressed in what appeared to be dark jeans and a dark leather jacket with a biker design on it. Wearing biker boots and a bandana, he looked an awesome sight. A long straggly beard covered the lower half of his face.

Linda had never seen a motorbike, but assumed he rode one because he was carrying a crash helmet.

One thing was certain, not only did he look out of place but he was beginning to spook her. It seemed no matter what time she looked out of the window during the evening, he was there seemingly just staring at her.

That evening as she pulled the lounge curtains; she saw him again, just standing there watching the house. Feeling a little unnerved she mentioned him to Derek, who looked surprised when she said he'd been there for the last few days.

Walking over to the window, he peered out through a crack in the curtain. Sure enough there he was, only unlike before when Linda had seen him, he walked away.

Derek suggested calling the police as he may be looking to break in at a later date and was probably watching to see who came in and out of the house.

Linda quickly assured him they didn't need to call the police. She wasn't sure how or why, but she knew he wasn't there to burgle them. Derek asked her to explain but all she could say was she didn't know, but she just knew she was right.

It was clear from the look on Derek's face he was becoming weary of the supernatural goings on.

The time was just before nine. They were talking about the house and Uncle Patrick's visit now only being days away when Derek shivered and said it had suddenly turned cold. Despite Linda saying she would check the heating, she had a strange feeling as to the sudden drop in temperature.

Just as she expected, the heating was working fine but the room was getting colder.

Then she noticed Derek staring at something and whatever it was, it was dark. Resembling a large black shadow it seemed to emanate up through the floor growing in size as it manifested.

It seemed to hover above their heads for several seconds before it flew across the room at speed and disappeared through the lounge wall.

"Whatever that was" said Derek looking quite shaken "it wasn't something good. I really think we should call off Patrick's visit and leave the house!"

The moment he said it, he wished he hadn't. The doors began banging, lights flashed, pictures fell from the walls and ornaments smashed. Derek had seen enough, he was leaving regardless of whatever she said.

To his surprise, she agreed.

Telling her they just needed to get out they hurriedly made their way towards the front door.

Derek looked terrified when on opening it a dark figure confronted him.

"You cannot leave, you will die if you try" said the man standing at the door.

"I don't know who you are, but I'm warning you, get out of our way" snapped Derek as he tried to push past him, "we'll die if we stay here!"

Blocking his exit, the man shouted everyone would die if they left.

"Why have you been watching us?" asked Linda "I've seen you!"

"My name is Louis" said the man looking less intimidating "may I come in?"

Instantly Derek said no, they were leaving, but Linda said let him in.

Surprised, Derek argued they didn't know him and they were leaving.

In a calm manner, Louis asked him to listen to Linda. He was there to help them.

It was then they realised the house was calm. Derek however was still unsure, but something strange happened. Joey appeared in the hallway and walking towards Louis held out his hand and taking Louis's led him past the others into the house.

Still shaking, Derek whispered to Linda he wasn't happy about it and suggested they left.

Reassuringly, she took his hand and said it was ok as she closed the door and they followed Louis into the lounge.

He was picking up a broken photograph as they entered the room. Joey wasn't there, he had gone.

Continuing to pick up broken items, Louis suggested Linda making a cup of tea.

"Hang on a minute" snapped Derek as Linda nodded. "Am I the only one who thinks this is strange? Our house is trying to kill us, this bloke turns up out of nowhere and now you're making him tea! I feel like I'm living in the fucking Twilight Zone."

Linda was stunned by his outburst and especially as he'd used bad language, but Louis said he understood how strange everything must seem. If they sat down he would explain everything.

Linda knew how badly the happenings in the house had affected her husband, but until then she never realised how much. Her mind went back to when he was so ill and she thought he would die. He was right, things weren't normal, yet she felt they were meant to be, almost as though her destiny had brought her to this point in her life. It wasn't the same for Derek, he didn't share her belief in the supernatural and he was right, there was a stranger sitting in their lounge who had been invited into their house by a spirit boy and they had no idea who or what he was. Despite knowing this, she suggested making tea and listening to what Louis had to say.

Reluctantly, Derek agreed but added if anything else happened they were leaving regardless.

Just as she reached the door to go and make tea, Louis asked if she had any salt. When she nodded he asked her to bring as much as she had back with her.

Derek never spoke to him while they waited for her to return, he simply sat opposite him and stared.

Ten minutes later, Linda returned with a tray of tea and biscuits.

Derek felt slightly angry with her for treating Louis like he was a friend when, in reality, he could be the total opposite.

There was a tall container of salt on the tray.

Without saying a word, Louis picked it up and walked to the edge of the lounge.

They watched curiously as he began making a trail of salt around the room, paying particular detail to the door or more specifically across the opening.

"That should help" he said as he placed the container back on the tray.

Seeing Derek wasn't comfortable with him there, Linda politely asked Louis to explain what was going on.

"Father Patrick asked me to come. I am part of a secret order of priests, few know about us. You won't find us in churches. We travel wherever God's work sends us to fight evil. For centuries we have known the day would come when Satan would rise. Several months ago we received a message telling us about you. We have been watching you to ensure what we were told had grounding and it does. I need to show you something."

Reaching inside his jacket, he took out a small plastic sleeve. Inside were a series of photographs of the night sky above their house.

There were five in all. Laying them out on the coffee table he told them to look closely at the dark clouds above the roof. The first was taken five days earlier and in truth it just looked like a night sky with the moon in the background, but when he pointed at the others in sequence all taken on separate evenings after the first one, they could see a pattern. It wasn't actually clouds, but one cloud which over the five days had grown in size and moved closer to the roof. More alarming was when he took another photograph from his jacket and laid it on the table.

"I had this one digitally enhanced. I took it last night. The naked eye would never see what you can see now."

They were both horrified to see dozens of demonic faces in the cloud and even more so when he told them they were making ready for the Apocalypse. The dark shadow they had seen earlier was a warning they were there and more would follow.

Derek stated they should leave as it was clearly madness to stay.

"You must stay" said Louis "don't you understand, Linda is part of this. At least wait until Patrick comes, he is the key to ending this. He's prepared to die to stop what is happening. We are all prepared to die because if we don't stop this the world as we know it will end! I have been sent to protect you until Patrick arrives and there are others close by should we need them."

Before he could finish what he was saying the children appeared. Mary was carrying a baby as she moved towards Derek. The others stood silently as she approached him and with desperation in her eyes asked him to help the children.

For the first time Derek seemed to appear comfortable with them. He didn't look afraid. Standing there, he was unaware of the little girl standing beside him until he felt her slip her hand through his. Dressed in rags; her hair tangled and her skin dirty, this pitiful little urchin was holding his hand as she said "Please help us mister," her beautiful liquid blue eyes full of fear and sorrow.

Moments later the children disappeared.

The little girl had clearly had a profound effect on him when he looked at Louis and said he would stay.

Thanking him, Louis did his best to sound confident they could beat the evil in the house, but only if they all stayed strong.

CHAPTER 25

Nathanial had met with Brother Daniel that morning for prayers. Despite no longer being a priest Nathanial still prayed every day.

It was as they walked through the grounds after prayer Brother Daniel expressed his concerns. Several monks were aware who Angel was and although they all appeared happy to help, there were some he didn't trust.

Nathanial confessed he had sensed hostility in the Abbey with some of the monks. Not that any of them spoke to him and Angel and the others had been kept hidden, but he felt all was not as it seemed.

Brother Daniel spoke of a meeting the previous day. The Abbot had decided to tell everyone who Angel was and how it was their duty, not only to her but to God, to help keep her safe. The majority had agreed she should be protected at all costs; however there were a few who had surprised him with their lack of faith. One in particular, Brother Shamus, who had only been with them for two months, had suggested Angel should not stay. His supposed reason was, it was a school and her presence could endanger the pupils. Fortunately the Abbot quickly dispelled his theory, but it was clear Brother Shamus wasn't happy about it.

As a devout monk, Brother Daniel knew their teachings were to help others and in the case of Angel, even more so because if the ancient teachings were correct, she was a chosen one and God had sent her to them for protection.

Nathanial asked if he believed Brother Shamus would harm Angel.

"As a man of God I would like to think not Nathanial, but since the day he arrived I'm ashamed to say I feel not all is as it seems with Brother Shamus. We know that unless our faith is strong the dark forces can manifest. We have both seen how easily evil can consume a man's soul, you more than most my friend."

Nathanial nodded, stating he would keep Angel and the others out of sight until they left the following day.

The two friends parted company as Nathanial headed off in the direction of their rooms.

Angel was talking with the others when Nathanial returned.

Not having seen her since the previous night, he instantly noticed the look of concern on her face as he entered.

As he sat down he asked how she was. He was shocked to hear of a vision she'd had the previous night of a dark entity that had tried to kill her. She had met this demon before; it was the night of the séance in which Joyce died.

Nathanial asked if she thought the vision was simply her mind playing tricks or could she have dreamt it.

Without hesitation she said no, it was a warning. It was as though she knew the dark forces were gathering and they would send someone to harm her. In the vision the demon said the master was waiting for her and this time he will not be denied.

Olivia had a fearful expression as she asked Nathanial if it was best not to return to the house. She was fearful for all of them and especially Angel.

"We must all return, it is our destiny. For so long I questioned why my faith had remained so strong. Many times I've thought about living as a man with a woman I could love for the rest of my life."

They all knew he meant Nancy, the love they felt for one another was obvious. They were soul mates destined to be together.

"I knew the day would come when my faith would be truly tested and that day is tomorrow. If I survive, I will no longer live by my vows, but it's God will that makes me strong. I have known all my life the day would come when that decision would be made for me. I just pray I'm strong enough to do what God wishes, because I am just a man and the forces we will encounter are powerful. I pray God will give us all the strength to do his will and stop this evil from engulfing humanity."

"We have all been chosen to do God's will. The events in our lives have brought us to this day," said Nancy in a gentle voice as she took his hand. "Once you were willing to sacrifice your life for mine Nathanial because your faith was so strong. Like everyone here, I am in no doubt why you were chosen. Your choice to leave the priesthood has no bearing on your faith or God's belief in you. I just want you to know the sacrifice you were prepared to make for me; I would willingly make for you."

For the first time since meeting him, everyone witnessed the emotions her words had given rise to when a tear ran down his cheek. Squeezing her hand, he thanked her.

The day passed slowly with the three woman spending time in their room and the men in theirs.

Brother Daniel had told them someone would bring their meals to their rooms. Breakfast and lunch had been brought by nuns.

Olivia looked at her watch and stating the evening meal was due, said she needed to use the bathroom before it came. Leaving the two women talking she left the room.

Barely a minute had passed when there was a knock on the door.

Nancy opened it, expecting to see nuns with their meal. She felt uneasy when two monks stood there; one was carrying a tray of food, their faces hidden under their hoods.

Quickly dispelling any bad or negative thoughts, she thanked them as she put her arms out to take the tray, but the monk carrying it insisted on placing it on the table. Both women sensed something was wrong when the second monk entered and closed the door.

Nancy gave Angel a look that expressed her fear.

"Thank you Brother" said Angel hoping he would simply put the tray down and leave, but she knew that wasn't going to happen.

Placing the tray down, he reached inside his habit and pulled out a large knife.

"You must come with us" he said threateningly to Angel.

Nancy tried to wrestle the knife from him as she told Angel to run. In the struggle the monk stabbed her and threatened Angel if she didn't go with them she would die too. With Nancy lying on the floor bleeding from a stomach wound, Angel tried to make her way to her but the second monk grabbed her and forced a piece of material across her mouth and nose. Despite trying to fight them, Angel passed out.

The monks hadn't anticipated Olivia returning from the bathroom. Just as the monk threw Angel over his shoulder and opened the door, Olivia returned.

Seeing what was happening, she shouted as the monk pushed her against the door frame knocking her to the floor.

With her struggling to get up, the monks made their escape.

Seeing Nancy lying in a pool of blood, Olivia made her way to her before calling for help. The room the men were staying in was further along the corridor and they couldn't hear her call.

Nancy was still conscious as Olivia applied pressure to her wound and asked if she could hang on while she got help. Nancy nodded as Olivia lifted her hand and placed it on the towel she'd used to stem the bleeding.

Moments later she returned with the men.

Nathanial ran straight to Nancy and cradling her in his arms begged her to hang on. Her eyes were heavy; she was losing consciousness as he told Martin to get the Abbey's doctor and call an ambulance.

Her consciousness was slowly ebbing away as they waited for Martin to return.

Olivia was distraught, not only for Nancy but for Angel.

Nathanial assured her they would find her.

"God please help me" cried Nathanial out loud as he held Nancy "I ask for nothing from you Lord except to spare her life. Take me! I know I have sinned with the love I feel for her, but she is innocent and not once have I broken my vows! I beg you in the name of Christ help us!"

The Doctor and Martin rushed into the room.

"Please help her" said Nathanial.

Kneeling next to her, the doctor did all he could before the ambulance arrived.

A nun came into the room; it was the one who had let them in the morning they arrived.

"Please Sister, go with her" said Nathanial "pray to God she lives. I love her."

The nun nodded and said she would pray for all of them.

As the paramedics inserted a drip in Nancy's arm and placed her on the stretcher, Nathanial kissed her head, begged her to hold on and said he'd see her soon.

The nun took her hand and walked alongside the stretcher.

Brother Daniel passed them as he entered the room and immediately asked what had happened.

Olivia tried to talk through her tears as to what she'd seen. Her belief was Nancy had been stabbed trying to protect Angel. She never got a good look at the monks, it all happened so quickly.

Nathanial asked Brother Daniel where they may have taken her.

"There are many secret places in and around the Abbey. I have no idea where they may have gone. Some places are out of bounds to us; maybe they've gone to one of them?"

Nathanial said he needed a map of the Abbey and its grounds.

They followed Brother Daniel to a huge library. There were no monks studying which was rare. They all assumed they had gone to find out what happened after hearing the ambulance arrive.

Brother Daniel moved the sliding ladder which ran along the vast shelves of books.

Climbing to the top shelf, he selected one.

Moments later he opened it on a table and took out some large sheets of folded papers from inside.

Opening it out, he showed the blueprints of the Abbey and grounds.

The Abbey was vast, sitting in seven acres, yet it was the areas and buildings in the grounds that interested Nathanial. One in particular wasn't shown as anything except a circle. He asked Brother Daniel what it was.

"It was once widely speculated the Abbey grounds held satanic circles. The most famous being the one you've mentioned Nathanial. It was originally used as a grain store, yet there was speculation it was used for devil worship. Of course we've not seen any evidence to collaborate this, but the Abbey is very old and most documentation referring to these supposed events date back over one hundred years ago. It's off limits to everyone and has been for years. There was talk of demolishing it a few years ago, but nothing came of it. I can take you there."

Nathanial tried to make James stay with the others and search inside, but his request was fruitless.

Brother Daniel led them out through the rear of the Abbey. They walked for almost thirty minutes. It was getting dark as Brother Daniel passed him a torch.

The old grain store was locked and it didn't look as though anyone had been there for a long time. James wasn't leaving anything to chance though. Breaking the door down, they entered. Parts of the roof fell down as they moved about inside; but there was no sign that anyone had been there.

Nathanial suggested checking the next empty building before returning to the Abbey. It was a type of barn which had probably been used for keeping animals. Looking derelict Brother Daniel told them to take care as it was unsafe.

After a thorough search, they agreed to return to the others.

It was as they approached the Abbey they spotted car headlights driving towards it. Brother Daniel expressed concern, stating it was unusual due to the late hour.

All three men had a strange feeling about it and ran towards the Abbey.

Just as they reached the main driveway they saw a car speeding off.

James suggested following it, but knew it would be long gone by the time he got to their car.

It was as they entered the Abbey that Brother Daniel spotted Brother Shamus and another monk hurriedly making their way past the main hall. He knew there was no reason for any of them to be there at that hour. His suspicions were correct when after calling out to Brother Shamus they didn't turn round, but moved quickly away.

James took off running to catch up with them followed by his friends, but the monks ran and disappeared before he could catch them.

"We need to find them" he stated "they know where Angel is!"

They searched every room in the area where they were seen running. The last room on that floor was the chapel; several monks were there for evening prayers. The three friends entered quietly and stood at the back. Several monks looked round at them, but remained praying.

James signalled for them to split up, walking the sides and the middle of the rows of pews.

With the monks heads bowed for prayer, identifying them would be difficult. It was as he neared the front of the rows James noticed what looked like footprints made by a black substance, maybe coal. Whatever it was, it was enough to fire his suspicions and tap the monk nearest to him on the shoulder. When the monk ignored him and didn't look up, he knew they were the monks he'd chased. Their presence in the chapel began to cause a stir when James said something to the monk; other monks began saying Sshh and whispers echoed around the chapel. Nathanial was now standing at the opposite end of the row. James indicated to him the monks they were looking for were there.

The two friends began closing in on them. Suddenly the monks made a run for it, jumping over the pew onto the monks in the row in front of them. A frantic scramble ensued as the monks tried to escape. One managed to slip out through a side door, but James managed to bring down the other. Holding him firmly so he couldn't escape, he marched him towards the chapel doors where Brother Daniel was waiting and told them to follow him.

He led them down to the basement where they wouldn't be heard. Once there he removed the monk's hood and was shocked to see Brother Dominic, a young monk who had been at the Abbey for five years.

Brother Daniel asked him where Angel was. When he refused to talk, James punched him in the face splitting his lip and making his nose bleed.

Brother Daniel asked James to let him talk to Dominic before using violence.

With the look of a killer, James stated he had two minutes.

Brother Daniel pleaded with the young monk to tell him where Angel was; but he refused to say anything except they were too late.

Horrified, Brother Daniel begged him to tell them where she was, but he refused.

They heard voices approaching and knew it wouldn't be many minutes before people came and realised what was happening. Brother Daniel told them to follow him; he knew a place they could go.

Placing one hand across Brother Dominic's mouth and twisting his arm up behind his back, James made him follow Brother Daniel.

Taking them through a small corridor and down some winding stone stairs they found themselves under the Abbey.

He led them to a small room that had once been used to store coal. The room was bare except for an old dining chair. James noticed a small barred window with no glass and a trap hatch that was once used to send coal deliveries down.

Throwing Brother Dominic onto the floor and pressing his knee into his chest, he proceeded to remove the belt tie from his cassock. It was as he pinned the monk to the floor he noticed something shining and picking it up, realised it was Angel's locket. Now he knew why the two monks had left black footprints, they had taken her there while they waited for someone to come for her.

Grabbing the monk roughly, James dragged him up and tied him to the chair.

Taking a penknife from his pocket, James cut the bottom of the cassock off and screwing it up stuffed it into the young monk's mouth.

"Don't want anyone to hear you screaming when I cut your eye out, do we" he said looking menacingly at the monk. "I can see by your face you think I'm bluffing, well believe me I'm not. You will tell me where she is or you'll die here, painfully!"

Before Brother Dominic had time to react, James cut his face. It was a deep cut going down to the cheek bone. The monk tried to scream out in pain, but his cries were muffled by the gag.

Brother Daniel protested, he didn't hold with torture.

"Then I suggest you look away" stated James arrogantly "because this piece of devil worshipping shit is going to tell me where Angel is!"

Brother Daniel begged him not to do it, but realising his pleas was falling on deaf ears, he said he couldn't be a party to what they were doing and began to walk towards the door. Nathanial took a firm grip on his arm and said he couldn't allow him to leave.

Knowing he would have no choice but to stay, he moved to the corner of the room, knelt down and began praying.

Nathanial nodded at James. It was the type of nod that gave the ok for him to do whatever was necessary to get the monk to talk.

James cut the monk's face and body time and time again. The monk passed out only to be slapped several times by him to bring him round.

After every cut, James asked if he wanted to tell them where she was, but every time the monk shook his head until James pushed the tip of the penknife just below his eye. Feeling the blade penetrating his skin, the monk thrashed around on the chair and tried to scream. Pushing the knife in deeper, James asked if he was ready to talk. This time the monk nodded.

Before removing the gag, James pushed the tip of the knife into the monk's throat and warned him if he called out he would kill him and they were taking him with them so if he lied they would kill him anyway.

The monk said she had been taken to Henrik's penthouse apartment in Mayfair.

Nathanial knew of it and told James they needed to go. He would call Martin and tell him to drive the car to the rear of the Abbey and pick them up. They couldn't risk being seen, especially with Brother Dominic.

Ten minutes later as they heard a car, Nathanial tried to open the hatch, but it was bolted on the outside. Calling Martin's phone, he gave their exact location and told him to open the hatch. A few moments later, Martin was pulling them up.

"We need to go" said Martin "they're looking for you. The Abbot told us not to leave when they searched our rooms. He said you had attacked two monks and had taken one hostage. They left one guarding our room, I hit him over the head, but he has probably already raised the alarm."

At the car, they threw Brother Dominic into the boot before Nathanial sped away towards the main gates. Just as he approached they began to close electronically. Hitting the throttle, he rammed them and through sheer force made it out onto the road.

Within a few minutes, he spotted car headlights coming up fast behind them. Quickly pulling into a field, he turned the headlights off and told everyone to be still. They watched as two cars drove past, both cars had been seen at the Abbey. Waiting until Nathanial deemed it was safe; they pulled back out onto the road.

Taking a different route in the hope of not being seen, it was almost two hours later when he pulled into a driveway of a coach house.

Nathanial asked them to wait in the car while he spoke to the owner.

They watched as he rang the bell and a few moments later a very elderly lady answered the door and embraced him.

They heard her say how wonderful it was to see him after so many years. They couldn't hear the following conversation as Nathanial stepped inside the house.

Several minutes passed before he came out and beckoned them inside.

Following him through the hallway they entered the kitchen. The old lady was making tea and sandwiches.

"I'd like you to meet my very dear friend, Sister Violet" he said introducing them, "she has very kindly agreed to let us stay here until tomorrow when we have to leave to meet Father Patrick at the house. James and I will find Angel and come back here."

When Martin asked if he wanted him to go with them Nathanial shook his head and stated it was safer for them to stay with Sister Violet; no one would look for them there.

Telling Sister Violet he and James wouldn't be staying for tea as they must find Angel; he kissed her forehead and thanked her again for helping them.

The two men removed Brother Dominic from the car boot. They took him to a large shed and after he was bound and gagged hid him in a large wooden chest that Sister Violet used for storage. James punched him in the face knocking him unconscious before he secured the chest. Leaving him there they would free him when Angel was no longer in danger.

Inside the house, Sister Violet invited the others to go through to the lounge; she would join them in a few minutes with tea and sandwiches.

Despite having had little appetite, Olivia was hungry. Thanking Sister Violet, she picked up a sandwich and encouraged Martin to eat one.

"You must try not to worry Olivia; Nathanial will find your daughter."

There was something about the way Sister Violet had spoken that made Olivia believe her; but she asked what made her so sure.

"I have never met anyone more honourable or true to his word than Nathanial and despite leaving the Church, he is the most dedicated man of God I have ever met. I feel privileged to call him my friend."

Olivia smiled and asked how long they'd been friends.

"We met when I was doing God's work as a nun at St Luke's Church. I'm still a nun, but I retired here. I felt the time was right for me to live in the world. Has Nathanial told you about the boy Peter?"

Olivia shook her head and explained they hadn't known him long.

"It was a long time ago. Peter's mother begged the Church to help; she believed her son was possessed by a demon. Back then the Church wouldn't readily accept such things, they needed proof. Father Michael and Father Nathanial agreed to see the boy. Young Peter was fourteen years old and in torment, haunted by a terrible demon. Despite all their efforts to exorcise the demon, Peter's possession was too strong and the boy's life was in terrible jeopardy. Finally Father Michael convinced the church hierarchy that bringing the boy to the Church was the only way to save him with round the clock religious intervention. I agreed to help. For almost a month the priests and I said prayers around the boy's bed before the demon finally left him. I witnessed Nathanial's dedication and belief that he could banish the demon and save the boy, even when everyone else gave up. On two occasions, I saw him offer his own life to save the boy. He never slept for days and nights. There were many times the demon attacked him, but still he battled to save the boy. He's a fine man and he will find your daughter."

While Sister Violet talked about Nathanial, several miles away in London he was parking the car a street away from Henrik's penthouse block.

CHAPTER 26

Despite his appearance and Derek's reluctance to accept Louis's arrival at the house, as the hours passed they both found themselves warming to him. Even Derek felt safer with him there. He seemed to have a calming effect as he talked about what had been going on in the house and how it had always been there, but it was Linda's decision to buy the house which had placed a large piece of the puzzle in place. He talked about her Uncle Patrick and how he was held in great esteem.

As the hours passed things in the house calmed down which in truth surprised even Louis, he had expected it to continue. It was after receiving a call he realised why.

Linda and Derek sat quietly as he spoke to the caller. It was clear from the urgency and panic in his voice something had happened.

When the call ended, he told them Angel had been taken. Linda was fearful and quickly asked if he thought she was alive. Of that he was in no doubt, she would need to be brought to the house. Derek looked scared and asked when.

"Not until tomorrow" said Louis "they will need to prepare her before she comes here. I have it on good authority that people are looking for her and I'm hopeful with God's help they will find her."

Linda asked what he meant by preparing her and looked horrified when he explained.

They both noticed Derek looked bemused by what Louis had said. Linda asked if he was alright.

"No not really love. I'm beginning to wonder is this really all happening or am I losing my mind. Here we are sitting chatting to a stranger who quite frankly looks like a hairy biker talking about demons and people of God. A few months ago I was dying then you found that bloody diary and now here we are waiting for the girl from that diary to appear and save us all. I'm sorry love, I've tried to believe it, but quite frankly I'm thinking what the hell is really going on. We should leave this house now and forget all about this fantasy that everyone except me seems to have bought into. Maybe we've been brainwashed?"

Linda looked embarrassed and wondered what Louis would think of Derek's outburst as she apologised to him.

"Please don't apologise Linda, I can fully understand where Derek's coming from. This whole thing does seem a bit farfetched, but unfortunately it's real. I wish it was all make believe, but it's not. The illness you suffered Derek was simply a means of keeping you here. It is Patrick who is the key to all this and this house has a portal to Hell; it's the perfect place for evil. Finding Angel's diary was no accident, she is the key piece in this puzzle, yet like you two, she was unaware until recently. Patrick has known for many years this time would come, but he didn't know where or how until you bought this house. Did you know when Father Angelo came to bless the house he came face to face with the demon?"

He watched as they shook their heads and then continued,

"Yes he did, it was the demon who tried to possess Patrick when you were a child Linda. So you see, everyone has not simply plunged into this, they have been chosen and soon we'll all know why."

Derek was still keeping an open mind; he was having a hard time believing what Louis said.

To Linda's surprise, he asked if there was any reason why he would need to be there after Patrick arrived.

Instantly, she stated he should want to stay for her and Uncle Patrick.

Begrudgingly he agreed, but quickly stated if things became really dangerous they were leaving. His reason was he remembered overhearing a conversation she'd had with Sophie about the night of the séance when Angel's friend Joyce was killed.

He was just about to say something to Louis when they heard tapping. Everyone sat silently, trying to pinpoint where the sound was coming from when suddenly Louis was thrown from the chair. Despite feeling afraid, Derek sprang to his feet to help him, but was instantly pushed back onto his chair. He tried to stand again, but something was pinning him down and whatever it was it had the strength of several men. He could actually feel whatever it was breathing on his face, its breath was rancid. Too traumatised to speak he continued to struggle. Then he saw it as it materialised, a grotesque creature with fanged teeth which had saliva dripping from them. Its body was half man half beast.

Linda screamed which brought Louis to his senses and, rolling across the floor; he quickly picked up his bag and took something from it. Throwing it at the creature he ordered it to leave. Whatever it was it exploded on impact with the creature's body. They all watched as a yellow cloud of dust seemed to engulf it. It began thrashing and screaming as it backed away from Derek and disappeared down through the floor.

"Oh my God" cried Linda "what was that Louis, I thought you said we'd be safe in here?"

Before he could reply, Derek said he was leaving but as he spoke the words the tapping started again, only louder.

"Stop it Derek! Louis told you it won't let us leave and you keep saying it will just make things worse!"

"Worse! Can it really get any worse! Whatever that thing was it could have killed me! I've had enough Linda, all this hocus pocus is getting to me. I'm leaving whether the bloody house likes it or not and if you've got any sense you'll come with me!"

Louis could understand how Derek felt but, regardless, he knew the house wouldn't let him leave. Ironically he had no idea why, Derek wasn't a key player and Patrick would come whether he was there or not. He tried to reason with him, suggesting he waited until Patrick arrived. Derek was having none of it, his mind was made up and he was going.

The very second he moved, the tapping got much louder. The door slammed with a large bang just as he reached it and at that moment the furniture began to move across the floor and pictures fell from the walls.

Feeling more anger than fear, he grabbed the door handle and shouted it was his house and he wouldn't be kept prisoner.

Louis shouted for him to stop, he knew the demon would retaliate. His words came too late; Derek was thrown into the air hitting the ceiling with force.

Linda was screaming as she watched her husband tossed around the room.

"In the name of God, STOP!" she shouted.

Suddenly everything stopped. Derek was lying deadly still on the floor, blood was pouring from a gash on his head.

They both rushed over to him. She was crying as Louis picked him up and laid him on the sofa. Nervously she asked if he was alive. To her relief, Louis said he was just unconscious, but they needed to stop the wound from bleeding.

Although he never said anything, Louis was relieved that Derek was temporarily out of action. His constant demands to leave the house were definitely having a very bad effect. His hope was once Patrick arrived, Derek could leave but he had his doubts.

CHAPTER 27

Henrik's penthouse was on the top floor, twelve storeys up. Inside the main lobby was a night security guard who checked who came in or out and sat at his desk watching the CCTV on the floors.

Getting past him could prove difficult. Luckily enough, Nathanial had studied the blueprints of the building after Henrik purchased the place a year earlier. He knew there was a rear entrance they could use.

Able to enter unseen, Nathanial knew there would be CCTV cameras on the stairwells, floors and lifts. They rotated so they would have a few seconds window in which to move unseen.

Nathanial believed God was on their side when they managed to get to the penthouse with little difficulty. Due to the nature of their being there, they weren't surprised to see a heavily built man standing outside Henrik's door. Staying hidden in the stairwell they discussed how to get to the penthouse.

James suggested he could simply walk up to the door and pretend to be an invited guest. Once the guard realised who he was it would be too late. He was confident he could take him down. There was no CCTV on the penthouse floor.

Nathanial had just agreed to his plan when they heard voices. Peering out through the door they watched as Henrik, Leticia and two other women came out of the penthouse. Henrik spoke to the guard in German, fortunately Nathanial spoke the language. Waiting until they heard the lift doors close, he told James that Henrik had said they would only be gone an hour. If anyone turned up early, the guard was not to let them in, they were to wait. A woman called Henrietta was staying with the girl. They were certain he meant Angel. His assumption was she was being or had been prepared and on Henrik and the others' return would probably be used in a sacrificial ceremony to prepare her for the next day.

Neither of them recognised the guard so they hoped they weren't known to him. Deciding that, once confident the others had left the building they would pretend they had arrived for the ceremony.

Fifteen minutes passed when they exited the stairwell. Instantly, the guard looked suspicious that they hadn't come from the lift.

Nathanial spoke in German stating the lift didn't seem to be working properly so they had decided to take the stairs from the previous floor. He even joked he was out of condition as it was only one flight yet he was breathless. Next time he would suggest to Henrik they met at a ground floor location.

For a moment the guard seemed to relax and told them they were far too early and he was under strict instructions not to let anyone in. They would have to come back in an hour.

"No this cannot be right" said Nathanial in German; "Henrik assured me he would leave instruction for me to be here. He knew I would arrive at this time. Is Henrietta here?" the guard nodded "Good then I would recommend you call Henrik and tell him Wolfgang is here and we will wait with Henrietta. Or tell her I'm here, she will sort this unfortunate incident out!"

They could see the guard was a little intimidated by Nathanial's words. The last thing they wanted him to do was call Henrik because their plan would be in ruins. When the guard took his phone out, Nathanial was quick to say he didn't want to be kept waiting a moment longer. In that moment the guard seemed to feel he needed to keep who he believed to be Wolfgang pacified so in a quick change of thought, said he would speak to Henrietta as he was certain it would be ok for them to wait with her.

Nathanial thanked him and apologised for his temper, but they'd had a long journey and they had been expected.

The guard nodded before knocking on the door.

The moment he turned around, James placed his arms around his neck and put him in a sleeper hold.

The two men held him up between them as a middle aged woman opened the door. Nathanial recognised her instantly. She was Henrik's spinster sister and, like her brother, a key player in the occult. They were often seen out together acting more like lovers than brother and sister. She was known to be fiercely protective of him and did not approve when he had other women. Nathanial's thoughts on the matter were simple, they were incestuous.

Before she had time to realise the guard was unconscious they pushed him onto her which instantly threw her off balance long enough for them to gain entry.

Despite getting up and attacking them, she was soon over powered after James punched her in the face to prevent her from screaming for help.

With her and the guard now both rendered helpless, the two friends bound and gagged them.

Time was running out, it had been thirty minutes since Henrik and the others had left and they would be returning soon. Finding Angel and getting back to their car was now of paramount importance.

Searching the penthouse they were surprised she wasn't anywhere to be found. Nathanial suggested checking the walls for a false panel. Within a few minutes, James was calling to him. He thought he'd found something after tapping the wall in the lounge, not only did it sound hollow, but he could hear something. It sounded like light banging with a muffled voice.

The two men looked for an opening and soon found a panel that moved along behind the adjoining panel. To their absolute relief they found Angel, bound and gagged, wearing a white robe. Her head had been shaved and there were cuts and bruises to her face and body.

James lifted her into his arms and placed her gently on the floor before untying her. He noticed her eyes looked glazed and assumed she'd been drugged; fortunately it had started to wear off which had enabled her to bang against the panel after hearing him tapping.

The moment her hands were freed, she threw them around his neck and hugged him. He looked curious when Nathanial asked if she'd been marked.

Still looking dazed, she said she thought so but they'd drugged her.

Nathanial asked James to look for a tattoo or mark somewhere on her body. Angel said her back hurt so for him to look there.

James lifted her gown and was shocked to see a tattoo of a ram's head with large horns between her shoulder blades.

Nathanial told him to carry her as they were leaving.

As they approached the front door he took Henrietta's coat from a coat stand and placed it over her. He opened the door carefully to see if anyone was in the hallway.

James suggested using the lift, but Nathanial said the stairs would be safer for two reasons. Henrik and the others could be in the lift travelling up to the penthouse and the security guard would be more likely to focus his attention on the lobbies than the stairwells.

They thought their plan had worked until they opened the door on the ground floor and the security guard was waiting for them.

Without a second thought, Nathanial rushed at him and, catching him off guard, managed to knock him to the floor. They wrestled for a few moments before Nathanial landed a fearsome blow that would render the guard unconscious long enough for him to tie and gag him. Dragging him to the stairwell, the friends made their escape.

Once outside, Nathanial told James to wait there for him but stay out of sight, he would fetch the car and pick them up in a few minutes. It was too risky to all go, in case anyone saw them along with the fact Angel couldn't walk as she was still woozy from whatever drug they had given her.

He helped James move Angel to some large rubbish bins at the rear of the block. Telling him to stay hidden, Nathanial left to get the car.

Ten minutes passed when James's phone buzzed. It was a text to say the car was outside.

Picking Angel up, he carefully made his way to the front of the building.

Spotting the car, he double checked to ensure nobody was watching. As he approached, Nathanial leaned over from his seat and pushed open the rear door.

Bundling Angel into the back and telling her to stay down, James quickly closed the door as he got into the front passenger seat.

They had to drive past the penthouse block as it was a one way road system. Nathanial checked his mirror as he passed by and thanked God no one saw them.

Angel stayed lying asleep on the back seat throughout the journey.

Before turning into the road where Sister Violet lived, Nathanial stopped the car and checked they weren't being followed. Once certain, he drove on.

Parking behind her house they exited the car.

James carried Angel to the house where Olivia was waiting at the door. Looking terrified, she asked if Angel was ok and looked relieved to hear it was simply because she'd been drugged.

Sister Violet told James to carry her straight through to the bedroom.

With Olivia sitting on the bed holding her hand, Angel began to wake up.

Nathanial stayed in the kitchen and called the hospital to inquire after Nancy. During the drive he had debated whether to go there, but knew by then people from the Abbey were aware she was there. He asked to speak to the nun who was with her.

His fears for Nancy were instantly calmed when the nun told him she was doing just fine and the doctors were expecting her to make a full recovery. The nun had the good sense to call the police and state Nancy's life could be in jeopardy as the men involved had not been caught. Nathanial smiled to himself when she said there was a policeman stationed outside Nancy's room. The only downfall was the police inquiries had led them to the Abbey where they had been told they were staying and that Angel and the others had been with her at the time of the stabbing. They weren't aware that Angel had been kidnapped.

Nathanial wasn't worried by this as he knew they wouldn't find them at Sister Violet's and after tomorrow it wouldn't matter. Olivia could simply contact the police then and make a statement. Not wishing to stay on the phone too long he sent Nancy his love, thanked the nun and ended the call.

The moment she gained her senses, Angel lifted her arms and placing them around Olivia's neck said how happy she was to see her.

Olivia began to cry just as Sister Violet entered the room and smiling at Angel said she'd made her some soup.

Thanking her, Olivia took the tray and placed it on the bed.

Angel was hungry; she hadn't eaten since she'd been kidnapped.

While she ate the soup, Olivia asked her what happened.

"It all happened so fast mum. Nancy tried to stop them from taking me. They stabbed her. They took me somewhere in the Abbey, but I don't remember anything after that until I woke up in the place James found me. Henrik was there with four women, one was Leticia. He told the women to get me ready. I was terrified. When they untied me, I tried to fight them. I tried to use my power to hit them with an object, but I couldn't make anything move. I think it was because I'd been drugged. They stripped me off and Leticia cut my hair off. They laid me naked on a table and did something to my back, it was painful. When they'd finished they bathed me in blood, but before dressing me hosed me down with clean water. They put that gown on me and left me bound and gagged on the floor. I tried to listen to what they were talking about, but Henrik came in and said they had to leave. He asked Leticia if I was ready. When she said yes, he told them to drug me again and hide me, his sister would stay with me under guard while he met the others from the airport. I don't know who he was meeting and I don't remember anything after that."

Olivia gently stroked the side of her face and introduced her properly to Sister Violet, explaining who she was and how she was helping them.

It was as Angel thanked her, Sister Violet sat down on the bed and touched her hand.

"Don't thank me yet child, there is still much to be done. Your faith will be truly tested tomorrow. Be strong and never let them see your fear. You will be safe here tonight and you are lucky you have people like Nathanial. He will die protecting you. I knew this day would come, but I never imagined it would happen in my lifetime. Have faith Angel and God will not desert you. If we fail then all will be lost."

They were interrupted by Martin knocking on the door. Olivia called to him to enter. Smiling at Angel and stating she looked better, he told Olivia that Linda had been calling her mobile.

Passing her the phone, he suggested texting her back, but not calling her so they couldn't trace the location.

Olivia simply texted 'hope all ok; can't phone.'

The reply was as simple, 'All ok, but I think something has happened to Alan. Watch the news.'

Olivia looked concerned and asked Martin to turn the TV on in the lounge.

A few minutes later everyone except Angel was watching the news.

They watched to the end, but nothing seemed relevant to what Linda had said until they watched the local news. They were horrified to see earlier footage of Alan's place cordoned off by police tape. A body was being carried to an ambulance. It was covered, but everyone's instincts told them it was Alan. The police were asking for witnesses to come forward after the body of a man was found mutilated at the address.

Olivia started to cry and said they should tell Angel. Nathanial disagreed, stating she needed to sleep and gain her strength for the next day. They could tell her after the day was over.

Olivia asked if he thought Alan's death was connected to what was happening. Nodding his head, he was in no doubt Alan had been tortured. He had died to protect them, although he couldn't have told them anything anyway, he didn't know where they'd gone.

James checked on Angel several times during the evening before joining her in bed later that night.

With him snuggled up next to her holding her in his arms, she slept soundly. At three o'clock that morning, James was woken by something heavy on his chest. Trying to focus as he scrambled his senses in the dim light, he could see Angel seemingly floating above him. As he tried to sit up to help her, something hit in in the chest, knocking the wind out of him. Again he tried to move, but the pain of whatever was preventing him was excruciating. He tried to call out to her, but in that second something hit him in the face. He could taste his own blood from a tooth that had been knocked out. His reasoning was telling him it was a strong, heavily built man who had him pinned down and was hitting him, yet there was no one there. Again he tried with all his strength, giving one hard push.

A piercing growl echoed around the room as whatever it was had been thrown from the bed. James was shouting for it to leave Angel alone as he scrambled off the bed. It wasn't until his feet hit the floor, he realised how much pain he was in. Barely able to stand, again he called to Angel, but there was no response from her. It was as though she was fast asleep as she continued to levitate.

Suddenly, the door flew open and Sister Violet burst in. In her hand she held a bottle of Holy water which she shook and sprayed out around the room. Although still unable to see anyone, they watched as furniture turned over and objects fell from the dresser onto the floor smashing. Whatever had attacked him was trying to escape from the Holy water. Gripping the bottle firmly and spraying it out, she shouted for the demon to leave. Every time the water hit the invisible foe, a loud rasping scream was heard.

With the entire house now awake, Nathanial was the next to enter the room. In that moment, he watched as Sister Violet was lifted from the floor and hurled against the bed.

Holding his crucifix, he commanded the demon to leave. Moments later all was calm and Angel slowly floated back down to the bed.

Instantly, Nathanial rushed over to help Sister Violet. Grateful that she seemed unharmed, be it a little bruised and shaken, he helped her stand.

Angel woke and asked why everyone was there; she was oblivious to what happened.

Nathanial suggested they went into the lounge as he suggested Martin making everyone a cup of tea.

Despite having grown accustomed to the strange happenings since leaving the army, James was concerned over the incident and he let them know his feelings.

Angry was how he felt when Nathanial stated he hadn't been surprised by what happened, he'd expected something to. His concern now was for Sister Violet if they stayed there.

The old nun surprised him when she stated that, like him, she'd expected something to happen and she needed to show him something before they left.

Curiously, Nathanial and the others watched as she removed a small wall picture and revealed a safe. Sister Violet was the last person you would expect to have such a thing. On opening it, she removed an old leather satchel type bag. Placing it on a sideboard, she removed some old papers and passed them to him.

As he began to browse through them, she asked if he remembered an old blind priest named Samuel from the time he spent at St Luke's Church with the young boy Peter, who was possessed.

Nathanial nodded. It was a long time ago, but he remembered meeting him once. The reason he remembered him was, according to Father Michael, he was over one hundred years old.

"I'm glad you recall him. Father Samuel lived to be one hundred and nine. I spent many years with him; he was truly a wise and devoted priest. The day he died, he asked to see me. He gave me those papers you're holding. Due to a stroke his speech was very limited, but that day he spoke with perfect clarity. He told me to guard them at all costs and that one day a man of God would come to me for help. It would be that man I needed to give them to. I have never read them, but he talked of the Apocalypse and how the faith of a few would save us from Satan and his legions. As time went on I forgot about them, but when you turned up, I knew the man he'd spoken of was you. So now we'll leave you in peace to read them."

Nathanial sat reading as the others left the room.

The pages were hand written by Father Samuel. In them he wrote of a vision he'd had when he was a young priest. In his vision, a beautiful lady dressed in a flowing white gown had appeared to him. She told him of a terrible time to come when Satan and his army would rise from the Underworld. A young girl, a descendant of Jesus would become Satan's bride and all life as we know it will end. The rivers and seas would run red with blood. Pestilence and famine would engulf the world. The girl will not know who she is, or the power she holds. A man will be sent to protect her; he will be a man whose faith will be truly tested. Should he fail, the girl must die at his hand to save humanity. Many will aid him in his quest.

Since that first vision, Father Samuel had been visited once every ten years by a messenger of God. Each time they had foretold of a time when Satan would rise. The last visit told of the child who had been chosen and the date of her birth and how she would be outcast.

The more Nathanial read, he felt beyond any doubt that child was Angel. There was reference to her facing her fears as a young girl when she would come face to face with evil. Many angels would be sent by God to protect her, but it would be a mortal who would sacrifice his own life to save her. The day of the reckoning she will go unhindered to the place where her destiny will be fulfilled. At that place a terrible battle between heaven and hell will come to pass.

For many years since his first vision, Father Samuel studied charts and writings. His findings were all written in the pages Nathanial was now reading.

For hours he sat quietly reading until he finally joined the others.

He was happy to see Angel was up and looking refreshed since the incident a few hours earlier. On asking how she felt, he noticed a smile come over her face when she spoke of a dream she'd had about her guardian angel, Johnathan. Despite the years passing since she'd seen him, he had not deserted her. In his absence, he had left others like Grace, to watch over her. For her, the best part of the dream was when he'd said he would be with her that day and she was never to doubt her faith.

Nathanial smiled to express his happiness for her. Sister Violet asked if the papers she'd given him had helped.

"Yes, they have Sister. Today will be a day we will all have our faith tested, but God will be there with us and we will overcome evil. I would like Martin and Olivia to stay here with you. They can join us later."

Instantly Olivia protested and stated she wouldn't leave Angel.

Taking her mum's hand, Angel told her how much she loved her and how she was the best mum anyone could wish for, but Nathanial was right, she should stay. There was no logical reason for her or Martin to risk their lives further. Seeing Olivia wasn't convinced, Angel used the ruse that if she was there, she would be worried about her safety and that would only make the situation worse. Finally, Olivia agreed, be it all reluctantly.

Nathanial suggested that after breakfast they left.

CHAPTER 28

Olivia cried as she hugged Angel at the door that morning. With a desperate look she begged her not to go, stating there must be another way.

"I have to go mum. Pray for us and God will hear you. Try not to worry. I have James and Nathanial looking out for me and remember my dream, Johnathan said he'd be with me. God willing this will all be over in a matter of hours and we can all get on with our lives."

Like any good mother, Olivia tried not to sound despondent, like everyone there she hoped it would soon be over. Her first thought was for Angel's safety. As her mother she knew just how afraid Angel really was. Her whole life had been a challenge and that day would herald the greatest challenge she had ever faced.

With Martin's arm around her shoulders, they watched as the three friends made their way to the car and a few minutes later pulled away.

Sister Violet tried to offer some words of comfort as the car drove out of sight and the friends went back indoors. The atmosphere was very sombre as Sister Violet placed a teapot and cups on the table.

Passing Olivia a cup she told her not to worry. Forcing a half smile, Olivia talked about the night of the séance when Joyce was killed.

Even Martin was shocked at the graphic detail she went into, he had never been told the truth and like everyone else, believed Joyce and Angel had fallen down the stairs. The demon they had encountered would have killed Angel had Johnathan not saved her, but what if he wasn't there this time. The thought of losing Angel was more than she could bear. From the day she entered her life as a teenager, Olivia had felt akin to her and the love she felt for her was real.

Sister Violet was in no doubt Angel was meant to go to Olivia's. Expressing her views, she talked about how everything was destiny and how God had a plan. Had it not been for her love and moving into number 16; Angel may never have known her capabilities or the courage to accept what she was.

Olivia knew Sister Violet meant every word, but she wasn't a mother. Nothing anyone could say would convince Olivia that risking her daughter's life was worth it.

Angel was quiet as Nathanial drove, despite James promising he would look after her.

Unlike him, she knew the evil they were about to face and all she hoped was they would survive.

Her promise to herself was if she was lucky enough to survive, she would try to put everything behind her, marry James and raise a family with him.

Her mind wandered back to her time in foster care when she was outcast. The day she met Olivia and how her life changed. Knowing her birth mother had been instrumental in choosing Olivia, she felt love for both of them, but Olivia was the one who had shown her how good life could be. Now she was grateful she and Martin were safe back at Sister Violet's.

Nathanial interrupted her thoughts when he said he had no idea what to expect when they arrived at the house, although he believed what Father Samuel had written that their journey would go unhindered.

Angel felt nervous as he announced they were approaching Albert Avenue.

James instantly spotted several cars which looked out of place. They were large saloons with tinted windows; he counted at least four as they drove closer to the house. More concerning were the three men standing at the house door, they looked like doormen, wearing jeans and T shirts. They were big, tattooed with a mean look.

James suggested him exiting the car first. In the event of trouble, Nathanial could simply drive away.

Nothing could have prepared them for what happened when Nathanial pulled in and moments later, a black taxi pulled in front of him.

Unsure who it was they stayed in the car, his foot hovering over the accelerator ready to speed away should anyone try to take Angel.

They watched as one of the three men walked towards the taxi and opened the door and helped elderly priest, Father Patrick, out of the car.

"Looks like they're on our side" said James as he opened the car door.

As the two priests were escorted to the front door, the other men made their way from the house to Nathanial's car.

Nodding at James to reassure him they meant no harm, one of them opened Angel's door. Placing his hand inside the car he helped her out. With a smile and a feeling of calm, she thanked him.

They heard car doors opening and closing as they walked along the pathway towards the waiting priests.

Father Angelo whispered something to Father Patrick as Angel approached them.

"I've waited a long time to meet you Angel" said Father Patrick as he took her hand, "I only wish it had been under different circumstances. If the scrolls are correct the battle between good and evil will soon take place. I can already sense eyes watching us and the evil manifesting in this house. I pray God will stand with us today and the prophecy will be fulfilled. Once we enter you must never doubt who you are or why we are here."

Before she had time to reply, James hurried them along as he spotted several people, including Henrik and Leticia, leave their cars and head towards them.

The moment Nathanial closed the door behind them, strange things started to happen in the house.

Louis quickly tried to usher them all into the lounge.

They could hear the sound of drums booming louder and louder. A wall mirror cracked and the foulest smell seemed to fill the air choking everyone.

Father Patrick was pinned against the wall by an invisible force. The already frail priest was fighting to breathe as Father Angelo quickly threw Holy water at him and recited a prayer. Moments later the evil was gone and Father Patrick slid down the wall.

Linda rushed over and, along with Father Angelo, helped him to his feet and into the lounge.

From there, James looked out the window. Henrik and at least ten others were just standing staring at the house. The three doormen were standing at the front door acting as a deterrent to stop them getting in.

Father Patrick looked shaken and pale as he sat in the chair. Linda was crying as she held his hand and said maybe he shouldn't have come. He was too weak to fight the evil in the house.

"If it's God's will that I die today my sweet Linda, then so be it. I am not afraid, but I am afraid what will happen if we don't stand fast and have faith in the Lord. I have waited many years for this day, the day when Satan will perish."

Suddenly the furniture began to shake and move, the lights flashed on and off and the banging began again, louder and louder. Blood ran from the walls.

"God help us!" shouted Father Angelo.

In that second, Linda was thrown across the room away from Father Patrick. Crashing against the lounge wall she laid unconscious on the floor. Furniture hurled across the room in a typhonic wind.

Surprisingly, Derek rushed over to Linda and shouted at whatever was doing it to stop.

Holding a crucifix, Louis told everyone to stand fast and recite the Lord's Prayer.

Father Patrick's chair began to spin and lift off the floor. It spun so fast nobody could get near it to help the priest. It came to a crashing halt as it hit the floor at speed.

Nathanial tried to reach him, but the wind was forcing him back.

Then the wind stopped as suddenly as it had begun and the foulest smell engulfed the room. Derek was nauseous from it and vomited. People were scattered around the room. James was still holding onto Angel. Not once during the great wind had he let her go.

Father Angelo stood reciting passages from the bible as the others regained their bearings.

Suddenly everything began to shake; it was like an earthquake. A crack appeared in the floor. Within seconds it had grown in size like a huge crater, cutting the friends off from each other.

Flames began spitting up from the crack as it grew. Moments later a huge beast with horns, claws, razor sharp teeth and cloven hooves stood in front of Father Patrick.

Time seemed to stand still as it laughed. It was the most sinister laugh, gravelly and low.

Seeming to grow in size the more it came from the abyss, it reached over and placed one clawed hand around Father Patrick's neck.

The already exhausted and battered priest barely had the strength to fight back as the beast's grip grew tighter.

"LEAVE HIM ALONE!" shouted Angel from across the room.

The others watched as a glowing aura appeared around her and rays of light which resembled sparks flew from her fingers as she pointed at the beast. Standing firm, she spoke clearly in Hebrew and commanded the beast to release the priest.

Releasing Father Patrick the beast spun round and focused his attention on her.

Like a fiery dragon, flames gushed from its mouth aimed at her, but like an invisible force field around her they couldn't penetrate to her body.

"COME FORTH MY LEGIONS" snarled the beast as its anger grew. Reaching out its claws it tried to grab Angel, but once again the force that was protecting her seemed to burn him as he tried to touch her.

Suddenly the beast flew up completely out of the abyss as the sound of a charging horse and a thousand screaming voices could be heard behind him.

Now it's huge scaly arrow-shaped tail thrashed around the room, knocking Nathanial and James off balance.

Linda began to come round as Derek held her and begged her to wake up.

As the beast thrashed its tail, Angel continued to thwart it and its rage grew worse.

Outside the others were still holding fast trying to stop Henrik and his cronies from entering, but more were arriving. Several people had joined them and they were chanting. The doormen were surprised they hadn't tried to rush them as they were outnumbered four to one.

Angel was growing weaker as she tried to hold the beast. Then to everyone's horror, something moved in the abyss and three smaller demonic creatures entered the room.

Father Angelo dropped to his knees and prayed for God to help them.

One of the creatures with tentacles protruding from its head and body moved towards him, snarling and thrashing its tail. Its face distorted as its yellow eyes fixed on the priest.

Father Angelo was terrified as the beast ordered his creatures to feast on their flesh and the creature grabbed hold of him.

"FIGHT IT ANGELO" cried Father Patrick as he heaved himself from the chair. "Show it no fear!"

Father Angelo took courage from Father Patrick's words as the creature bared its teeth to strike.

At the same time another creature had made its way over to Nathanial. It resembled a troll with a short stout body, its flesh made more repulsive by its colour, a dull green and what appeared to be warts and open sores. It was wielding a large spiked club which it swung around its body.

Nathanial was ready for it. Taking the dagger of St David from his jacket, he caught the creature off guard and plunged it into its eye. Its shriek was deafening as it thrashed in agony and slid hurriedly across the floor before disappearing down into the fiery abyss.

The beast was angry and ordered more to come.

The edge of the abyss came to life as grotesque demonic creatures clawed their way out into the room, increasing in their numbers and each one more grotesque than the one before it.

Picking their prey, they moved towards it.

It was a large demon that picked out Father Angelo; it was the size of a large man with horns and black body armour. Around its head it swung a spiked flail ball. The priest knew he had met this demon before and without God's help he could not defeat it. It roared as it approached the priest, knocking him over with the flail. With Father Angelo wounded and stunned the demon made its move. With one hand it dragged him up from the floor and sank its fanged teeth into the priest's neck. Father Angelo knew he would be done for as its teeth began to penetrate deeper into his flesh, but unexpectedly it suddenly dropped him and gave out a deafening shrill from pain as it sank back into the abyss.

Stunned and badly wounded, Father Angelo questioned why the creature had suddenly left. Staggering to his feet he could see Father Patrick lying on the floor, a bloody crucifix in his hand which he'd used to stab it in the back.

Still weak from his encounter a few minutes earlier with the beast, the frail priest had collapsed after saving his friend.

Several more grotesque creatures came up from the abyss as the beast moved towards Angel.

"You grow weak mortal" snarled the beast looking at her "soon you will belong to me and your kind will be no more! Your God has failed you."

Angel tried to hold him off but her powers were diminishing. Yet his words had an effect on her and, summoning all her strength and courage, she pushed him back.

"Your legions will fail Satan; my God will not desert us. For centuries you have lain hidden in your abyss, today that will end!"

James watched in amazement at the bravery of the woman he loved. Seeing she was struggling to keep her footing, he moved around behind her and, placing his arms firmly around her waist, held her steadfastly.

Despite everyone's efforts the creatures were growing stronger as more and more came from the abyss.

Nathanial was backed into a corner by two of them. He lunged at them with the dagger, but still they came at him. Linda was barely conscious as another grabbed her leg and tried to drag her away from Derek, but he picked up a silver candle stick which had ended up on the floor and without hesitation brought it crashing down on the creature's skull. It lay on the floor twitching and screaming. Sheer exhaustion was taking its toll on everyone, especially Angel. She sounded desperate as she told James she couldn't hold the beast much longer.

Just as she felt all hope was lost, a bright shaft of light came down from the ceiling and celestial bodies seemed to float down inside it.

The beast backed away from Angel and, like her, watched as four angels, including Johnathan, manifested.

Angel felt a surge of relief at seeing him, one of the angels was a female and she looked familiar. It was her mother, Evelyn. Each angel had a golden sword which seemed to glow.

Despite their help the battle was far from won when more creatures came from the abyss. The appearance of Johnathan and the other angels gave the mortals a renewed hope and each of them fought with renewed strength and courage, but the beast wanted Angel. With her power weakening, he saw his chance and with a powerful swipe of his hand broke through the force field and threw her and James across the room. In that moment, James lost his grip of her. The beast saw his chance and swiping at her again pushed her across the floor into the abyss.

James and the others tried to save her, but she was gone and they were badly outnumbered, weak and injured.

James threw himself to the edge and looking down into the endless sea of darkness frantically called her name. In his desperation to save her, he hadn't seen the creature now standing behind him. In that moment it seized the opportunity and struck. James could feel its claws ripping into his back as he tried to get up to fight, but the creature was big and too heavy to throw off as it stomped down on him to hold him firm.

With the creature overpowering him, he hung over the abyss, his strength and life ebbing away. Looking down into the darkness, he saw a bright light which grew bigger and brighter the nearer it came. Bleeding profusely from his wounds, he wondered if his eyes were deceiving him; was this the moment of his death. He tried to focus on the light; he believed he could see Angel moving towards him, she was shrouded in a light. During his Army years, he'd heard stories that when someone dies a loved one comes for them, maybe this was his time. It was as she reached out her hand to him, he noticed someone was holding her, it was her mother.

"Get up James!" said Angel as their fingertips met, "you cannot die. I love you."

Just as he rallied his strength to fight the creature, he felt it move off him. Turning his head, he saw Nathanial holding the dagger, it was dripping with blood.

While the battle raged inside the house, outside Henrik, Leticia, Henrietta and Damian had managed to get past the doormen. Despite this they were still holding off the others.

Louis tried to prevent them from entering the lounge by throwing Holy water around the door, but he was attacked by a creature.

In all the chaos the beast hadn't realised Angel had been saved, he had now focused his rage on Father Patrick. The frail priest was grabbed by the neck. Despite Father Angelo and Derek trying to help him, the beast plunged its claws into his chest. It laughed as its hand pushed into Father Patrick's heart. It was just about to inflict the final blow and rip his heart out when suddenly it turned as Johnathan plunged his sword into its thigh. In its anger it swiped at Johnathan knocking him across the room, ripping the flesh from his chest as its claws made contact.

Angel, although weak, made a valiant effort to keep the beast at bay, but she was failing. It was just too strong. As the battle between good and evil raged, she could see her friends bleeding, mortally wounded. All hope was fading. In desperation she cried out.

"Forgive me Lord, I have failed you."

Suddenly, there was a loud deafening bang like thunder and a light so strong it was blinding. As the light filled the room, time stood still. Several of the lesser demonic creatures scurried back into the abyss.

Henrik and his followers dropped to their knees as Nancy and Sister Violet appeared before them in the doorway. Nancy seemed to hover as the light emanated from her.

Raising her arms she pointed at the beast. Instantly it tried to shield its eyes and cowered as it moved back towards the abyss.

"How easily you were deceived Satan" said Nancy in a calm, but powerful voice. "Today you will feel the true wrath of God."

With the beast temporarily blinded from the light, the angels flew into the air with their swords raised. In an instant, and with the precision of great warriors, they each brought their swords down plunging them into the beast.

It spun and shrilled as it writhed in agony. Hitting the floor with a mighty thud and mortally wounded, it crawled to the edge of the abyss.

Nathanial passed the dagger of St David to Nancy.

Holding it firmly with both hands, she thrust it into the beast's head as it slipped into the abyss, followed swiftly by its legions.

Flames leapt at her from the blackness as the most chillingly loud shrill echoed from its depths. Nancy stood unscathed by the flames as she commanded the legions back to Hell.

Just as the abyss began to close the angels attacked Henrik and the others before hurling them into the abyss. They watched as Henrik clung to the edge and his body changed. His face distorted into that of an old man, burnt and disfigured.

Henrik's body was trapped as the abyss closed, cutting him in half. It was Louis who inflicted the final blow as the abyss closed for ever. Despite Henrik being severed in two, his torso was still alive writhing and twisting. Having taken the animal skin pouch from Nathanial, he held the pouch above Henrik and poured the Holy water over him. Henrik turned to ash.

Moments later all was calm. The abyss, along with the evil, had gone.

Nathanial looked around at his friends, the battle had been won and although victory was sweet, it had come at a terrible price. His friends had all fought bravely and selflessly, but for some they would pay with their lives. One question laying heavy on his mind was Nancy, but now was not the time. Helping his friends must be his first priority.

Attempting to get up from the floor was difficult, he was bleeding badly from a chest wound and his strength had gone. Staggering to get to his feet, he felt a hand take his arm. Looking up, it was Nancy.

Without saying a word, she smiled and placed her hand on his chest. In that moment the pain disappeared and he felt his strength return.

Standing, he held her and asked what was going on.

"Sister Violet will explain everything soon Nathanial, but first we need to help everyone."

One by one she moved round the room, healing their wounds.

Father Patrick was dying and she knew she couldn't help him as she knelt down beside him.

"So you were the chosen one?" he said as she held his hand.

Before she could reply, a shaft of light came down from the ceiling. Johnathan and two of the angels moved towards it, but Angel's mother stopped and spoke to her.

"I am so proud of you" she said as she gently touched her face "be happy Angel and always know how much I love you."

Angel cried as her mother kissed her cheek.

With Johnathan and the others waiting, Angel's mother moved over to Father Patrick and gently took his hand.

"Come dear Patrick. The prophecy is complete, your work is done. You have earned your rightful place next to our Lord."

The old priest smiled as his eyes closed for the last time and his life left his body.

They watched as his soul left his mortal body and floated towards the light. After entering, he manifested into the man he'd once been. Looked healthy and happy, he smiled at Linda and said goodbye.

Angel's mother began moving towards the light; just as she reached it she turned and spoke.

"The world will not know of this day or the sacrifices you were all prepared to make to prevent evil from conquering, but, God knows and your efforts will not go unrewarded. Nathanial, you have watched over Nancy and kept her safe. The love you have for one another is unbreakable and God wants you to be together. He relinquishes both of you from your vows so you can marry."

Walking into the light, she called to Angel that she loved her and along with her brother Johnathan, they would always watch over her and the beautiful children she and James would have.

The shaft of light disappeared.

Father Angelo knelt by his friend Father Patrick. The wounds to his body had disappeared and although his life was gone, he had a look of contentment on his face as Father Angelo leaned over and kissed his forehead.

Nathanial stood with his arm around Nancy. Turning she smiled and kissed him.

God was right, they loved one another unconditionally, their bond would stand the test of time and their love would never be in doubt.

Curiously, he asked her again how she had been the one. He grinned with her reply.

"Sister Violet will explain everything, but first we need to move Father Patrick's body into the bedroom and clear up because the police will be here shortly. One of Linda's neighbours called them an hour ago."

Derek barely said a word as they all began putting the furniture and ornaments back in place. Angel had just finished sweeping up all the broken bits when one of the doormen entered and told them the police had just pulled up.

Linda invited the doormen in to join them for a cup of tea after he said everyone who'd been outside had gone.

A young constable and a WPC rang the doorbell. Linda answered it.

She smiled when they said a neighbour had reported a disturbance.

Inviting them in, she explained how they were modernising the house and some friends had come over to help. The disturbance was probably due to the amount of noise they made when moving the furniture.

The WPC didn't look convinced, especially as the neighbour had stated there was a crowd of people who had been chanting outside.

Nancy walked over to her and gently placing her hand on her arm, stated that it had been a mistake and as she could see everything was fine.

In a complete change of thought, the WPC smiled at her colleague and said they could leave as there had clearly been a mistake and there was nothing to report.

Five minutes later, convinced all was well, the police left. They had no idea what had really taken place.

Aside from the furniture which was broken, the lounge looked normal an hour later as they sat drinking tea.

Angel called Olivia to tell her everything was fine. She could hear the relief in her voice when Olivia stated she'd see them later.

Nathanial sat holding Nancy's hand as Sister Violet spoke.

"Firstly I want to say what a pleasure it's been spending time with you all, but unfortunately my time here is nearly spent, so I'll keep this brief. I'm sorry we had to make everyone believe that Angel was the chosen one and to a degree she was, you've all seen what she can do. However since the day she was born we knew Nancy was. Father Samuel changed the birth dates of Angel and Nancy to protect her, so when you read his journals Nathanial, you would believe it was Angel. God chose you to watch over and protect Nancy and I must agree it was a fine choice. I'm sure you will have a long and happy life together. Oh and I don't want you to think that Nancy knew, she didn't until a few hours ago, we all agreed it was safer that way. Never doubt the love she has for you Nathanial. Like you, everyone here was selected to do God's work and none of you failed in that quest.

Father Angelo when your time comes you will join Father Patrick. There is a place ready for you, but that will not be for many years, there is much for you to do. Now to you Angel, I know there are so many things you want to know about Evelyn. Your mother was a real angel who was sent here to help people, unfortunately she fell in love with a mortal, your father. Sadly he was killed and your mother's heart was broken so she was called back to us. It was the only way they could be reunited. Johnathan is the child she was carrying. They will always be near you. Your friend Alan was murdered by Damian and Hermann. His sacrifice has not gone unnoticed and he's reunited with his loved ones.

Linda, buying this house was no accident. We knew Father Patrick would come and that had to be. Derek was a worry to us;" she added with a grin "we felt he may force you to leave after his illness, but today he showed his love for you and hopefully a little faith."

"There is one last thing for me to do before I leave. Come along children it's time to say goodbye."

They all watched as the children manifested in the centre of the room.

Joey ran straight to Angel and embraced her, followed by Mary and the others.

They hugged Linda and Derek too. He looked tearful as he hugged Joey and said goodbye.

"Ah I believe our escorts have arrived children," said Sister Violet "we must go."

Angel felt happy as her friends, Joyce and Alan, along with Olivia's late husband Charles manifested and the children ran towards them.

Joey took Joyce's hand just as the shaft of light appeared and they all walked into it as they waved goodbye.

"Remember" said Sister Violet "God works in mysterious ways and things are not always as they seem."

They watched in amazement as she began to fade as she walked into the light.

"So was she an angel?" said Derek looking totally confused.

The others laughed as Nancy nodded.

It was later that evening when Linda called the ambulance, stating that her elderly uncle who was staying with them had taken a nap and they feared he'd had a heart attack because they couldn't wake him.

CHAPTER 29
(Three Months Later)

Olivia called up the stairs for Angel and Nancy to hurry up; they didn't want to be late.

Moments later she, Martin and Derek stood patiently waiting at the bottom of the stairs. Angel appeared first. She looked beautiful wearing a silk wedding gown; her hair, although having grown was short. It was swept up and held by tiny flower pins.

"Best not forget these" said Martin as he handed her a bouquet of stunning red roses. "You look absolutely gorgeous sweetheart. Your James is a lucky man."

Nervously she smiled and, after thanking him, stated she was the lucky one.

Olivia felt her trembling as she kissed her cheek.

It was to be a double wedding with Nancy and Nathanial. Nancy had spent the night at Olivia's being that she and Nathanial didn't live near. He had spent the night at Linda's.

Nancy came out of the bedroom and down the stairs.

Olivia handed her an identical bouquet and told her she looked stunning. The two men agreed as Derek put his arm out for her to take.

Looking at his watch, Martin suggested they should leave or the grooms might think they're not coming.

Martin felt proud as Angel took his arm and they made their way to the door, followed by the others.

The wedding limo was waiting along with a second car which would take Olivia, Linda and James's mum.

Neither bride had wanted a big fussy wedding so there were no bridesmaids, just their closest family and friends.

Derek had felt honoured to be asked to give Nancy away as she had no contact with her own father since going to live with Nathanial after her possession.

The two brides held hands in the car to try and settle their nerves.

Father Angelo was waiting for them when they arrived at the church. The Pope had given his blessing for him to marry them.

Olivia and the ladies made their way inside and sat down moments before the brides entered.

The two grooms looked as nervous as any men could and more so when they saw the beautiful women they were about to marry.

The church was half empty with just a few family and friends. Linda's sons and their families were there, along with several priests who were friends of Nathanial and Nancy.

Just as Father Angelo completed the service and pronounced them men and wives, he leaned forward and whispered they had visitors as he nodded towards the rear of the church.

When they looked around they could see clearly Father Patrick, Father Michael, Alan, Joyce and all the angels, including the children.

Momentarily forgetting where she was, Angel waved at her mother, causing the congregation to turn and look. Only the people who had seen them before could see them and no doubt everyone else thought she had waved at someone sitting at the rear of the church. When Linda smiled at Joey, she had a tear in her eye.

There was no big fancy reception, just a meal at a local hotel.

James and Nathanial did however make a small speech thanking everyone for sharing their special day with them and stating how much they loved their wives. James's father made a short speech, along with the grooms' best men.

They had booked a honeymoon together in the Caribbean, but that night they would stay in the hotel, courtesy of Father Angelo. Like everyone there the priest knew they would all live long and happy lives and that the angels would always watch over them.

ABOUT THE AUTHOR

All my life I've been passionate about writing, even as a child. Little did I know then I would have to wait until I was 50 to fulfil my dream and actually publish my novels.

My family have always been of paramount importance to me, so it seemed natural to put my life, as a would-be writer, on hold until my children were settled and happy. There never seemed to be enough hours in the day, especially when my girls were growing up. Time was the only thing I could never control and between fostering teenagers, raising money for worthy causes and rescuing guinea pigs, I never seemed to have any left for me! Often I would write during the night hours so as not to upset my family's routine. I still do, old habits die hard.

I felt confident enough to try and secure an agent, but I quickly realised I probably stood more chance of becoming the next Prime Minister than actually getting signed up! Everyone loved my books and constantly said I should publish. So, with the help of my lovely 'little' Ian (a young man who we all consider family), we looked at eBooks and print publishing.

Despite having to fit my writing around my working life, I always run two books together. Fortunately, I never get bored with writing or suffer from writers block, but there are, on occasion, times when I feel the need for change so I write a few chapters in one book then switch to the other and repeat the process. I also love writing poetry about real topics. Some are funny some are sad. I was thrilled when, after entering a competition, two of my poems were selected for publication.

I have written several novels in different genres which I'm told is quite unusual. Truth is all of my writing comes from the heart and from some of life's experiences. One question I'm always asked is where my story lines come from. My answer is simple. Like most of my friends I attended the school of hard knocks, but I feel truly blessed to have a large extended family and to have met so many people from so many walks of life, some good, some bad and some decidedly dodgy, but never dull. Without any doubt they have helped to inspire some of my characters, but for the story lines my colourful imagination has come into play.

Earlier this year, I was asked to ghost write the autobiography of a bona fide, old school, London bad boy and I must admit, I'm loving every minute of it. I felt honoured to have been entrusted to write this amazing story, along with flattered as an author to do the book justice. No sugar coating no fancy words, just writing it as it is. Ironically it's like writing a non-fictitious book for my Ruthless series!

OTHER AVAILABLE TITLES

Ruthless Series 1

• Book 1: Jimmy's Game
Addictive, obsessive, sexually driven and all consuming; Jimmy's Game is a book that will dominate your darkest desires of control and power.

• Book 2: Maria's Journey
Compelling, brutal and stretching every boundary of love and loyalty to its limits; Maria's Journey will leave you wondering how she ever survived and remained the lady she is.

• Book 3: Mickey's Way
Touching, loving, merciless and unforgiving, only a father knows how far he will go to protect the ones he loves.

• Book 4: Billy's Move
Sexy, passionate, body pulsing, when you find true love and someone has wronged them, there has to be revenge and it's always served best when it's unexpected.

• Book 5: Tony's Business
Totally absorbing, a boss driven by power, control and greed. Now he has to make the toughest decision of his life, but can this king relinquish his crown?

Ruthless Series 2 - The Next Generation

• Book 1: Carlo's Law
When you double cross the king of London, be prepared to pay the ultimate price.

• Book 2: George's Ascent
Can a man kill to prove himself?'

• Book 3: Vito's War
His greatest fight will be for his life.

• Book 4: Shaun's Call
Some fights you just can't win.

• Book 5: Coming Soon…

Other Standalone Titles by Karen Clow:
• The Angels Are Dying
• Brassick